NEIGHBOURS

NEIGHBOURS
Laurali Wright

Macmillan of Canada/Toronto

Canadian Cataloguing in Publication Data

Wright, Laurali, 1939–
Neighbours

ISBN 0-7705-1791-9

I. Title.

PS8595.R566N45   C813'.5'4   C79-094108-2
PR9199.3.W75N45

Printed in Canada for
The Macmillan Company of Canada Limited,
70 Bond Street,
Toronto, Ontario
M5B 1X3

This book is for my father,
Sidney Victor Appleby
. . . and for John;
my critic and my love.

Acknowledgements

The author wishes to acknowledge the help and encouragement of: the Creative Writing Division, Banff School of Fine Arts; the *Calgary Herald*; James Cardwell; Suzanne Zwarun; Katey Wright; and Johnna Wright.

NEIGHBOURS

Chapter
1

From her bedroom window she saw the car drive up, and she was astonished. Later, Jack told her that she should have expected him, but she hadn't. She never ever expected him; he always took her by surprise.

He arrived just before suppertime and, although it had startled her, she was extremely glad to see him. He called out, "I'm home," and Heather went running to him from the living room, shouting "Daddy! Daddy!" and Betty came bouncing down the stairs.

She tried to look calm, even though she was flustered, and as she came down the stairs she wondered what she looked like; and then she saw in his eyes that she did not look pretty.

He put his suitcase down, and his briefcase, and grabbed Heather in his arms. He reached out and gave Betty a hug around her shoulders and a kiss on her cheek. She felt his moustache against her skin, like coarse fur. She saw the two thin people there in the hallway and didn't know how she had gotten so fat. She never thought about it except when she saw the two of them together.

She left Jack with Heather and ran into the kitchen to find something to make for dinner. Feelings jangled around inside her. She tried to ignore them as she looked through the cupboards. For a while she looked without seeing anything at all; for a moment she thought the cupboards were empty. That bothered her, to be so unprepared. But then she found some cans of stew. She called Heather to help her and they made dinner together, stew and bread and butter and tea and some canned peaches for dessert.

Jack seemed quite content.

Afterwards, she asked Heather to help with the dishes. It had been surprisingly pleasant, making dinner together. Heather had done most of the work, actually; Betty just set the table and made the tea. She had told the child what to do, of course—supervised. It was, yes, pleasant, working there in the kitchen with Heather, she thought, while Jack unpacked and put his things away upstairs. But after dinner Heather went to play outside.

So Betty put the kitchen in order by herself, and then she went into the living room where Jack was reading the newspaper.

"Shall we have a chat, then? Did you have a good trip? Was the weather good? How long will you be home this time?"

One question just led to another, she found, and she wanted the answers to them all, and was afraid she would forget if she didn't ask them all at once.

"Everything is fine, just fine," he said, and went on reading. As though one of us isn't really here at all, she thought. She watched him as he read, and saw that he was pursing his lips to nibble at the inside of his mouth. She thought he looked a little like a rat, nibbling away.

"And when do you have to go away again, do you think?" she said, patting her fuzzy hair. "Will you be home for long this time?"

He rattled his newspaper. He was getting impatient, she could see that. But shouldn't a husband and wife have a conversation together, she asked herself? Shouldn't they? Asking him things was the only way she knew to start a conversation. She could have told him about what she and Heather had been doing. But they had talked about that at dinnertime. There was nothing left.

"Jack? When will you have to go away again?"

"I just got here, Betty," he said, and she saw that he was tired. "Do you want to get rid of me again already?"

Betty said nothing.

"You've been getting more headaches," he said, putting

down the newspaper. "Heather says you've been getting more headaches."

"I don't want to talk about that." She hurried upstairs, and he followed her.

"And you haven't been over to the school yet," he called, coming closer. "You said you'd go, Betty. For God's sake, it's almost the end of the year."

She turned around to say something, but his presence near her in the tiny hallway was smothering, so she scurried into her room and sat on the bed.

He came to the doorway and looked around. "Jesus Christ." He went down the hall and looked into the bathroom and Heather's room and he kept on saying, "Jesus Christ!" She sat on her bed and cried. He banged his feet as he went downstairs. The sliding door to the back yard rolled open, then closed.

Soon she felt better. She combed her hair, which sprang right back from her head in fuzzy spirals. Her eyes had almost disappeared into her face. Just a small amount of crying made them swell. And her face looked splotchy and bloated. If he had only told her he was coming home she could have changed her dress, which she saw was stained, and put some stockings on her white, pudgy legs and dabbed some makeup on her eyes and maybe washed her hair. But he never tells me, she thought. He just suddenly arrives.

She went downstairs and pulled back the kitchen curtains to peek outside. Jack was there in the back yard, getting out the lawnmower.

Heather appeared over the back fence and lifted herself up from the other side until she was hanging over it, head resting on skinny arms, laughing. Jack began to smile and there they were, talking together, so relaxed, like there was nothing to it.

Betty let the curtain fall back into place. She sat on a chair. There were brown spots on the table from the stew they had had for dinner, and tiny grains of salt, and

3

greasy smudges of butter, and white circles left by Jack's mug.

He insisted on using a mug for his tea or coffee, and it always left a white circle on the wooden tabletop. If he would use a cup and saucer she knew that wouldn't happen. But he said he preferred mugs and he told her to get some cloths for the table. She meant to do that, but she forgot. She used to have tablecloths.

The two of them were laughing out there. Heather had come through the back gate into the yard. The lawnmower started up. It had a very loud sound, like a dentist's drill, only much, much louder.

There was a lot of sunshine coming into the kitchen through the curtains. It wasn't even summer yet, but the room was hot and stuffy. She could have gone into the living room, but she didn't move.

The kitchen was terribly messy.

Peeping out from around the curtain, she saw Jack put the lawnmower away, winding the long, long cord around its handle. Heather was raking the grass into a pile. Jack wheeled the lawnmower back into the little tin shed and got a big plastic bag from in there and began scooping the grass into it. The two trees in the back yard hovered over them.

They were so confident; Heather sweeping the rake over the cut grass, Jack piling it into the bag. Soon there was no more grass lying around at all. Heather put the rake away and Jack carried the plastic bag out to the garbage can. The yard looked fresh and gleaming, framed by its tall fences, splotched by tree shadows.

Jack got out the hose and began to water the lawn. Heather stood beside him. Through the soft hiss of the spraying water Betty could hear the murmur of their conversation, and she could hear the shouts and laughter of children playing in the yard next door, and the mother there called out, "Shelley!" in a full and happy voice.

Betty got up and pulled the glass door open. They

4

both turned to look at her, startled. She thought they looked guilty, standing there.

"Heather, come in here and help me clean up this kitchen," she said.

Nobody moved.

"You're supposed to help me," she went on. Tears spurted into her eyes.

Heather said, "I helped you with dinner. I practically made the whole dinner. And then I helped Daddy with the lawn. It's not fair." She glanced at Jack, who had turned his back and was continuing to water the grass. "Do it yourself."

Betty was shocked. She waited for Jack to say something.

"Jack! Don't let her talk to me like that! It's not right. I'm her mother, she must treat me with respect. . . ." He whirled around and aimed his voice at her.

"You can't do a goddam thing, can you, you can't wash a dish or sweep a floor or do a goddam thing!" She tried to interrupt him but he just kept on, getting more and more angry, shouting now.

"That house is a pigsty! It's a pigsty every time I come home! You can't even tell what colour the floor in that kitchen is supposed to be; you couldn't get all the filth off those counters now if you tried! You want help?" He came towards her, still holding the hose. "You want help? I'll give you help!"

He pushed her aside, threw wide open the glass door into the kitchen, and pointed the hose inside. Betty heard Heather shriek and start to cry.

"There! That'll get it clean! That'll get the stinking place clean!" Jack's voice was shrill. He waved the hose wildly around inside the kitchen. The harsh spray struck pots and pans and dishes piled in the sink, bounced off the toaster with a twanging sound, zinged viciously against cupboards and stove, splatted against the walls. Salt and pepper shakers were knocked to the floor and they rolled frantically as the jet from the hose hit them again and again. Water continued to pour in and gradually piled up, grey and gurgling, on the floor. Jack pointed the nozzle like a machine gun at the table and chairs, at the sticky-fronted refrigerator. The strong spray roared.

Betty watched it all, fascinated. Her red slippers were sodden. The front of her purple dress was drenched. She watched, thinking about hurricanes, and hardly felt the cold water which flew sideways from the nozzle of the hose and struck her. Heather ran across the grass and through the gate and disappeared.

After a while Jack stopped. He turned off the water and threw the hose down on the small patio and without even stopping to shake the water from his clothing and his face and his hair he walked quickly around to the front of the house. In a minute she heard his car start and drive away.

She squished up to the door, peered into the kitchen, and shook her head sadly. She walked around to the front and went upstairs and took off her dress and her slippers and put on her robe and lay down on her bed.

I really must do something, she thought. I must do it soon, so that eventually, when he comes home, I can be prepared.

Help was what she needed, and she resolved to find some. She would go to people who knew about these things and she would ask for their advice. It won't be too hard, she soothed herself, stroking her heart. Grown-up people are not cruel on purpose. At least, they are not usually impolite.

Later, when it was quite dark, Betty heard Heather come back and go into her room and close the door.

Much later, Jack came home. He was downstairs a long time, and Betty heard muffled bangings and sloshings. Then he came up and went into his den. He closed his door, too, and she heard him moving around in there, and then it was quiet.

A long, long time later Betty tiptoed downstairs, avoiding the steps that squeaked. She went into the kitchen and turned on the light.

The floor was still damp, but there were no puddles. She wondered if the toaster would still work. The whole room looked very clean. She smiled with pleasure, it looked so fresh and gleaming, and she turned off the light and went upstairs to bed.

Chapter
2

A cat came to her house. It was grey, and had long fur and large green eyes.

She opened the front door to see if the milkman had come and there it was, sitting on the porch in the May morning. It looked at her. She tried to shoo it away, but it just moved down the walk, then stopped. She went inside and looked out through the curtains, through the window, through the greening tree branches, and it was still there. Sitting. It didn't have a collar on. She wondered, do cats wear collars?

It made her nervous. She walked around the house for a while and when she looked out again, at first she thought it had gone, and she was relieved. Then she saw that it had moved back to the doorstep and had lain down there.

She expected it to go away, and waited all morning for that to happen; she got a headache from waiting. But it didn't go away.

It must have left eventually, because when Heather came home from school Betty asked her, "Did you see the cat out there?"

"There isn't any cat out there," said Heather, and went into the kitchen to eat something.

But the next morning, when Betty opened the door to get the milk, it had come back. She jumped when she saw it; she had almost forgotten about it. All day it stayed there, but when Heather came home, again it had left.

On the third day she decided that she had been inhospitable. It had come to visit, to visit her, only her, since it was always gone when Heather came home, and for two days she had left it outside while it waited patiently and politely.

So on the third day she opened the door wide and said, "Come in."

He sat still for a moment, looking into the house. Then he walked inside, looked around, and walked on through the living room and the dining room and into the kitchen. She was amazed that he knew where it was. He sat down on the floor and looked up at her expectantly.

"Now what shall I offer you?" He continued to look at her.

She was nervous. She did not know what one gives to a cat. She put a bowl of water on the floor. He sniffed at it, and his small tongue touched the surface of the water and began to go in and out of his mouth.

She got down on the floor to watch him. He raised his eyes to her, but his tongue kept going in and out of his mouth, in and out of the water, quickly, delicately. He was silent as he drank, staring at Betty and then at the bowl.

He had a short face, the top half of it filled with his green eyes, which did not blink but just looked back at her. She could not tell what he was thinking. His ears were small, and there were tiny hairs inside them. He had long whiskers around a small, almost invisible mouth, but when he yawned, his mouth was filled with small teeth— a jagged white line of sharp little teeth.

He sat there, propped up calmly on his front legs. She put her hand out towards him. She could see no change in him, but she could feel a change, as though he were suddenly filled with electricity.

He got up and began to walk around the house. She followed him. He stopped to look over his shoulder at her now and then, one of his front paws raised.

He walked all around the kitchen, under the table and the chairs, and all around the living room, arching his neck as he lowered his head to sniff quietly at the carpet or a newspaper. He went upstairs. Quickly he ran, soundlessly up the stairs; but as Betty hurried after him the steps squeaked in the usual places.

He was looking down the hall towards the rooms she had there. When she came up quickly behind him he didn't jump or move out of the way but turned his head around and stared at her. She stood still until he began to move, down the hall towards her bedroom. She ran ahead of him, when she saw where he was going, and opened the door for him.

He walked in and moved around her room with curiosity. She stayed at the doorway and watched, and was proud that there were so many pretty things for him to see: the photograph on top of her bureau, her soft and pretty slippers, the bedspread—it was slightly soiled, she noticed, but still so pretty, yellow with pink flowers growing in it, soft and warm. The cat looked at all these things, and at her magazines on the table beside her bed, and the lamp there, with the yellow shade and the base which was a china girl holding an umbrella. He looked approvingly at her small pink carpet and the big brown stuffed chair and then he walked out the door and down the hall to the bathroom.

The cat didn't see all of her things, of course. She saw no reason to show him everything. He probably wouldn't have been interested anyway, she thought. Not in my tools.

He didn't care for the bathroom.

The other doors were closed, so Betty opened them for him. But he didn't want to go into Jack's room. He stood in the doorway and lifted his head, and his nostrils moved. Then he walked away and into Heather's room.

There was a bed and a chest of drawers and a bookcase and a big box filled with toys Heather had outgrown. It was a messy room. Betty was embarrassed as the cat stood there looking into it. Heather hadn't made her bed again, and there were clothes strewn about. Betty thought about rushing in and hanging things up and making the bed, but realized it was too late. Besides, he was only a cat, after all. He walked around Heather's room. He was soon bored with it and went out and down the stairs.

He walked to the front door and sat down, looking up at the doorknob. Betty was pleased that it was so easy to understand him. But she was disappointed that he wanted to leave.

"Have I done something to offend you? Wouldn't you like some more water?"

But he just looked steadily at the doorknob; so she opened the door and he walked outside without even glancing at her.

She was hurt, and a little bit angry.

"That isn't the way you do things," she called after him from the porch. "You have to say, 'Thank you. I did enjoy myself.' "

The next-door neighbour looked up curiously from the garden she was weeding. Betty pulled herself back into the doorway. She watched the cat as he crossed the street and disappeared between two houses.

He was only a cat, and couldn't speak, but he could have done something, she thought. He could have done something gracious and polite.

Chapter
3

Betty paced restlessly the length of her house, back and forth from the window in the empty dining room, which overlooked the back yard, across the mustard-coloured carpet to the window of the living room, which overlooked the street. Here she reached behind the old sofa and pulled back the curtain to look out, through the thick-leafed branches of the big tree in her front yard. She had always wanted to chop off some of the lower branches, the better to see out, but Jack wouldn't hear of it.

Back and forth, back and forth she paced, and each time that she found herself turning to head for the opposite end of the house, it was surprising to her. She wished to be purposeful, and striding the length of the house over and over again was not purposeful, she knew.

This was the day she had chosen to go out and seek advice. If a cat could go visiting, unannounced, then surely she could, too. It was a morning in the middle of the week; children would be in school, men would be at work. The sun was shining; it was important to be warm. Here was the day, then. The morning. But she was not ready for it.

She had decided, broadly speaking, where to go for her advice. If a cat could go visiting, unannounced, then surely she could, too. She had decided to combine this venture with something else she was supposed to do. She was supposed to try to make some friends. This notion made her impatient; yet, if she had to go out for advice, she had decided, she might as well try the other as well.

The only place she could think to go was to another house. She did not like people in large bunches, like grapes. She only liked them one at a time. At least, she could *bear* them, one at a time. Or maybe two together.

The only houses she was familiar with were those grouped around her own. Obviously, then, she had to go to one of these houses—one of the houses in her neighbourhood.

But to actually carry out her plan she had to be purposeful. And this morning she was not purposeful. She paced fretfully. It is not fair, she thought. It is really not fair. It is difficult enough to make plans. To lack, once they are made, the energy and resolve to carry them out —it is simply not fair.

She went out onto her porch and sat down on the top step. She looked around the neighbourhood. The houses did not match. If they had been all the same it would not have made any difference which she chose to visit. But since they were different from each other, she had to do a lot of thinking before picking out one door to knock upon.

She studied them—those she could see. The one directly across the street made her nervous. It was almost completely hidden by lilac bushes, which had grown as tall as trees and reached out to clasp hands all along the front of the house. There was barely enough room in the middle for a person to get through. Betty seldom saw anyone go through there. Soon the bushes would send strong shoots over the walkway, and then nobody would be able to go in or come out ever again, she thought. Above the bushes the top of the house appeared, craning its peaked roof and one small window. Only that one window could see anything, Betty thought sadly.

On either side of that house was a newer, smaller one. The one on the right was painted yellow; the other, light brown. There was a white picket fence in front of each. No trees grew in either yard, but there were lawns, and one of the houses had flowers planted under its windows. The springtime flowers always grew better on that side of the street, Betty noticed.

These two houses, bracketing the big, old one, were short. They looked uncertain, as if afraid they might be picked up in the dead of night and moved away somewhere. Like Betty's house, they didn't have any basement windows. In both houses lived small children and their parents. In one of them also lived a dog, a big red-brown dog, which loped lazily throughout the neighbourhood whenever he pleased. Betty did not like dogs. From the other house, the family clambered into a car and left together every morning, early.

There were other houses up and down that side of the street, but Betty wasn't interested in them because she couldn't watch them well.

Her favourite house on the whole block was beside her, on the left as she sat on her porch. There was a high white fence around three sides of it, and a hedge along the front. The house sat on the far side of its wide lot. Two tall evergreen trees grew in the front yard. The porch was painted white and had two lawnchairs on it. A broad, white banister edged the porch, and upon it sat big pots with red flowers in them. The lawn swept around the front and the sides of the house and into a back yard, which had more trees. An old rubber tire hung on a heavy rope from one of them. Betty had seen children swinging on the tire, and their yelling sometimes bothered her. But she was fond of the house. A family lived inside it. There were no animals there. The woman went out every day, but not early, as did the man and the children. The house was light green. It looked as if it had grown there, Betty thought.

To her right as she sat on her rickety porch was a house which looked about the same as her own, except that it had been recently repainted and gleamed white in the sunshine, with dark green shutters. Lilac bushes grew along the front of its yard. They were sitting there neatly, waiting to bloom.

This house, too, was surrounded by a fence, but it was

not as high as the one on the other side of Betty's house. Betty's back yard, therefore, looked peculiar, with a short fence on one side and a tall one on the other. Jack had put up a fence at the end of the back yard, from the garage on one side to the high fence on the other, so that actually two of the three fences were the same height. Still, it did look peculiar. But Betty didn't spend much time in her back yard anyway.

The woman who lived alone in the house to the right of Betty's had come outside. Betty watched her curiously, feeling hidden. The woman came out every day about this time and dug around in the flower bed underneath the windows. There were small green shoots poking up from the soil, and the woman smiled at them and muttered things as she fussed with the dirt.

She walked oddly. She rolled, jerkily, lifting the right half of her body in the air, not bending it at the hip, then putting it carefully down, moving the left half of her body forward, then jerking the right half up again and putting it down.

It is certainly an awkward way of getting about, Betty thought, watching intently. The woman made very slow progress. Betty had observed that before.

She had a thought. Why didn't she try this house? The one right next door? Surely people who live in houses which sit beside one another must have things in common. She became excited. She stood up and crept over to the fence. The woman was still poking in the dirt, muttering. I'll just open my mouth and see what happens, Betty thought, her heart slamming in her chest.

"Helloo!" she sang out loudly.

The woman turned. She shaded her eyes with her hand. She was a short woman, with grey hair pinned on top of her head—and not pinned very securely, since wisps of it were coming loose. Betty could not see her face clearly; it was hidden by the hand over her eyes. But she saw that the woman wore a blue-and-white striped dress

15

with a grey woollen shawl over her shoulders, and that there were stout oxfords on her feet. Betty noted the oxfords with approval.

"Hello there!"

Betty started. What happens now? she wondered. She opened her mouth again. "May I come over to visit you?"

As soon as she had said it she was mortified. Her energies began to gather themselves to propel her back inside her house. Then the woman laughed heartily and shouted back, "Sure! Come on over!"

Betty was amazed. She let go of the fence. She went around it and squeezed between the fence and the lilac bushes and walked slowly across the woman's lawn. The woman came to meet her, body lurching, a hand outstretched.

Betty took the hand. It felt strong. The woman's skin was almost brown; there were darker brown spots on the back of the hand; the hand was wrinkled; some of the fingernails were broken and there was chipped nail polish on them. Red, it was.

Her neighbour's face reminded Betty of a chipmunk. There was a small round mouth and a small nose and two eyes that were blue-green like the nearby river, and the cheeks were puffed out, as though she had nuts in there. The skin of the cheeks and neck was loose. Wrinkles spread out from the corners of the eyes and mouth and along the forehead. But nothing could make the face droop, because of the pudgy cheeks.

"I wondered if I was ever going to meet you," said the woman. "Come on in." She stomped unevenly up the steps and into the house. Betty followed the woman inside.

"What's your name?" said the neighbour, in the hall.

"Betty. And my last name is Coutts."

"I know what your last name is. You're Heather's mother."

Betty sagged. So that's why she wanted to meet me, she thought. Because I am somebody's mother.

"We're friends, sort of, Heather and me," said the woman. "Sometimes. She doesn't come over much any more."

"Why?"

"I don't know. She's got other things to do, I guess." The woman laughed. "You tell me." She looked at Betty expectantly.

"I don't know. I don't know why she came here in the first place."

The woman raised her eyebrows, which Betty thought made her look more than ever like a chipmunk. "Do you feed the birds?" she said.

"No," said Betty.

"Well I do. That's why she came. To help me feed the birds. Do you have a garden?"

"No," said Betty, frowning.

"Well I do. She helped me weed, too." Betty could feel the woman's eyes running over her face and body. She started to itch.

"Come on into the kitchen," said the woman, struggling down the hall. She told Betty to sit at the kitchen table and began making some coffee.

"How long have you lived next door now? About a year?"

"Yes. A year."

"Funny," said the woman. "Time was I used to know everybody on the block. Well, almost everybody. I've lived in this house for twenty years," she said proudly. "Aren't many of us left now." She sat down at the table. "You know that old place across the street from you? The Sharkeys live there. They've been around here even longer than me. Poor old folks. They're getting on now; can't keep the place up like they used to."

"My favourite house is the green one on the other side of me, the one with the big trees and the white porch. It's so pretty, don't you think?" Betty crossed her legs, but the top one kept slipping off, so she uncrossed them and sat flat-footed again, a space between her knees.

"That's the old Crawley place," said the woman. "Maisie died about four years ago and Herb didn't want to live there without her so he sold it. People's name is Dryer, or Dyer; something like that. They seem nice enough. Got two kids. The woman—her name's Sheila, I believe—she's an energetic little thing. Always digging or weeding away out there; bustling up and down the street to the bus." She began to hum a tune. Betty didn't recognize it. "People come and go so fast now, it's hardly worth the bother getting to know them." She stretched her right leg out in front of her.

"Is there something the matter with you?" said Betty.

"I've got arthritis in my hip."

"Oh. Is it very painful?" said Betty, warily.

"Sometimes. It'll probably get worse. So I'm told. I don't let it bother me. Not any more than I can help." She got up and poured coffee.

"What do you do all day?" she asked.

"What do you mean?" said Betty, feeling sweat on her forehead.

"I mean, do you work, or what?"

"Didn't Heather tell you about me?" said Betty cautiously.

"Nope. Heather didn't talk much. Well? Do you work?"

"No. I don't."

"I figured as much."

"How? How did you figure that?"

"You're here, aren't you? In the middle of the day? Besides, I hardly ever see *you* trooping up the street to the bus stop."

"It's not nice to spy on people," said Betty coyly, wagging a finger.

"Oh, I don't spy," said the woman. "I just like to know what's going on." Betty drank some coffee.

"My goodness me," said the woman suddenly. "Here we've been sitting here for ages and I haven't even told you my name!"

"That's right," said Betty reprovingly. "You haven't."

18

"It's Perkins. Poinsettia Perkins." She waited. Betty gawked, and the woman exploded with laughter. "Oh, you should see the look on your face! My, my!" she roared, tears in her eyes. "Oh my, I enjoy doing that to people!"

"You've got to admit," said Betty, indignant, "that that is a very odd name, an extremely strange name. It's no wonder that I've got a strange look on my face hearing it. How could anyone name anyone that? It's dreadful." She took a slurp of her coffee. She felt comfortable.

The woman looked at her musingly. "I was born on Christmas. But you're right, you know," she said after a minute. "It's an awful name. I've always hated it."

"I shall call you something else," said Betty. "What would you like me to call you?"

The woman thought. "Bertha," she said. "Bertha, I think."

"Very well, Bertha it is. How do you do, Bertha."

"How do you do, Betty," said Bertha, and burst into more laughter, her eyes almost disappearing as her cheeks thrust upwards.

"I did have a job once, you know," said Betty abruptly.

"You did? What kind of a job?" said Bertha, wiping her eyes with a napkin.

"Oh, office work. Office work. I worked in an office, in a photography shop in Vancouver which had an office behind it. It was a good job, a very good job. When I left, to get married, to Jack—he is my husband, Jack—when I left there the people at my office gave me a large card which they had all signed, and it was a good-luck card. Wasn't that nice?" She beamed.

"It certainly was. Very nice," said Bertha happily.

Betty looked around her at the floor. "I didn't bring my handbag," she said, distressed. "If I'd brought my handbag I could have shown you the card."

"You carry it around with you?"

"I keep it in my handbag, of course I do!" Betty drank

19

some more coffee. She wiped her mouth daintily on the back of her hand. "There were other girls in my office, too, of course. One day one of them invited me to come up to her apartment so that she could do my hair." Her hand went up to her frizzy head. "I hadn't thought of that for such a long time. My, it's pleasant to have memories, isn't it. Isn't it? You have memories too, don't you? Pleasant ones?"

"Oh yes, I've got some good memories," said Bertha. "But I like my life better than my memories." She winked at Betty.

"What kind of a life do you have?" said Betty, her small blue eyes gleaming palely.

"Oh, a quiet one. Don't see many people. Just my family, mainly. I feed the birds, garden, look after my plants." She gestured around her. Betty became conscious of hanging ferns and ivies clustered above the table, close to the window, reaching down for her. She ducked. Bertha laughed. "They won't bite. And I sew a lot. And I collect things. Stamps, coins, things like that."

She looked at Betty calmly. "Heather said your husband's away a lot. Do you get lonely?"

Betty brushed at her lap. "Oh no, not really, I have many things to keep me occupied, many things. There's the house, for example. It's quite big, bigger than this house. And I'm supposed to keep it clean, of course." There was a pause. "But I don't," she went on. "That is my largest problem, I find. Cleaning. Housecleaning. I don't do it well, and Jack gets quite upset. I've resolved to get some help." She glanced at Bertha hopefully.

"Not here you won't," said Bertha. "I'm probably the world's worst housekeeper." She sipped her coffee and began to hum again.

Betty looked around her neighbour's kitchen. It *was* untidy. There were plants all over the countertops and on the little table under the wall telephone. The floor was dusty. Even this table, the kitchen table, although covered by a cloth, looked untidy because there was a heap of mail sprawled all over it, pushed aside by Bertha when she'd put down the coffee cups. And there were dirty dishes in the sink. It made Betty feel better to see another untidy house. But there is a difference, she thought, between this house and my own—between an untidy house and a dirty one.

"I just don't know what to do about it," she muttered.

Bertha hummed, and occasionally drank some of her coffee. Her hum vibrated strongly, wishing it knew the words. It was quiet in the kitchen, except for Bertha's humming and coffee cups clicking in saucers every now and then.

"I've never come to see anyone like this," said Betty. "Do you think it was a good idea?"

Bertha stopped humming. "D'you mean coming over here?" Betty nodded. Bertha wrinkled up her forehead. "That depends on why you came."

"Mainly," said Betty, surprised at herself, "to see if I could make a friend."

"I think it was a good idea," said Bertha briskly. She pounded herself sharply on the chest. "Well. What shall we do now?"

"Would you show me the rest of your house?" said Betty.

"Sure." Bertha winced as she got slowly to her feet. "The downstairs, anyway. I don't like to go upstairs any more than I have to."

She led Betty into the adjoining dining room, whose window was filled with plants hanging at various heights from the ceiling. "Southern exposure," she said to Betty, who nodded blankly. "I don't use this room much," Bertha went on, indicating the table with four chairs and the matching china cabinet. "Except when my family comes for dinner."

"What kind of a family do you have?"

Bertha led the way into the living room. "It's not a big

one. Just my son and his wife. No grandchildren yet." The room had a sewing machine in it, with a large table near by spread with a pattern and some bright blue fabric. "I'm making myself a pantsuit," said Bertha. She stopped to eye Betty critically. "You shouldn't wear polka dots," she said. "Makes you look bigger." Betty looked down at herself. "And here's my piano," said Bertha, stroking the keys. The top was strewn with sheet music and books of music. "I'll play something for you some time, if you like."

"Oh, I would, I'd like that!" said Betty. "Oh, I do admire this room," she said, looking around. "It is a very comfortable room. There is sunlight in it, and music. And you probably have some books in here somewhere, and of course there is a carpet, showing some of the wood of the floor around it." She touched the hardwood with the toe of her shoe. "This is how rooms are supposed to be," she said, hugging herself.

"And this is my chair," said Bertha, lowering herself into it. It had a high back and was well cushioned. There was a footstool in front of it and a table beside it. There was a lamp on the table, and on the floor on the other side of the chair stood a knitting bag. Wool and knitting needles protruded from the top.

"You knit, too?" Betty said excitedly.

"Oh yes. And crochet. And I do petit point, from time to time."

So much had happened in this room that the activity of the days and evenings still hung restless in the air.

"You have this room just the way you like it, don't you?" said Betty, dreamily.

Bertha grinned, and her cheeks were shoved up under her eyes again.

"Yes, I do, just the way I want it. Drives my daughter-in-law crazy."

"Would you mind if I came to visit you again?" said Betty.

"Of course not. Didn't I tell you I'd play the piano for you some time?"

Betty looked around the room. "Maybe we could have our coffee in here the next time?" she said. "I feel very comfortable in this room." She touched the back of Bertha's chair.

"Maybe we'll do that," said Bertha, struggling to her feet.

"Good!" said Betty. "I'll come again, then. Good!"

They went to the front door and Betty waved vigorously as she went down Bertha's walk and back to her own house.

Chapter 4

As he entered the lobby of the office building, Jack felt a stab of self-hatred. The place always did this to him: his breath tasted sour in his mouth, he was sure there was dandruff on the shoulders of his jacket, he knew his tie was the wrong colour.

He looked up at the clock on the wall beside the bank of elevators. It was twenty minutes to nine. He went to one of the pay phones and dialled Jessup's number.

He cupped his body inwards around the phone. "How's she doing?" he said inanely, and heard the heartiness in his voice. It was a salesman's voice; but the doctor had one, too, he told himself.

Jack interrupted Jessup's murmurings. "She's been getting more headaches," he said. "That's why I'm calling. Heather says she's been getting more headaches." He returned the wave of a fellow worker heading for the elevators.

"Let's see," said the doctor. "When was the prescription renewed last? Let me see now . . . yes, she did get more pills after she was here last time. It's a bit early, but nothing to worry about, Mr. Coutts. I wish we could persuade her to lose some of that weight. . . . "

"She's been going to see you for a year now," said Jack. Fifteen minutes to nine. "It's been a year," he said quietly into the telephone. My kid probably can't remember her any other way, he thought. He heard the water striking the interior surfaces of the kitchen, saw Heather's face slacken in shock, watched her disappear through the back gate. "Jesus," he muttered. "I lose my temper sometimes. I get home and I lose my temper."

"It's very difficult to be patient with Betty."

24

"The place is just so goddam filthy." He laughed at himself. "I should be used to it by now, but sometimes it gets to me."

"It's hard for you to live with the symptoms of her problem," said the doctor. "I understand that; it's perfectly normal. Try not to blame yourself. Although of course it would be more helpful to Betty if you could manage to be calm and supportive. The root of the thing . . . " He droned on to Jack about fixations and tendencies and complexes.

Jack watched the minute hand on the clock stutter towards nine o'clock. He heard men behind him exchanging jovial greetings.

He knew about the importance of determining "the root of the thing". He knew Jessup figured it lay somewhere with Betty's parents. It wasn't that he was uninterested, or didn't care; it just didn't seem to have much to do with him, or with the filthy house he went home to, exhausted, for two or three days every two weeks.

" . . . and her lack of friends," he heard the doctor say, "the lack of people she can relate to, confide in, of course this exacerbates things. You're really the only one she has. I'm sure you see that."

"When you move as much as we have," said Jack sharply, "you don't make many friends. Listen, I've got to go."

"It might be a good idea if you gave more thought to changing your job," said Dr. Jessup. "We might make progress more quickly if . . . "

"Look, forget it. I'm a salesman. That's all I've ever been; that's all I know how to do. I have to earn a living." Jesus, he thought, I'm going to be late. Christ, I can just see him: *So you don't want to go on the road any more, eh Jack?* eyebrows rising, pale hand reaching to take off his glasses, staring at me remotely, looking up my record. . . . "Got to go, Doctor. Thanks."

He half ran to the elevator, made it inside just as the

doors were closing, and, in the crush of silent passengers, took some unobtrusive deep breaths as he rode to the twelfth floor and his assignments for the next two weeks. The doors swished open and he stepped out into the hall. He stopped to brush at his shoulders, pull at his tie; then he walked towards the glass doors and pushed them open, putting on a smile.

Chapter
5

I've done it before and I can do it again, she thought as she stood on a porch and aimed her finger at a doorbell.

Only last time it was easier; last time I was outside and she was outside and I just opened my mouth. Things went well, after a while, really quite well, Betty thought, and smiled, remembering her new friend. But that friend couldn't help her, couldn't give her the advice she needed.

I've done it before and I can do it again, she told herself, her finger wavering in the air in front of the doorbell.

The porch ran the full width of the house, and the end of it was in shadow. Betty smelled the strong, sharp odour of the red flowers in the pots.

Just ring the doorbell, just ring it, she whispered to herself, and then open your mouth like last time and things will be fine, just fine.

She couldn't persuade her finger to move any closer to the doorbell.

She looked out upon the lawn, at the shadows cast there by the giant evergreens. It is really very hot today, she thought.

Inside the house, Sheila sat on the sofa. Why don't I feel any different? she thought. It didn't feel as though anything bad had happened to her at all. I'm smart, though, she thought, and I know that this will not last, this definitely will not last.

Her hands started to shake and she reached out for her sunglasses. They were lying on the coffee table where she had put them when she got in, maybe fifteen minutes ago.

The whole world was looking at her, waiting for her to do something. She didn't want to be looked at. She reached blindly for her sunglasses.

Ed went over to her, uneasily. He tried to take her hands, which were attempting to get the sunglasses wrapped around her entire head. He accidentally knocked them to the floor; and that's when she felt the first gush of humiliation, as though she were on the bus in the morning and suddenly realized she had nothing on but her see-through panties.

She tried to get her sunglasses back, but he grabbed her hands and held them tightly.

"You knew there was something wrong, Sheila. You must have known."

"Shit. Piss. Fart."

Was he deliberately trying to keep her from getting her sunglasses on? She lunged at the floor to capture them, but he held her tight. He looked worried. What else is in his eyes? she wondered.

Wave after hot wave of humiliation swept over her, and he became just one among many, staring at her.

"Fuck."

She pulled away from him and the heat that was shame turned itself into rage, and with rage came physical strength, too much for her to keep inside her. She threw up her right arm and swung it like a club into his face.

"You sonofabitch!" she screeched, and ploughed him one. All that vicious, lovely strength in one blow. It felt wonderful. It took some of the attention off her and put it onto him, where she thought it belonged.

He sprawled on his heels, on his backside, and the doorbell rang.

"Leave it," he said from the floor. "Leave it!" he shouted as she got up and trembled to the front door.

"Ding-ding," it sang out cheerily. "Ding-ding." My God, this feels like a French farce, thought Sheila.

28

She opened the door a crack and said, "What do you want?" Promptly an eye appeared at the crack: small, blue, with eyeshadow rubbed all over the lid, hastily, carelessly. There was no mascara on the pale lashes.

"It's me-ee," said a voice, sounding exactly like the doorbell.

"Who?"

"Betty. From next door."

Sheila had never met Betty from next door. She remembered seeing her, that was all. She remembered that the woman was large. The very idea of neighbours appalled Sheila, who thought she really ought to live on a farm somewhere.

The door was shoved gently against her foot—once, twice, three times. Sheila looked down. There were three things her foot could do, as she saw it. It could continue to hold the door open just a crack; it could kick the door a tremendous blow and slam it closed on that wheezy blue eye; or it could step back and let the door open.

Why am I thinking about this? thought Sheila. What am I doing?

There was another shove, less gentle, and the foot shot back so as not to get injured and there she stood, Betty, all of her, all two hundred and forty pounds or whatever.

They looked at each other, Betty beaming and Sheila shocked.

"May I come in?" Betty asked coquettishly.

And Sheila said, "Why sure."

She had figured out what would happen next, but it hadn't happened yet. The words he had poured out were a bunch of bees, a whole hive of bees which were still up there in the air above her head, buzzing, circling, waiting to land. She could hear them—could almost see them. She knew that when they landed she was going to get stung, and she was waiting for that with detached interest. Once there is real pain to deal with, she told herself confidently, something can be done.

"Why sure," she said to Betty, and drew the door back the rest of the way with a neat gesture and a small bow. "Come on in."

Betty minced across the threshold, carrying her great weight as if pretending it weren't there.

"Sit down; have some coffee," said Sheila expansively, waving towards the dining room.

"Would you have tea?"

"Pardon?"

"Would you have some tea?"

"No, I don't have any tea. You can have coffee, milk, or orange juice. Take your pick." She heard Ed coming down the hall and rage surged inside her.

"I'm going out for a while," he muttered with a brief glare in Betty's direction, and he kept right on going past them and out the door. It shut loudly behind him. You couldn't really call it a slam, Sheila decided. She laughed out loud and wondered if he'd be back before the kids. He goddam well better be, she thought, there is no bloody way I'm going to make dinner for the goddam kids, I'm going to have a bath and go to bed right now, right as soon as this woman leaves. . . .

Now that he was gone the house let out its breath somewhat, and the bees dropped closer. She knew she should get busy and think about all this, but that damned buzzing was so distracting . . . come on come on sting for Christ's sake let's get it over with start start start . . . maybe I'll forget the bath, just go to sleep, just curl up under the covers with the sun still seeping through the curtains like melted honey dripping all over the floor, and in the warmth and the quiet I'll go to sleep before those bees can land and I'll sleep right through until morning I'm always better in the mornings. . . .

She had poured two cups of coffee and taken them and cream and sugar to the table. She looked out the window. The car was out of sight. She thought, he goddam well better get back before the kids.

" . . . and you live such a busy life, don't you," Betty was chattering. "I saw you come in just a few minutes ago, home from work I suppose, eh?"

"Yeah. Home from work."

"And your husband comes home every day, too."

Sheila laughed. "Yeah. He comes home. Not always at the same time."

Betty gurgled merrily. "And you have two children, not just one, but two, I've seen them. My! What a lot of work!"

"They're not so bad."

"And this house, too, you keep this big house so clean, don't you? Don't you?"

"Yeah," said Sheila. "I keep it clean. And the clothes, too."

"It's very clean, very clean indeed, I can see you must spend hours tidying up, polishing, sweeping."

Sheila looked at Betty incredulously. "What are you talking about?"

"You don't have any problems of that sort, I can see that, no, everything is in order, everything is in its place. And you have so many things to keep in order, too, you really do have a great many things, don't you, what with four people here and all."

Sheila got Betty in focus. She sat brightly at the dining-room table. She was huge. Her neck bulged, much too big for the tiny head which sat upon it. Her bust thrust itself eagerly before her, shapelessly. There was no waist there that Sheila could see. The woman's hips rocketed out from under a checked dress. It has food stains on it, my God, thought Sheila, food stains all down the front, right where you'd tie a bib if she were a baby.

She had cocked one fat knee over the other and was bobbing her right foot up and down. She held her coffee cup with enormous care, buried as it almost was in her fat hand, and took delicate little sips from time to time. Her brownish-blonde hair was short and frizzy, and it shot up from her scalp in agitation. Mascaraless eyelashes fluttered apologetically in front of the blue-smudged lids. Her mouth was small, and she had crooked teeth. Had she ever been pretty? Sheila wondered. What could she look like, minus seventy-five or a hundred pounds?

"Now I myself, I have some difficulty with housecleaning," Betty confided, leaning towards Sheila. The coffee sloshed around dangerously in her cup. Sheila's hands darted across the table and took it from her and put it back in its saucer. Betty nodded graciously, thanking her. She entwined both hands around her knee and sat back.

"I don't know quite what it is," she said, eyes buzzing busily from the prints on the wall to the plants in the bay window and into the kitchen, empty and sterile. No sign of dinner, thought Sheila as she followed Betty's gaze. I'll be goddamned if I'll make dinner let him make dinner himself the sonofabitch let him feed his own kids for once.

"I look around me," said Betty, "and sometimes I can find nothing wrong with my house at all, nothing, it's such a dear house, especially parts of it, you always like some rooms better than others, don't you, some rooms are just part of you, a solace, a comfort, a cave, if you like.

"Other times, though, when Heather—that's my daughter—comes home from school or Jack—that's my husband—comes home from a trip, other times I look around me and see that it really is a dreadful mess, dreadful."

Sheila watched her, lazily. She was occupied with waiting—waiting for the bees, waiting for the children, waiting to go to bed.

"The problem is that I don't quite know what to do about it," said Betty. "That's why I've come here. Do you understand me?" She leaned earnestly towards Sheila, blue eyes blinking.

Sheila could see the pores in her skin. Her face was

grimy. Sheila wanted to get some cleansing lotion and pour it all over her face and scrub and scrub with one Kleenex after another until there was a mountain of Kleenexes and that face was clean. Then she'd release Betty from the stranglehold and let her get up from the floor where she'd lain sprawled, fat thighs flapping against the tiles, while Sheila scrubbed industriously away.

"No."

"I beg your pardon?"

"No. No, I don't understand you. I don't know why you've come."

Betty's eyes blinked rapidly a few times. She looked around the room. "I suppose you couldn't be expected to understand. You have things under control here, don't you, all under control. . . . "

Sheila had started to laugh and couldn't stop. She felt Betty watching, but when she looked back there was no uneasiness in Betty's face, no surprise, no embarrassment. She was just looking on calmly, as Sheila laughed until tears poured down her face. Sheila got up and went to the kitchen sink. She splashed water all over her face. She got a paper towel and slapped her face dry.

"Sorry," she mumbled.

Betty nodded and reached for her enormous beige handbag, scuffed and stuffed. She walked out of the room to the front door. Sheila remained slumped in her chair.

"Perhaps I'll come again," called Betty. "When you're feeling different."

"You do that."

Sheila heard the door close.

The bees hadn't landed and she was damned if she'd give them another minute. Her body was as heavy as Betty-from-next-door's. She dragged it upstairs, where she pulled off all her clothes, put on a nightgown, dumped her clothes into the laundry hamper, closed the bedroom door, pulled the drapes, turned down the covers, and got into bed.

Her mind was in a safe pink lull. She left it there. The bees weren't going to get her until morning. She went firmly to sleep.

In the night she awoke to hear a child crying and Ed soothing him, and she smiled behind closed eyes and snuggled contentedly down into her pillow.

She remembered like a slam in the stomach and the pain had arrived.

He came back to bed and crawled in carefully beside her, resuming his wakefulness.

She couldn't go back to sleep. She'd never fall asleep again except alone, she was sure. She wanted to think; she needed some logic, some order in her head. But the deep wound that had sprung somewhere inside her was immobilizing. She was convinced it would never heal, that it would stay within her, festering, until it destroyed her. She wondered what world existed outside this room where the bedroom furniture formed shadows in the moonlight.

"You asleep?"

She waited to see what she would do. Did nothing. Said nothing.

They lay there all night, quietly, and sometimes perhaps they dozed, but they didn't really sleep. Sheila didn't dare change her position. He might find out she was faking and grab her or something. She didn't want to be grabbed. She'd slug him again if he grabbed her. She lay, becoming cramped, trying to think but getting only a jumble of images she did not welcome, until finally it was seven o'clock.

The clock radio came on and she got quickly out of bed and went into the bathroom. Locked the door. Waited until her muscles stopped whimpering. Set to work removing the makeup from the day before and putting on new makeup. She didn't think she looked any different than she had yesterday, and that was strange. She combed her hair and looked at it fearfully as she did so, but there were no grey hairs there. Not yet, she added grimly to herself.

She had to go back into the bedroom for her clothes.

"We've got to talk," he said from the bed, and his voice sounded very loud. She took her clothes into the bathroom and got dressed there. Talk. Talk. Bastard, talk to yourself. Call a friend.

She woke the children and went down to make breakfast. Let him lie there, she thought. Let him stay in bed all day. Why the hell should I care whether he goes to work or not. I don't give a damn what he does. Let him call a friend, yeah, and fuck the day away out in a meadow somewhere I don't give a damn.

She couldn't see the frying pan because there was a sheen of tears in the way; not pain, not sadness—anger. Anger. That was the way. That sonofabitch . . .

The kids came down. How do you keep things from kids?

"Feeling better, Mommy?" said Shelley.

"Yeah, fine, honey, thanks."

"We missed you at dinner."

"You have a nightmare last night, Peter?"

"Yeah, we missed you at dinnertime. We had Kentucky Fried Chicken. You would've liked it a lot."

"I didn't feel well. I'm fine, now, though. I asked if you had a nightmare, Peter."

"Just a little one. Daddy fixed it."

"Good. Eat up, both of you, so you won't be late."

He's better with them than I am, she thought. He should take the kids. I'll take the records. We can trade on weekends. He can listen to music while I take the kids to a movie or something. I don't believe this.

She drank some coffee while they ate, then got them out the door to school. She heard Ed calling, exasperated, from upstairs. She got panicky, grabbed her purse and her jacket, and left the house.

She scurried up the street to the bus stop. I'll get there too early, she thought, hours too early, but what the hell, I can't stay in that house. Things will never be the same again.

That came as a shock. I will never be quite the same person again, she thought.

The sun shone benignly and the lawns on both sides of the street were lush and green, but today she couldn't look for new flowers, couldn't stop to inspect the buds on the lilac bushes that hedged some of the yards she passed. She was stuffed full of a great ache; she wanted to cradle herself in her arms and soothe it until it went away.

And what about the kids, those kids, she thought. Oh Christ I love them so much what am I going to do. Tears blinded her as she neared the bus stop and saw there was no one else there—tears again, like an extra skin across her eyes. I brush it away, forget about it, then it's grown over again, goddam it, screw him screw him oh shit how could he do that to me! That's funny, really funny. People do it every bloody day, every single day, but not to *me*, not to *me* how could he hurt me like that! I can't live with him any more. . . .

She glimpsed the bus, quivering like a mirage. She blinked, shook her head. The bus pulled up and she got on. Nobody noticed her. She dropped a quarter and a dime into the slot and went to the very back of the bus and curled up into the corner of the vacant back seat. She looked out upon the day and didn't see it.

I can't live with him any more. Where will I go, what will I do, what will I say to him you sonofabitch I want to kill you I want you to die that's the only truth I can say, the only thing that's true. . . .

Chapter 6

Sunshine piled into the dining room. Sheila sat waiting until it was time for her to leave for work.

She was also waiting to see whether things had changed; whether there were more new feelings to astonish her or if yesterday's new feelings had become more comfortable, capable of having logic applied to them. She sat there quietly until the doorbell rang.

"Helloo!" trilled Betty, her fixed beam like the undeterred light from a lighthouse. "How are you feeling today, any different?"

"Not much," said Sheila.

"Ah. I wondered if we might continue our conversation. May I come in? I know you're terribly busy but I'll just take a minute—oh my, having a cup of coffee, are you, before starting your chores? Isn't that nice. I enjoy a few moments to myself now and then, too. May I come in, then?"

"I'm having a cup of coffee before I go to work."

"Oh yes, you have a job, don't you." Her birdlike eyes twittered around the entrance hall, the door to the dining room, the hallway leading to the living room. "You go off to work every day, just like I used to. Why haven't you left yet?"

Her feet darted across the tile floor of the dining room. Her eyes moved constantly, fingers spasmodically clutching her handbag. It's worn and grimy like her, thought Sheila. She's all worn and grimy. How depressing. Yet I bet her husband doesn't muck around with other women, I bet he doesn't, goddam him.

"I have a part-time job," she said, following Betty to the dining-room table. "I only work from ten in the morning until two in the afternoon."

37

Betty plumped herself into a chair, clutching her handbag in her lap. "Then you have the best of both worlds, don't you? You go out to work and earn money and see people and feel important, and then you come home, not too tired, and you have your family to take care of. Yes, the best of both worlds. But I don't know quite how you do it."

She stopped and looked at Sheila expectantly. "Your house is still so tidy, you see," she said. "Even though you aren't in it all day long, even though you don't have all day to keep it clean and neat, it's still tidy."

Sheila dreamily watched her coffee, watched the sun shine on its beigey surface, watched the liquid move as she stirred the spoon back and forth. She tapped the spoon slowly on the edge of the cup to get rid of the drops that clung to it and put the spoon in the saucer.

"Do you want some coffee?" she said, remembering her manners.

"No. No I don't want any coffee I came here to ask for your advice."

The words burst out all jumbled up, but Sheila heard them and looked up in surprise. "Advice about what?"

"Cleaning."

"Cleaning? Cleaning what?"

"My house. Cleaning my house. I don't know how to do it." She watched Sheila warily.

"I don't understand you," said Sheila.

Peals of laughter trilled from Betty's open mouth. She leaned back and gently slapped her fat thigh with one hand. "I knew you would say that. You said it the last time I came. I didn't think you would understand, of course I didn't!"

Sheila waited, confused. Betty watched her, head cocked to one side, fingers tapping her knee.

"It's such a silly thing, really, so silly," she said. "Yet there it is. I can't seem to clean my house, and Jack doesn't like that—Jack's my husband, you see—and of course Heather is too young to help much. She keeps her own room tidy, of course, children must learn responsibility, but she can't do very much to help me with the rest of the house. . . . "

"You mean, you want me to clean your house for you?" Sheila was amazed.

"No no no no of course not, of course I don't want you to clean my house, my goodness whatever must you think of me," said Betty, banging her feet upon the floor like an impatient racehorse or a trapped thief desperate to flee.

"No no no I said I wanted your *advice*, your *advice*, not your actual *help*, certainly not, certainly I had no intention that was not in my mind oh my goodness . . . "

"Hey, calm down. I was just trying to understand what you meant, there's nothing to get so upset about. Are you sure you won't have some coffee?"

"No, no coffee, thank you. I know it must be nearly time for you to leave for your work, I only wanted your advice." Her face quivered, and she struggled out of her chair and up on her feet, her so-small feet, so small for the rest of her.

"Now don't go yet. I don't have to leave for another five minutes," said Sheila sharply. "Sit down. Describe your problem."

Betty sat. She looked down at the floor, shuffling her brown oxfords along the pattern in the tiles. "My problem is . . . my problem is . . . I can't clean my house." She looked up, miserable. "I don't know what it is, but I simply can't do it. I don't know how, you see. I keep doing things wrong, in some way. I do not understand it. It is getting worse. And Jack is becoming more exasperated. Of course I don't blame him. All I have to do, my only responsibility really, is to clean the house. And I can't seem to do it. I thought that you might be able to tell me what I'm doing wrong." Her fingers played with the handle on her purse.

"I don't know if I can," said Sheila thoughtfully. "I mean, I've never thought much about housecleaning, you know? I just do it."

"I know, I do see, your life is so busy, so full. You're preoccupied with everything you have to do; you just do it automatically. Oh goodness you're lucky to do things automatically; I don't think I do anything automatically!" Betty pealed out her laugh again, and Sheila grinned.

"Hey look," said Sheila. "All you do is take a few swipes around with a duster and shove the vacuum cleaner back and forth . . . what's the matter?"

"Oh nothing, nothing. It's just that you make it sound so easy, you see, whereas actually it is not easy at all."

Sheila sighed. "I'll tell you what. I've got to go now, or else I'll be late, but—"

"Oh yes, I do apologize . . . " Betty sprang up and hurried towards the front door, Sheila following.

"Now just a minute, just a minute." Sheila took Betty's shoulder, it was warm and huge, and turned her around. Betty looked absorbedly at the floor. "I'll be glad to help you—to give you some advice." Sheila smiled, and Betty looked straight into her face.

Sheila saw the eyeshadow, smudged brightly all the way up to the brows. She saw the faintly dirty face, flesh pasty, near-grey, except for the orangey lipstick scrawled upon the mouth like an alarming message. Saw the kinky brown-blonde hair standing up stubbornly from the head. Saw the crooked teeth, smelled the breath. Maybe if she learns to look after that damned house, thought Sheila, she'll have more time to spend on looking after herself.

"One night next week I'll come over . . . unless . . . maybe you don't want me to come while your husband's there?"

"He won't be there, he's away again, he's often away, you see, so I should have lots and lots of time to do things but I don't, or rather, I do, but I can't. No, no can you come? Can you? That would be wonderful!" She clutched at her handbag with one hand and at Sheila's arm with the other.

"Yes, I'll come," said Sheila, and nudged Betty out through the door into the morning sunshine. "I'll be over after dinner. I must rush now, really. Goodbye."

Part of her mind scurried down the sidewalk with Betty, the remainder tried to think what she had to do. Find my purse, get my jacket, and what's the time my God five minutes until the bus leaves I'll have to run.

She grabbed her things and ran outside, slamming the door behind her. She pelted up the street, walking fast when she got out of breath, running again when she could. Near the corner she saw the bus pass the intersection and zoom into the stop. She ran full tilt, waving her arm and shouting. Someone inside pulled the cord just as the bus was about to leave. She climbed on and gave a weak smile of thanks to the driver, who, for once, smiled back. There's something to be said for sunny days, she thought as she weaved down the aisle, panting and dishevelled. They put people in a good mood.

Under it all, the breathlessness, the searching for a seat, the finding of one next to a window, the settling down to watch the familiar, sun-drenched landmarks go by—underneath it all she knew there was trouble. And then there it was, total recall, the clout in the stomach, and she wondered how many more times she would feel it over how many more weeks and months, until finally, finally, maybe one day she would remember with at most a pang. A pang of what? hurt? bitterness? jealousy? what?

She felt very tired. And she didn't feel young any more.

Betty watched from behind the curtains as Sheila ran for the bus. She waited patiently for five minutes and then she walked out of her house, down her walk, turned left, continued to the next house, turned up that walk, kept

41

right on up to the porch, climbed the steps, turned the knob, walked in, and closed the door behind her.

Betty's heart was beating very hard. She heard it, felt it in there. She stood in the foyer waiting for her heart to calm itself and, as it did, she drank in this house, this clean house that wasn't hers.

She opened the hall closet. The door squeaked, sounding very loud in the quiet of the house. Oh my goodness, she thought, what if someone is here? What if someone has come home while I wasn't watching?

"Helloo!" she trilled, and waited, holding her breath. Nothing. Just the faint echo of her own greeting hung in the air.

She peered around the open door of the closet. Winter boots still on the floor in tidy pairs. Winter hats asprawl on the shelf. But from the rod hung only spring things, light coats, light jackets. Several empty hangers were there. She could see them moving slightly, just slightly, as though the jackets or sweaters which had hung from them had just then been removed. She nodded, satisfied, crept into the dining room, and tiptoed through it into the kitchen.

All was sparkling clean, counters shining, refrigerator and stove shining, no dishes to be seen anywhere. She opened cupboard doors and saw stacks of clean china, rows of glittering glasses, coffee mugs all in a row, hanging from hooks. Sunlight angled inside the cupboard, bounced off the glassware, and hit Betty in the eyes.

She closed the doors and squatted down. More cupboards. Pots and pans, measuring cups and spoons, baking dishes.

She stood up and tugged at the lip of the dishwasher. It wouldn't open. She saw a handle, pulled it, and the door flew open and released a cloud of steam. Betty leaped back. When she saw that the steam was dissipating she edged closer to look inside. It was filled with plates and glasses and knives and forks and spoons and a platter, and they were all clean, clean and hot. She touched a big bread knife and jerked her hand away; it stung, it was so hot. She had to close the dishwasher door; reached out with a long arm, slammed it shut, pushed the handle in. Nothing happened.

She went out of the kitchen, crept through the dining room and down the hall to the living room. The curtains were open. She could see through the window large trees and the back of a garage. Grass covered the yard and pink petals were heaped on the grass beneath one of the trees. Some clung still to its branches.

In the living room Betty looked at things. She looked at books on bookshelves and records in a record holder next to the record player and lamps here and there and a big leather chair. It wouldn't hurt to sit down, she thought. She held her arms outstretched in front of her and lowered herself, grunting, into the chair. There's nothing hard about this room, she thought. Or edgy. It's a soft room, a very pleasant room. . . .

There were other rooms down there, but Betty went along the hall and up the stairs, stealthily—these steps did not creak—listening, listening, although she knew there was no one up there. Not in this house. Everyone in this house had a place to go in the daytime, and everyone could be depended upon to go there. That's the kind of house it was. She could feel it. She crept softly up the stairs and came to the upstairs hallway, where there were several doors. She made her way to the one at the end of the hall.

Sunlight poured in through the window, which faced the street. It was a huge room, with white walls. A large fern hung from the ceiling in front of the window, above a long, low chest of drawers. No mirror above the chest; just the fern, and the window, with flowered curtains, bright flowers on a white background. Betty gasped, it was so beautiful. The bed was huge, to match the room, and it had a spread so large that it met the floor on three

43

sides. It was a green colour, the same green as the leaves around the flowers in the curtains. She moved towards the bed, cautiously, and ran her hand over the spread. Warm, from the sun.

There was a carpet all over the floor, she noticed. A white carpet. Betty thought it looked like white grass—an albino lawn.

She went into the bathroom. She turned on the light. Everything gleamed so. There was nothing on the counter next to the sink except a toothbrush-holder with four brushes in it, a soap dish with soap in it, a tube of toothpaste, a plastic glass. Everything was light brown or green: the towels, the shower curtain, the bathmat. . . .

She opened the medicine cabinet. Lots of things in there, she noted with satisfaction. Aspirin and mouthwash and scissors and Eno's Fruit Salts. She chuckled. Eno's Fruit Salts! What a silly thing!

Then she saw three pairs of tweezers. She reached slowly for one pair and held them in her fingers, twirling them delicately, clamping them shut and letting them open. Three pairs. Three pairs. They'll never miss one pair, she thought. Let me see, are they all the same? All the same. She dropped the tweezers into her purse, closed the cabinet, and turned off the light.

Hurriedly she glanced into the children's rooms, one for each. One was messier than the other, both were jammed full of colour and things. It was a good thing the sun was not shining into those windows. She would be blinded by the jumble of colour from toys and bright patchwork quilts and little plastic building-blocks all over one floor and dolls wearing costumes all over the top of a bookcase and books crammed into shelves and red curtains at one window and white ones at the other and wallpaper with stripes and wallpaper with roses. . . .

She left the house, went down the walk, turned right, continued up the street, turned right down another walk, up the steps, and through her own front door.

Nobody had noticed, of course. She had known they wouldn't. She hurried upstairs into her yellow room, all bright with the sun, reached up into the closet for the box, put the tweezers inside, replaced the box, sat on her bed, and saw that she was trembling—more than trembling, she was shaking. She lay down on her yellow bedspread and looked at the yellow curtains, upon which the bright yellow sun flung the shadows of tree branches. She lay there shaking, and gradually it slowed down, then stopped.

Chapter
7

Ed started the motor and nudged the car up to the end of the pathway along which she would walk. I feel like a bloody prowler, he thought, although it was broad daylight and there were people streaming along all the walks. Maybe he should have stayed where he was, the car hidden by bushes. She'd see him now, when she came out of the building, and maybe she'd go right back inside and out another door and take the bus home. Christ, he thought, what a stupid situation. He put the car in reverse and looked behind before backing up, and as he did, he saw her. Too late now. He watched her spot him, hesitate, half turn . . . then she stalked along the path and up to the car. He opened the door, and she got in and looked out through the windshield.

Then she turned and looked straight at him, and he found her gaze unsettling. It was accusing, but he was getting used to that; it wasn't that which shook him. She looked different. There were tiny lines in her face which hadn't been there before, and he wondered if there were some in his face, too. She looked soft, sitting there, despite the grimness in her face. Her skin was soft; he found he loved the new lines in it and wanted to say so, but even he wasn't that stupid.

"Hi," he said.

"Hi."

"Do you want to have some coffee somewhere?"

"How is it that you're here to pick me up?"

"I wanted to."

"Have you given up your job, or what?"

"I told Bill I had to leave early. Personal business. Do you want to go somewhere for coffee?"

46

"Sure. Why not." How many times had he done that, she wondered—left school on "personal business"? She congratulated herself on her detachment. She wondered if he'd screwed up his career as well as his marriage. She thought about asking him, but her throat hurt.

They drove off. She had to direct him; he wasn't familiar with the campus. She was very polite as she told him where to turn. It was hot outside and hotter in the car. Sheila rolled down her window and took deep, furtive breaths.

She was glad she had her job. It was like going from one world to another. She had to ignore the things that were going on inside her private head while she was in the office, and that was good. She liked to hear the students moan and groan about having to take spring-session courses when they could be out playing tennis, or sitting around drinking beer, or earning money. She liked the feeling of dealing competently and efficiently with minor crises brought on by professors misplacing grades, or finding they had too many students—or worse, too few —registered in the upcoming summer session. She liked the people she worked with, most of them, and she thought they liked her, too. But she didn't know any of them well enough for them to realize she had troubles. Thank God.

And this had been a day stroked by summer. People had glanced frequently towards the windows, knowing that the blue sky outside was breathing warmth, and the trees were shaken by a wind that was warm, and the leaves on their branches were slowly, sensuously opening themselves to the promise of summer. Soon there would be dust and sudden thunderstorms and heat hanging heavy over the city. It was Sheila's favourite time of year, the brief moment just before hot, deep-blue skies. This year it brought her no joy, but there was comfort in it. She burrowed into the day like a gopher into its hole, and she hadn't started twitching until she walked out the door and saw the car. She wondered if Ed could see her twitching.

He drove them to an A & W. It was ridiculous to have ordered coffee, Ed thought, as the two mugs squatted in their hands, tossing steam into the air. Why the hell didn't we ask for root beer? Sitting inside this stuffy car drinking coffee, for God's sake, while the sweat gathers under my arms and between my shoulder blades. He knew that when he finally got out of the car his shirt would be stuck to him, cold and clammy.

"Sheila I want to talk to you and I want you to sit there and listen until I'm through."

"I'm not one of your goddam students."

"I know you're not, Sheila, I know that. I just want you to try to understand, for God's sake."

"What's to understand? You got itchy; you went out to screw around."

His determination seeped away. What the hell. What could he say. She'd been blunt, and she'd been right. But there ought to be a way to explain it to her, he thought.

Sheila wished she hadn't made that crack. She should listen to him, at least. Hear whatever he had to say and think about it and let it do something to her. But he didn't seem to want to talk any more. She saw the carhops bustling past and the tray sticking out from Ed's window and his coffee sitting on it and other cars driving in, mostly high-school kids. . . .

My God, she thought. What if some of his students come here. They'll see that something's wrong, I know they will. Maybe they've already seen it in his face in class, or in the halls, or going in and out of the school. They probably already know, they probably do, and I wonder what they think. Do they think Jeez that Dwyer, he's something, eh? Getting action on the side, that's pretty good for an old geezer, his wife must be a real turd. . . . I bet that's what they think, and I bet the rest of the staff knows, too, at least some of them, probably the ones who've been to our house for parties and dinners my God, my Christ I bet they know and what do they think of me, what do they think of me. . . .

"Who is it."

"It doesn't matter," said Ed, startled.

"Who is it."

"Sheila, for Christ's sake it doesn't matter. I told you, it's over."

"If you could tell me about it in the first place you can tell me who it is. Who is it!"

"Nobody you know."

"Who."

"Somebody at school."

She stared at him. "A student?"

He was outraged. "No for Christ's sake not a student what the fuck do you think I am?"

"A sonofabitch that's what I think you are. Who then, a teacher? A teacher. How convenient." Ed flushed, and swore. "That's really convenient. You must have felt like you were back in high school yourselves . . . " Ed felt a flash of anger. " . . . holding hands in the hallway and sneaking out for a quick whatever the hell you did together at lunchtimes and then sneaking out after school— to her apartment? Is that where you went?" He started to sweat heavily. "Her apartment? I can't imagine even you sneaking off to a motel. To her apartment, then, for a quick . . . fuck and sometimes not such a quick one sometimes you'd be very late, time for a really long one or two or three short ones . . . " Her words were all scrambled up together and her face was shiny with tears.

He grabbed for her. The coffee slopped out of the mug and into her lap. "Shit!" he said as she jumped. He got a handful of napkins from the tray and started mopping up the coffee on her skirt.

"Don't touch me!" she hissed, and yanked the napkins from his hand. She sobbed and vigorously pounded the coffee into her lap with the napkins.

"Sheila Sheila Sheila don't do this."

49

She jerked her head up. There were tears all over her face. "You want to laugh," she said. "You think it's funny." He could feel a grin begin to grow and desperately he tried to prevent it, but she was dumping as many tears into her lap as there were drops of coffee already there.

"You bastard," she whispered viciously, and stopped crying.

He stopped smiling, too. "I'm sorry, Sheila. Really."

He pushed the button outside, and they waited in silence for the carhop to collect the tray. Then they drove home.

"I'm going out," he said later.

"Go ahead. Have a terrific time."

She watched him put on a sweater.

"Have a hell of a good time."

She shut her mouth sharply so she wouldn't say another word.

"I won't be late." Pause. "I think I'll go to a movie." Pause. "Alone." She kept staring at him. The harder she stared the easier it was to keep her mouth shut. He looked very sexy. Tired, but sexy.

She waited until she'd heard the car drive away, and then she threw the pot she was holding. It crashed onto the table, taking plates and glasses and silverware down like rows of bowling pins—except that some of them broke.

Peter and Shelley ran in to see what was going on.

"What happened?"

"An accident. I dropped a pot."

"Boy, you sure did," said Peter admiringly. "Look at that!" He whistled at the mess on the table. "Boy, that's some mess!"

"How did you do that, Mom?" asked Shelley. "Did you throw that pot there, or what?"

"No, I didn't throw it, of course not. I just stood there looking out the window and I dropped the damn thing."

When they were in bed and probably asleep, she took a glass with two ice cubes in it and a half bottle of Scotch and she went into the living room. She didn't turn on the lights and she didn't pull the curtains, but she opened the window a little bit. She wanted to watch the sky darken and listen to the sounds of the evening.

Next time she would do it first, she decided. Next time she'd be the one to say, "I'm going out," and she'd run out and get in the car and drive to the mountains. Looking at the mountains was good for the soul, and hers certainly deserved a treat.

She sat in the leather chair. She put the bottle and the glass on the small table beside her. She was enjoying herself; she darted a look around the room to see if anyone was watching. She poured herself a drink and took a sip. She grimaced, took another sip, and felt the Scotch plummet down her throat and into her empty stomach, where it gurgled around, probably surprised to find itself alone in there.

She had intended to get drunk. Half a bottle would do it. But now she didn't feel like getting drunk. It was likely that getting drunk would make her throw up, and she loathed throwing up. She was depressed to realize that she couldn't even get drunk.

Ah, what the hell, let's just call it quits, she thought. She looked around the living room and tried to imagine sitting here with him, dividing up their possessions. It could be done, she thought. Christ knows, enough people do it. She didn't want it to happen in this house, to this family. But what else is there? she thought. What can I do with all this crap in my head?

She stood up. A mild surge of nausea came and went. She closed the curtains, fumbled around in the dark for the glass and the bottle, and took them back to the kitchen.

She didn't want to read, didn't want to watch television. She went to bed. And fell asleep. And didn't wake when Ed came home and looked down on her and sighed.

Chapter 8

"I have to go out tonight," said Sheila.

"Where to?" said Peter.

"Next door."

"To the Coutts' house?" asked Shelley.

Sheila stopped halfway to the kitchen, hands filled with dirty dishes. "Is that their name? I never asked. Yeah. Just for a while."

"Can I come with you, Mommy? Maybe Heather wants to play. I haven't played with Heather for ages."

"I'm going over there on business, sort of."

"What kind of business?" said Ed.

"She's asked for some advice. I'm going to give her some advice." She began loading the dishwasher. "I hope you don't mind too much staying in tonight," she called to him frostily. "At least for an hour or so. Naturally you're free to go wherever you like when I get home. But I don't want the kids left alone."

"I don't mind," he said. "I wasn't going anywhere."

Sheila slammed the door of the dishwasher closed and turned it on.

Outside, she shook her head disbelievingly as she headed next door. The woman can't really mean she doesn't know how to clean a house—she's just lonely, Sheila thought. How the hell did I end up doing this? I always say no when someone asks me to have coffee; I don't even let the Avon lady in, for God's sake.

She tramped down the sidewalk and turned in towards Betty's house. She spotted something red sticking out from behind one corner. It was moving. She went closer.

"Heather! Hi! I just wondered what you were." She laughed. "All I could see was a red spot."

52

"It's my jacket," said Heather. She was sprawled face down in the grass, looking up at Sheila over her shoulder.

"What've you got there?" A grey cat lay on its back, all four legs in the air. Sheila could hear it purring. "Oh, isn't he pretty," she said. She rubbed his stomach and the purring grew louder, the paws waved like seaweed under water. Sheila looked at Heather and they smiled.

"His name's Tommy."

"Is he yours?" The cat had turned over and arranged itself sphinxlike, flat face lifted to Heather, eyes half closed.

"No," said Heather, rubbing him under the chin. "I don't know who he belongs to. Are you going to see my mother?"

"Yes, I am," said Sheila, standing up and brushing grass from her slacks. "Is that okay?" She smiled down at Heather.

"Sure. Did she ask you?"

"Yes. I'm invited."

Heather stroked the cat's back. "Well, then," she said.

Sheila went across the lawn to the front porch. She rang the bell.

The house remained silent. She rang the bell again. Still no sounds from within.

"Heather," she began, but Heather and the cat had disappeared.

Sheila glimpsed something moving behind the curtain. She knocked impatiently at the door. It flew open.

"Come in! Come in!" cried Betty.

Sheila went into the hall.

Along its walls were stacks and stacks of newspapers.

"You should tell the school about this," she said.

"About what?"

"The newspapers. They have paper drives. You know. The kids go around the neighbourhood collecting newspapers, and they sell them and use the money to buy extra things for the school." She looked around the hall. "They could make plenty out of all this. And then these papers would be out of your hair."

53

"Oh no. Oh no, I couldn't. I very seldom answer my doorbell. I don't like to give things away."

"Pretty hard to clean your way around stacks of newspapers," said Sheila.

Betty ran into the middle of the living room and stood there, smiling. Sheila followed.

"Are you moving or something?" she asked in surprise.

"Moving? No. No, we're not moving." Betty looked around the room, bewildered.

There was very little furniture. A chesterfield under the window, dark red, almost purple. The cushions sagged and showed their stains defiantly. Large splotches of the indeterminate fabric covering it were worn through, and it was missing one leg, which caused it to lurch drunkenly towards the wall. Against that wall slumped an old card table, dark green, with stacks of comic books piled on top of it.

"Look at this, isn't it pretty?" Betty ran across the room to a blue-and-white-checked hassock covered with a furry material, and she stroked it with both hands.

"It's very pretty, yes," Sheila stammered.

The only other thing in the room was a large ashtray on a stand. And there were drapes at the windows, made of grey, meshlike material, and yellowy-brown carpeting covered the floor.

"Come!" Betty skittered across the empty dining room that connected with the living room and disappeared around the corner into the kitchen.

"Jack sometimes helps me clean this room," she laughed, as Sheila entered.

There was a round wooden table with three wooden chairs, a stove, a refrigerator, and the usual counters and cupboards.

Dirty dishes overflowed the sink and were piled precariously high over every square inch of countertop.

The floor was sticky: grease and dust mixed together in a gluey film that obscured the pattern of the linoleum.

"Personally, I think you should start right here," said Sheila.

"But don't you want to see the rest?" said Betty, standing on one foot and then on the other.

She tore out of the kitchen, down the hall, and up the stairs. Sheila followed, helplessly.

Betty stood at the open bathroom door. Sheila looked in. The rings around the tub were at varying heights. The counters on either side of the sink were cluttered with bottles—hand creams, body creams, deodorants, bath oils, shampoo. My God, thought Sheila, I never would have thought she used all this stuff. Each bottle showed signs of having been handled many times and never wiped off: there were solid streaks of goo on all of them, and most of the labels were almost invisible.

In the medicine chest, which Betty flung open for Sheila's inspection, were many little vials of pills, nail files, tubes of ointments and small bottles of cream, eye shadow, lipsticks—everything crammed in so tightly that when Betty whisked back the glass door half of the contents toppled out and disappeared into the forest of bottles on the counter. Betty laughed gaily and squatted down to open the cupboard doors under the sink. Here were still more bottles, rolls of toilet paper, half-used tubes of toothpaste, large bath sponges, their holes clogged with dust. . . .

"What you should do in here is throw out a whole bunch of stuff. Just throw it out," said Sheila, dazed.

Betty stood up and nodded, soberly, her head going up and down, up and down, and Sheila stared back at her until she could feel her own head start to go up and down, up and down. She noticed a sore on Betty's lip.

"What's next," she said, tearing her eyes away from Betty's face and letting them fall upon the sink, which stared at her sullenly through its grime.

Betty darted back into the hall.

"This is Jack's room, Jack's den," she said breathlessly,

holding open a door. "I don't worry about this room; he likes to care for his things himself. Perhaps just a run-through with a duster, a touch-up with the vacuum cleaner. I have a new one, you know."

Sheila looked inside nervously.

Everything was extremely neat in that room: pens and pencils in a proper holder upon the desk; glass top on the desk shining; leather chair glowing; throw rug a splash of red on the hardwood floor; sofa neat, with blanket and cushion unwrinkled. There was a glass-fronted bookcase, too, which held the only books Sheila had seen in the house so far. The whole room was so clean, so spotless, she felt she was looking through glass at a room in another house altogether.

"That's a very tidy room," she said to Betty. "He should send you off on the business trips and stay home himself to do the housework."

Betty laughed and looked at Sheila appraisingly. "Oh no," she said, smiling slightly. "That would never do. Never." She closed the door to the den, hard, and stood looming in the narrow hallway.

"There's no need for you to see Heather's room," she said thoughtfully, looking Sheila over. "It's just a little girl's room; she hasn't made her bed and there are clothes all over the floor."

She turned and walked to the end of the hall. The door there was closed. She stood with her back to it, hands behind her.

"This," she said slowly, "this is my own room, my very own room." She half turned around, then stopped and turned back to Sheila.

"I don't think you need to see that, either," she said abruptly, and headed down the stairs.

They stood in the middle of the living room. Betty was preoccupied.

"Listen, Betty," said Sheila urgently. "You know what I

think you ought to do? I think you ought to get in a cleaning company. Servicemaster, one of those."

"What for?" said Betty distantly.

"Well, to clean. They've got these machines—they can vacuum out all the dirt from your rugs, and from that chesterfield. They clean them with a really powerful soap. And they can strip all the floors and get them all clean for you. The whole house could be as clean as that den."

Betty stood quietly in the living room, looking around vaguely.

"The thing is, Betty, that this place is pretty dirty. I hate to say it, but it's really terribly dirty. It would be very, very hard for you to get it really clean. Even if I were to help you, I don't think we could do it."

Betty sat down slowly on the blue-and-white hassock and rubbed the sides with her hands.

"If you got those people in, Servicemaster or somebody, to do it for you, then you could manage to keep it clean yourself from then on."

Betty smiled and nodded. "Would you like a cup of tea before you leave?"

"No thanks, I've got to get home." She started to move towards the door. Betty remained on the hassock. "I really think that's the best thing to do. You need professional help in a situation like this."

Betty smiled again. "Yes, it's a good idea, a very good idea. Thank you so much for your kindness."

"I haven't been kind," said Sheila. "I haven't helped you at all, have I?"

Betty smiled and nodded.

"You're not going to get anybody to come in here with a goddam machine, are you?"

Betty stopped smiling, but she didn't speak.

"Betty, my God . . . I'll come over and help you do it. You'll see, between us we'll get the place shining, really we will. . . . "

Betty stood up. "No. We can't get it shining. I know that. Go home now."

Sheila backed towards the door. Betty smiled again. "Go home," she said gently. "Go home."

Sheila went home.

Chapter 9

Sometimes she liked going to see him, Betty thought as she sat down in a black chair by the window in his office. But sometimes going to see him made her need the pills even more—the green headache pills. She wondered if things were planned that way; if he made her have headaches so she would have to take pills, and then she would have to get more, and then she would see Jessup again, and he would give her more headaches. It didn't make any sense. I would stop coming to see this man, she thought, except for Jack. Jack wants me to keep seeing him, so I do.

And sometimes I even like it, she thought again as he came in with a smile and sat behind his desk, holding a folder she knew contained much inaccurate information about her. She smiled back.

"It's good to come here and have someone to talk to," she said, still smiling, and he told her she should have other people to talk to, as well.

She said she did talk to other people—people in the drugstore and the supermarket, sometimes people on the bus. He shook his head.

"That isn't what I mean. I mean you should have friends."

"Well of course I should have friends, everybody should have friends, but that's easier said than done, now, isn't it?

"Jack doesn't bring people home, people he works with. He says he's home so little that when he is in town he just wants to be with Heather and me. Well you can't argue with that, can you? That's a very nice thing to hear. It's very nice indeed that he doesn't want to share his home with other people." She shifted her weight and wondered irritably why chair-makers assumed all people were the same shape.

She had been trying to decide, on the way downtown on the bus, whether to tell him about her new friends. She had not been able to decide. Now she thought, as she gazed at him calculatingly, that he didn't deserve to be told. Not until he had become observant enough to realize that a larger chair was required.

Her irritation with him disappeared. "I don't have anything to say to you today," she said absently, looking out the window and down on the traffic in the street below.

He started to speak; she interrupted, with a sly and sudden smile, to say, "Well—maybe *one* thing." He leaned towards her, and she thought wryly, what kind interest fills his face. "I had a visitor. It was only a cat," she added, holding up her hand to deflect his enthusiasm. "But that's something, isn't it?"

"I suppose it is," he said, smiling. "Do you like animals?"

"I don't normally enjoy unexpected visitors," she went on. She remembered that he always wanted her to talk about things from the past, and thought she could do him that favour today, because to talk about the present without mentioning her neighbours would be difficult. "I remember another unexpected visitor I had once," she began indulgently, and for a fleeting second she felt like her mother. She could remember her mother telling her stories, and here she was about to tell this man, this doctor, a story; and, just for a second, time cracked and she was her mother. She opened her mouth quickly and began.

"It was raining again, but then I never minded that, never minded the rain. It sprinkled down outside endlessly, as though someone had forgotten to turn it all the way off. It would rain like that for days and days in Vancouver, sometimes—absentmindedly, just a little bit, like a mist, a gentle spray, and then with a start, off it would go."

She sneaked a look at him. He was listening. She continued.

She remembered that it was raining that night. She could hear the drops land gently upon the hydrangea leaves, slide gently off, plop onto the mucky soil below. She couldn't actually hear all those separate sounds, but she imagined that she could as she lay curled up on her sofa under the light with a book open. Half reading and half listening to the rain she was, the grey rain falling from a now-black sky, and she realized that she hadn't had any dinner, even though it was already evening. She began to think about what she had in her cupboards, what treats were there for her to munch on as she read, when there was a soft knocking at her door.

She was extremely startled.

At that time she didn't know that she didn't like unexpected guests—she even sometimes secretly hoped to have one—but so far they were something she never ever received.

How did this person know where she lived? How did this person know she was home? Who was it out there, anyway? She wondered all these things in the seconds after she heard the knocking at her door.

Through the square, clouded glass pane in the top of the door she could see only a smudge of a person.

She jumped up and called out, "Who's there?"

"Alan," said a muffled voice.

She was incredulous. The only Alan she knew was Alan the office boy at her work. But what would he be doing there? And what was the proper thing to do? It was raining outside; he would be wet. He would bring wetness into her neat and tidy small apartment. He would bring an entire strange person—himself—into her neat and tidy small apartment. But he knew she was in; he had heard her call out. Now what was she to do? She couldn't leave him outside in the rain.

She went to the door and opened it a crack. "What do you want?"

He stammered when he answered. "Well, j-just to see you, for just a minute."

She was relieved. "All right, for just a minute, then," she said, drawing the door far enough open for him to come in.

He brought with him the sharp scent of the outdoors, musty and green and breathing. Too strong, too raw. It was the rain that did it. The Andrews, who owned the house in which she lived, should have all their back yard in grass, she thought, and none of it dug up for a vegetable garden. That's so old-fashioned, anyway, nobody has vegetable gardens any more, nobody has that raw beating earth lying there all dug up, breathing, exulting, exuding that too-strong smell of earth into the air for people's noses to bump into.

"Come in, come in," she told the boy irritably, as he hung there on the doorstep.

He came in clumsily, showering Betty and half the room with raindrops, mumbling an apology, trying to shed his raincoat. She was horrified. "Just for a minute," he had said, and here he was trying to shed his raincoat in her living room!

"What do you want," she said sharply, and he looked up at her, amazed, from the half-crouch in which he was trying to divest himself of his coat, peering at her ridiculously through glasses getting cloudier by the second, smudged as they were by grime and rain and now vapour. He hunched there awkwardly, one sleeve hanging, and began some jerky movements, trying to decide whether to take the coat all the way off, or put it back on while at the same time pretending he'd never meant to take it off in the first place.

"I j-just wanted to ask you something."

She thought of offering him some tea, but she didn't. She wanted to be alone again. The surprise of his visit had left her; she realized as she stared at him that she had hoped he might be someone else. She didn't know who. Seeing him there in her living room wasn't interesting at all. He was as dull in her living room as he was in her office. She wanted him gone.

"What?" she demanded. "What do you want to ask me?"

She was becoming quite irritated. He really was quite irritating, standing there dripping all over her carpet, one sleeve hanging embarrassed from his shiny coat, glasses all smudged, ears sticking out, brushcut hair gleaming, scalp beneath gleaming too, ugh, he was ugly, ugly, pimples all over his nose; she just wanted him out,

out, to let her settle back down on her sofa, reading and eating and listening to the rain.

"If you'll go out," he blurted.

"Out? Out where?"

"Out with me?"

"Don't be silly, it's raining."

"No, not n-now, I mean another t-time—to a movie, or a restaurant, or someplace."

By now he was red all over his face and down his neck. It was a most unpleasant sight. Betty couldn't believe that this person was asking her for a date.

"A date? A date? Is that what you mean? A date?"

"Y-yes, a date, yes," he said, nodding his head vigorously, trying to move it so quickly through the air that she could not see his face's colour.

"I don't think so," she began. She wanted to try not to hurt his feelings. Then she saw hope in him because she had spoken tentatively, and she was enraged, and felt trapped. There was only one way to get out of her tiny apartment and he was blocking it with his skinny awkwardness. Why should she feel trapped in her own apartment?

"No," she said firmly. "No!" she shouted. "I do not want to have a date with you! Go home!"

She groped behind him and found the handle of the door and flung it open, inward. It almost struck him and he moved quickly aside, nearly knocking over a vase of flowers she had placed on a small table to the side of the door—flowers to be appreciated by Betty and whatever unexpected guests might arrive, flowers which he had not even noticed.

He backed out through the door, making sounds of some kind, and quickly she slammed it closed behind him. She locked it, too, for good measure. She leaned against the door, listening to him stumble along the gravelled path that led to the side of the house and around it to the street. She listened until his footsteps had dissolved in the sounds of the rain.

"I thought about telling the other girls at the office about it," Betty said to the doctor. "I thought about how we would laugh together.

"This was the first time he had asked to date me.

"I decided not to tell the others. He never asked me again, of course. I was glad of that.

"He never talked to me again at work, either."

Betty drew a long breath.

"Did you have a telephone in your apartment?" said the doctor.

"What?"

"A telephone. Did your apartment have one?"

Betty glared at him from beneath her brows. "Oh yes," she said grimly. "It had a telephone, all right. A black one."

"Then why do you suppose he went to see you, instead of phoning?"

"I don't know," she said. "I don't know why he came to see me, for heaven's sake how should I know."

"Maybe he thought it was important to talk to people face to face."

Betty sniffed and adjusted her handbag in her lap.

"It's hard, sometimes, to visit people. To go places."

She gave him a small smile. "Yes. But it can be done."

"Yes, it can, Betty. It can," he said, pleased. "Do you think, for example, that you could go to a meeting at the school? I mean, after the summer holidays are over, of course."

Betty grew still. Rush, rush, rush, she thought precisely. She looked at Jessup coolly. There are not many clever people in the world, she thought.

She saw herself putting on her good blue dress and her good blue coat and walking to the school, into the auditorium, where there would be crowds of mothers and fathers—walking in there and watching all the heads turn around to see her. She would pretend not to notice, but she would notice. And there would be no more seats left, all the chairs would be filled. She would have to stand there inside an empty space at the back of the auditorium while everyone looked at her with foreign faces. She couldn't do that. There would be no point, no point.

She said some of this to the doctor, impatiently.

"Why would it have to happen like that?"

"Because I would have to go *alone*, without *Jack*. That's just the way it would *happen*."

Her time was up. She wished it had ended earlier. She gathered her handbag into her arms and wrenched herself from the chair. She was depressed now, and angry with the doctor. She mumbled goodbye and hurried out of his office and through the waiting room, feet scuffling quickly towards the elevator.

On the bus she thought hard about her new friends. She might already have lost one of them. She knew that, and was dismayed.

She had not seen Sheila for a long time. When Sheila came to her house, the children were still in school. Now the days were midsummer hot and she had not seen Sheila again. Oh, she'd seen her—seen her bustle out to her garden wearing shorts. Once Betty even ran outside onto her front porch and called, "Helloo!" and Sheila had stopped weeding and looked over and said hello back. But that was all.

It was so stupid, such a stupid thing to do! Betty scolded herself. I don't know why I did it, except that's what makes Jack angry, the house being dirty. As soon as I had asked her to help me, I wished I hadn't.

But Sheila had really tried to help her, Betty realized. It wasn't her fault that she had expected Betty's house to be like her own, only maybe a tiny bit dirtier. Betty had tried to warn her, but it wasn't Sheila's fault if she had misunderstood.

She looked around the bus at the people sitting near her.

She would visit Sheila again. Yes, that's what she would do.

She smiled at the people on the bus, showing them her crooked teeth.

Chapter
10

Bertha got to the door as quickly as she could because she didn't like them to know that she couldn't move around well. She knew how foolish that was. They could see perfectly clearly that she couldn't move around well.

When they were in the hall she put up her cheeks to be kissed, the right one by Arlene, the left one by Bob. Then she rubbed her hands together cheerfully and ushered them into the living room, following after them slowly, not allowing pain in her face.

"Oh Mother," Arlene sighed.

"Same mess as always," said Bertha. "Clear something off and sit yourselves down," she said, lowering herself carefully into her chair.

Arlene's perfume filled the room. Bertha refrained from coughing. I wonder if that girl owns any slacks at all, she thought, observing Arlene's tightly fitting green dress. She wore high-heeled shoes, which Bertha thought ridiculous, and eyeglasses with rhinestones embedded in the frames. Her red hair—not auburn, but red—was done up in curls, as usual, and she wore a great deal of makeup. She outfits herself, thought Bertha, as though she thinks there's something in particular she ought to look like.

"I see you've had the lawn cut," said Bob.

Oh my goodness, I've done it again, thought Bertha. "A little boy did it. He lives across the street and down a bit. He charges a quarter for the front and a quarter for the back and it's worth it, let me tell you."

"I could have come and done it for you. I was going to."

"I know, I know. I'll call you next time it needs it. Promise." She winked at Arlene, who smiled back indecisively. "Bob, go get us some sherry from the china cabinet."

66

Every time they came she was more nervous. As if they came to inspect her, not to visit.

"See my new dress there?" she said to Arlene, pointing to the table beside the sewing maching. Pieces of a pattern were pinned to some pink fabric. Bob edged himself next to his wife on the loveseat and put the sherry and the glasses on the coffee table.

"It's going to be beautiful, Mother."

"Yes, I'm a pretty good sewer. When you two decide to have a baby I'll have a grand old time, sewing and knitting."

"Oh Mother," said Arlene, embarrassed.

"I'm not trying to rush you. Just want you to keep it in mind."

"So how are you getting along, Ma?" said Bob, passing out the glasses. His tall, heavy body was thrust into blue jeans and a light sweater. They look a most unlikely couple, thought Bertha.

"Me? Just fine, like always." She noticed that her heart was speeding up. "Busy, of course, what with the garden and my sewing and all."

"Seen any of your friends lately?"

"You know perfectly well that most of my so-called friends have died or moved away." I've got a tongue just a little faster than is good for me, she thought. She hurried on, before they could jump in with all four feet. "But as a matter of fact I've made a new one. Very interesting woman. Lives right next door."

"And how's your hip?" said Arlene, too bluntly for Bertha's taste.

"No better, no worse. I've got some painkillers when I need them."

"I worry about you, Ma," said Bob heavily. "We both do."

He looks just like his father, thought Bertha. Same brown eyes, same thick dark hair—though Sam's wasn't dark when he died.

"I know you do, Bob," she said, wanting to pat his hand but afraid to try reaching over that far. "I'll let you know if I get worse. I promised I would, and I will."

"It's the winter we worry about." Arlene took off her rhinestone glasses and held them in her lap. There were lines in her forehead.

"My goodness, child, if that isn't silly," said Bertha. "Here it is only July and you're worrying about the winter!

"Let me tell you something." She rested her head on the back of her chair and looked out the window across the room. The lilacs were long over, but the sweet peas were coming up in the back yard; she wished she had some in the front, too. "Being old, like me, is kind of like being real young. When it comes to time. A young girl or boy on the first day of summer holidays just can't see to September, the summer stretches out so long, so far ahead. That's the way I am." She raised her head. "It's July, and I'm living in July, and I'll be damned if I'll think ahead as far as November."

"You're right, Mother," said Arlene after a minute. She put her glasses back on and hugged Bob's arm. "She's right, hon."

"How about some more sherry?" Bob shrugged and smiled.

Betty pulled back her living-room curtain and stared at the car sitting in the street in front of Bertha's house. It was a small yellow one. She had seen two people get out of it and walk straight up to Bertha's door. Betty knew they must be Bertha's son and his wife.

They were not small people, and she wondered how they fit themselves into that little car. After all, she had trouble even fitting into her house, sometimes.

She was tired of lying on her bed and had come downstairs, and now she stood restless on her front porch, looking up and down the block. From somewhere not far away she heard the harsh whine of a lawnmower. She looked down at the grass in her front yard. It was time that Jack came home again, to cut it. Perhaps he would clean the kitchen again, too. She laughed, then grew sullen, remembering that she had planned to do that herself.

She did not want to go to the shopping centre. Sometimes she knocked things off the shelves, and people turned to stare at her.

She could not visit Sheila. It was Saturday, and her husband would be home.

It was too late in the day to walk up and down the streets and alleys looking for things. She only did that in the early mornings, when no one else was about.

There must be somewhere she could go!

Of course there was! Betty laughed happily. She would go next door to Bertha's house and meet her children! Perhaps Bertha would offer her tea, and maybe even play the piano.

She went to Bertha's door and pushed the buzzer with her thumb.

Bertha struggled up from her chair. She pushed down on the arms with both hands and hoisted herself up using her left leg; the right one she held out awkwardly in as straight a line as possible. Bob and Arlene watched as her eyes squeezed shut with the effort. Arlene pressed her hands into her lap and forced herself to remain seated. Bob was halfway out of the loveseat when she poked him. He sat back down. Bertha lurched to her feet, grinned at them in triumph, and limped towards the front door.

"She's getting worse," said Arlene wearily. "She is."

"But she'll be all right until winter," said Bob grimly. "Sure."

"My goodness," said Bertha at the door. "Hello!" Bob and Arlene looked.

A figure loomed in the doorway, not much taller than their mother but a great deal bigger around. It advanced into the hall. Its head peeked around the beaded curtain that partially separated the hall from the living room. Bertha had made the curtain.

"This must be your family!" said Betty.

The head is too small for the body, Bob thought. So are the hands and the feet.

Betty lumbered into the living room. She bent down and, with her hands on her knees, peered intently at the faces of Bob and Arlene. Bob made a move to get up but subsided when he realized that she was not going to move and that their heads would crack together if he stood. He felt uncomfortable and annoyed as the woman stared at him, light-coloured hair askew all over her head, nose shining, a smudge of something on one of her cheeks.

"This must be your son and his wife," she said triumphantly.

Bertha came into the room behind her. "That's them," she said shortly. "That's Bob, and that's Arlene. This is Betty Coutts."

Betty straightened up. "I live next door!"

"This is your new friend, Ma?" Bob said doubtfully.

"This is her," said Bertha.

"Arlene!" said Betty loudly. Arlene said nothing as Betty leaned down, gazing at her intently. She was afraid the woman would lose her balance and topple onto her, crushing her and getting sweat all over her.

"What pretty glasses!" said Betty, reaching out to touch them. Arlene flinched.

Betty whirled around and went to stand beside Bertha. "They are a very nice-looking couple," she said. "All grown up. That's lucky. It's too bad," she said merrily, "that you have to wait until you get old to have grown-up children."

Bertha sniffed.

"What are you having?" said Betty, brightly, as her eyes came to rest on the sherry.

"Sherry," said Bertha. There was a small silence. "Do you want some?"

"Oh no, I don't think so," said Betty. She smiled at the three of them. "Do you have any tea? Some tea would be very nice."

"Go get her some tea, Arlene," said Bertha. "Come on, come on, sit yourself down."

Betty sat down heavily on the loveseat, beside Bob. Arlene disappeared around the corner and a loud clattering began.

"Now isn't this nice," said Betty, her feet together, hands primly on her knees. "I was feeling a bit lonely over there, so I thought, Why don't you go over and say hello to your friend Bertha? I thought, and so I did."

"Bertha?" said Bob.

Betty looked at him inquiringly. "Your mother. Bertha."

"She's given me a new name," said Bertha.

"Bertha?" Bob looked at her.

"Stop repeating yourself, Bob, for heaven's sake. Bertha. That's what she said. Bertha. I like it."

Arlene came in and handed Betty a cup of tea. She sat on the piano bench.

"Thank you so much; that was so kind of you." said Betty, and began sipping. "We agreed, didn't we, Bertha, that that is such a ridiculous name—Poinsettia, really!—it didn't suit her at all, and I said I refused to call her that and I asked her what she would like her name to be and she said Bertha. That was when we first met."

"But you can't change a person's name, just like that," said Arlene, bewildered.

"Of course you can," said Bertha, trying to look at Arlene over her shoulder. "Move that bench around here where I can see you. A person's got a right to call herself anything she pleases. Or to call anybody else anything she pleases, for that matter. Now Arlene, for instance, happens to suit you. But if it didn't, well then, I might call you something else." She grinned.

Betty put her cup down. "It's time for me to go now,"

71

she said, getting up. "I was going to ask you to play the piano for me, but I see that she is sitting on the piano bench, so I will wait until the next time I come."

Arlene jumped to her feet, but Bertha motioned her to sit down again.

"That's just fine, Betty. Next time. Can you find your way to the door all right? I don't feel like getting up again just now."

"I'll see her out, Ma," said Bob.

"My gosh!" said Arlene when Betty had left. "That is the strangest woman I ever met!"

"Is she all right, Ma?" said Bob. "I mean, is she always like that?"

"Like what?" said Bertha. She looked at their shocked faces. "Well, she is a bit strange, I guess. But interesting. Very interesting. Like I told you." They remained doubtful. "I like her," said Bertha firmly. At least, she thought, I hope I do.

Bob shook his head. "She's probably up and down like a yo-yo," he said glumly. "I just hope she keeps to herself when she's down."

"I am perfectly capable of sending her away if I don't want to see her," said Bertha.

"But, giving you a new *name*!" said Arlene.

"You've got to admit," said Bertha with a grin, "it is an improvement." She winked at them.

Chapter 11

Sheila hurried home from work, went straight to the telephone in the bedroom, and called her mother in Saskatoon.

"Mom? Listen, I've got to talk to you. Have you got a few minutes? Can you just sit down and light a cigarette and listen to me for a few minutes?"

"Of course, Sheila, what's wrong? Is it one of the children? Ed?"

"It's Ed. Nothing's wrong with him, I don't mean that. I mean . . . " She rubbed her head, sat on the bed.

"He's been screwing around, Mom. Ed has. Mom, what should I do?" A mother's presence hummed across the telephone wires and Sheila began to sob. "Ten years, Mom, and he comes to me and says he's been sleeping with some broad. What the hell do I do, Mom? What do I do?" Tears flooded her face and she reached blindly for a Kleenex to sop them up.

"My God. Sheila. I can't believe it. Sheila? Calm down! Calm down or we can't talk, can we? How serious is it?"

"How serious? How serious? I just *told* you, Mom, he's been *sleeping* with her! That's how serious it is!"

Mrs. Pennington lit a cigarette as she cradled the telephone receiver into her shoulder. She took a long puff.

"I know, Sheila, I understand that," she said, worried. "But does he . . . love her, does he say? Or is it just . . . a casual thing?"

"Mother!" Sheila shouted into the telephone. "How can it possibly be *casual*! What could be casual about tearing off all your clothes and jumping into bed with someone for the purpose of sexual intercourse!"

She took a deep breath. "Listen, Mother, I know what

73

you mean. Yes, I suppose it's casual. He says he's broken it off."

"Oh, Sheila, dear. I know this is very difficult for you, but if it's not serious, then your marriage is not in danger, dear. You get over something like this—like it's the flu, dear. Look at it that way. I know Ed would never do anything to hurt you. . . . "

"Well what the hell do you call this, then?" she shouted into the phone. "Just what the hell do you call this? It's been two months since he told me and still everywhere I go, everything I do, I keep imagining him in bed with that . . . with that *tart*, whoever the hell she is. It's not a goddam bit like the goddam flu, I feel like my insides are being torn out!"

"I know, dear, I know how much it must pain you. But I meant that your marriage is just as important, just as precious to Ed as it is to you. I see every time I see you together how very much he loves you, Sheila. You must know that, too, my dear." Mrs. Pennington thought about offering to fly out to Calgary. She discarded the idea. They would be much better off working things out between them.

"I don't think you understand yet, Mom," said Sheila dully. "What I'm trying to do is decide what to do. Whether to leave him, or what. I keep thinking about dividing up the stuff here, that sort of thing. Who'd get the house? The kids? I know some people I could ask to recommend a lawyer. But I don't do anything. I just get mad, and then depressed, and then mad again; and through it all I hate him, Mom. I hate him. I can't live with someone I hate."

"What people?" Mrs. Pennington asked sharply. "Divorced people?"

"What the hell difference does it make?"

"It doesn't make any difference, I suppose. Except that divorced people might . . . well, they might be inclined to encourage you in that direction, and I really think that would be a tragic, a terrible mistake, Sheila. You and Ed have so much together. You've been so happy for so long, dear. And then there are the children, aren't there? What would you do about the children? Oh Sheila," said Mrs. Pennington, "how could you possibly explain it to the children?"

"I'd just tell them I hate their father and can't live with him any more because he's been screwing another woman." Sheila crumpled on the bed and began sobbing again. She had been astounded to discover how quickly her body could manufacture more tears. Even faster than that sonofabitch can make more sperm, she thought with a spasm of pain, wondering how often he'd been in somebody else's bed in the afternoon and hers at night, servicing them both with equal glee.

But it wasn't equal, she thought wearily, for the hundredth time. Hadn't they made love, she and Ed, less frequently in the past year or so? Certainly they hadn't done anything at all since he'd told her. She couldn't bear to have him touch her. . . . But had he become gradually less interested in her, sexually? He must have; otherwise why would he wander off to look for someone else?

She'd lost her sexuality. She'd known it for months now. It had oozed out of her and vanished. And here she sat, a huddled shell of a woman who would never again appeal to anybody. She was mortified, and terror-stricken. She was only thirty-four!

Her sobbing intensified, and she realized her mother was trying to make herself heard through the din. Sheila took another handful of Kleenex and pressed it to her face until the tears stopped.

"Sheila? Sheila? Are you still there? Sheila!"

"I'm sorry, Mom. I'm just so upset." She took a deep breath. "Oh Mom, I wish you were here!"

"Don't you have any friends you can talk to about this, Sheila?" Mrs. Pennington asked gently. "I feel so far away. And what about a holiday?" she said hopefully.

"Are you going away on a holiday? That might be such a good idea, dear. Perhaps you and Ed can work things out if you get away together. I'd be happy to take the children, dear, you know that. Sheila?" There was no response.

"Oh, Sheila," said her mother despairingly. "It's hard for you to believe, I know, but really, this thing isn't very important. Ed loves you and the children and wants you to stay together, that's what's important." She strained her ear to the receiver and shook her head impatiently. "Sheila. Remember, Sheila, that he broke it off with that woman—and he told you about it."

"Why, Mom?" Sheila wailed into the phone, which was salty wet and getting hard to hold on to. "Why did he tell me? Why didn't he just break it off and say nothing? I didn't know what was going on! I would *never* have known, if he hadn't told me!"

"I don't know, Sheila," said her mother, tired. "Why don't you ask him?"

There was another pause. Mrs. Pennington let it hum.

"Maybe I will. Maybe I'll just do that. But I can't talk to any of my friends, Mom. Christ, I'm humiliated. I just can't let any of my friends know about this; I'd die if they found out. They think Ed and I have such a happy marriage. . . . " Tears began to flow again.

"And no, we're not going away on a holiday. I don't want to go anywhere with that goddam . . . I'm working and the kids are going to day camp and Ed's teaching summer school and oh Christ it's such a lousy summer!" She blew her nose furiously. "Listen, Mom, I'd better go. Thanks. You've been a big help."

"I don't think I've been much of a help at all," said Mrs. Pennington uneasily. "I want you to phone me again, Sheila. Or I'll call you. I'm worrying about you."

"Yeah, okay Mom, thanks. Don't worry. I'm gonna go now. I love you, Mom."

"And I love you. Goodbye, dear. Good luck!"

"Yeah. 'Bye, Mom."

She hung up the phone and blew her nose again.

She thought about starting dinner but saw from the clock radio that it was much too early. Nobody else would be home for a couple of hours.

She looked vaguely around the bedroom, thought vaguely about watering the plant, and then lay down on the bed.

She was exhausted. Her shoes hurt. She kicked them off. Her underwear felt like chains around her bust and waist and thighs. She squirmed around, trying to get comfortable. Gradually she let herself settle into the bed and heard the buzz of summer and watched the curtain blow gently in the light wind from the open window. She'd make a cold dinner, she thought fuzzily. It was too hot to turn on the oven.

She heard her instincts again. She was getting very tired of them. They wanted her either to get out and never see him again, or to have an affair. She'd gone all through it before, dozens of times. She tried to imagine herself packing up and leaving, ignoring the tear-stained faces of her shattered children as she loaded suitcases into a taxi and left—for where? That's where that fantasy came to a shuddering halt, every time. Where would she go? She tossed restlessly on the bed and, staring at the ceiling, worked her way through Fantasy Number Two. An Affair.

She went down the list of all the men she knew. The only one who appealed to her at all was her doctor, who, of course, was forbidden. She thought about the professors in the English department, where she worked. One had dandruff. One had skin like the inside of a fish. One was fat and perpetually wiped his face with a huge grey handkerchief. One, she was sure, was gay. One smoked a pipe and even in the summer wore jackets with leather patches on the elbows. He thought he was extremely sexy. Maybe he was, to some of his students. Sheila thought he was funny.

Oh Christ, she thought, abandoning the list halfway through it. There's no one. Not a single bloody one! And besides, even if I did want to go to bed with somebody, who says he'd want to go to bed with me?

She threw herself around, wished she smoked, propped her head up on one elbow, and stared towards the window. Out there are a whole lot of men, she told herself. Some of them are sure to want to go to bed with me.

She jumped up and went over to the full-length mirror on the back of the closet door. She stared critically into it. Five feet six inches tall; curly brown hair; brown eyes; getting a little lined in the face, but that's all right, she thought defiantly, that's character—Christ, am I going to have a lot of character by the time this is all over; getting a little thick around the waist, but not very damned much. She pulled in her stomach muscles. That's better, she observed with satisfaction. Then she watched her eyes fill once more with tears.

She turned away from the mirror and looked helplessly around the room. She snatched up her handbag, shoved her feet into her shoes, and ran for the front door.

Outside, she strode purposefully down the street in the direction of the shopping centre.

Sheila did not eat her dinner. When she got up to take her plate into the kitchen, her meatloaf was still on it, and the potatoes and the broccoli, too. It made her sick to look at it.

"Hey, Mom! You make us eat *our* dinner." Gravy outlined the edges of Peter's mouth.

"I'm not hungry. Besides, I've stopped growing and you haven't."

"Be quiet and eat, Peter," said Ed.

Sheila got her handbag and fished out a package of cigarettes and a book of matches. She opened the cupboard and took out an ashtray. She sat back down at the table and began, casually, to open the cigarettes.

"What the hell are you doing?" said Ed.

"What does it look like I'm doing? I'm going to have a cigarette." She got one out, put it between her lips, struck the match, held the match to the end of the cigarette, and began to puff, energetically.

"I can see that," said Ed. "But *why* are you having a cigarette? You don't smoke."

Sheila coughed.

"You'll choke to death, for God's sake!"

"It will be a little difficult," she said, with some effort. "But I'm sure I can do it. A lot of people have learned to smoke." She coughed again, took another drag on the cigarette—more cautiously this time. "I'm sure I can learn, too. I bet I could learn how to do all sorts of things, if I tried." She puffed again, and gazed calmly around the dinner table, where three pairs of eyes stared at her in horror.

"Mommy, it's dangerous," said Shelley. "You can get lung cancer and die from that."

"Mommy!" yelled Peter, shooting up from the table and knocking his chair over. "Mommy! Don't!"

"Oh, for Christ's sake," said Ed disgustedly, and left the table for the television room.

Sheila stubbed out her cigarette hurriedly and calmed the children.

"Smoking a few cigarettes a day doesn't give anybody lung cancer." They looked at her doubtfully. "Good grief, everybody knows you have to smoke a whole package of the damn things, or two packages, every single day for years and years and years before you're in any danger of getting lung cancer."

"I'll ask my teacher at camp tomorrow," said Shelley.

"You do that," Sheila snapped. "Besides," she said more gently, "even if a person has smoked a lot for years and years, if that person stops smoking, then after a while the lungs are all clean again and it's as though you never smoked at all. I've read that. It's true."

"But if you never *start*," said Peter earnestly, "if you never *start*, in the *first* place, then your lungs *never* get dirty and you *never* have to wait for them to be clean again."

"Yeah, well . . . don't worry about it."

Ed stayed in the television room while she tidied the kitchen and waited until it was the children's bedtime. He put them to bed. She was watching television and smoking her second cigarette when he joined her.

"Why are you doing that, Sheila? It's stupid."

"I know it. Maybe that's why I'm doing it."

"It doesn't make any sense to do something that could hurt you," he said rationally, sitting on the couch beside her.

"It doesn't make any sense to do something that could hurt someone else, either. But you did that." Her hands were cold. She resolved not to crack up this time, no matter what.

Ed leaned against the back of the couch. "I didn't do it to hurt you." He sat up and reached to take her in his arms, then jumped back. "Put that damn thing out, will you?"

Sheila put it out. She sat tensely, hands folded in her lap. The summer sun was browning him even though he spent most of his days indoors. His teeth looked whiter. There was grey in his hair, she noted with satisfaction. But there had been grey in his hair for years. It made him look younger, not older. She looked at him carefully. He was still in pretty good shape. Still had the cleft in his chin. His smile still flashed, delightedly, as though surprising him.

Not that he was smiling now. He looked grim just now. Hadn't smiled in quite a while, except sometimes at the children. Let's face it, she thought, the bastard still gets you all hot and bothered just sitting there glaring at you. Oh for Christ's sake. There are other men, lots of other men, millions of them. They all must have the strength beneath the skin that makes you shiver, the alien feel of flatness, of slumbering muscles—well, not all of them, some of them are skinnier than I am, and pasty white or pop-eyed, or they have bellies that plop around obscenely over their belts. But some of them, young or well cared for, they must have that spring in them—the thing that's different—the lines and slopes and hollows and thrusts that fit so well with the body I live in. . . .

"There was none of that crap about my wife not understanding me."

"Good."

"I like being married. I like being married to you."

"Good."

"I like the way we live together. I like the way we fuck together."

A buzzing started in her stomach. "Fucked."

He looked at her, his mouth half open, thinking.

"Fucked. Past tense," she said to him.

"What's that supposed to mean?"

"We haven't done it lately. Won't do it again. Probably."

"Oh Christ." He got up and started walking around the room. "You're going to punish me, is that it?"

"I just can't."

"Can't what?"

"Can't . . . sleep with you. Every time I think about it I think about that tart how did you do it how did you end up in her bed for Christ's sake that's all I can think about."

"Sheila. Oh shit." He sat down on a chair and rubbed his face. "Oh shit. I noticed her. She was pretty. She has the kind of body, the kind of walk . . . I got her a cup of coffee in the staff room one day. I touched her hand." He looked up at Sheila. She saw the misery in his eyes, but that only made it worse. "I wanted to sleep with her. And she wanted it too. So we did."

"And how was it?"

"It was okay. It was different," he said quietly. He

turned away, but she could feel him moving through the air towards her.

"Different. What? What did she do that was different?"

"Not like that, Christ, not different, I mean, not *you*."

"How old is she?"

"Oh for God's sake. Not *better*, not *younger*, I don't give a shit about all that, I just got horny for her for Christ's sake so we did it but I didn't want it to go on I tried to stop but for a long time I couldn't stop," he said loudly, walking around the room again.

"Why did you tell me about it?"

The television special was still going on. It was about Jane Goodall and how she lived alone in the jungle with the apes.

He sat down and looked at her. What do I want to see there, she wondered. Repentance? Not there. Guilt? Not there. Sorrow? A little bit, maybe. But mostly there's anger.

"Why are you angry with me?"

"I'm not angry with you! I'm just trying to get through to you! I love you, for Christ's sake!"

"Love me love me shit you love me, you sure kept it a secret all right while you were doing it, didn't you, you sure kept it a secret while you were screwing around with that broad, didn't you?"

"I told you, I didn't want to tell you about it while it was still going on. I couldn't tell you until it was all over with, goddam it!"

"I bet you slept with her and me on the same day sometimes didn't you? Didn't you?"

"I haven't slept with you since it started," he said.

"You bastard." A hot, searing pain started from the inside and worked its way through her body like a frantic flame. But her hands were cold. Pictures popped into her head. Blonde hair, a fat ass, big juicy boobs, all the things Sheila didn't have, and she was probably totally free, too, about ten years younger than Sheila with lots of affairs before this one and lots and lots of fun in bed she probably had *The Joy of Sex* in her bookcase and tried out everything she could first alone, to practise, as much as that was possible, and then with Ed, oh Christ, she squeezed her eyes tight to try to shatter the pictures but they kept coming, faster and faster, glimpses of unfamiliar breasts big and firm with huge nipples, and blonde hair sprawling around her crotch and legs outspread and sweat on her forehead and Ed there, too, Ed's cock big and twitching to get in, Ed's face buried in those breasts his cock coming closer and closer to that coarse blonde hair between the wide-open legs—she shot up and shook her head.

"I won't listen to you any more. I won't listen. I'm getting out of here." She started for the stairs. Ed caught her and turned her around and forced her back into the chair. She kicked at him and kept her eyes shut because she didn't want to see him watching her cry, her face all screwed up with pain and hate.

"Let me go you sonofabitch I hate you, don't you know that? I'll hate you until the day I die let me go." She felt that she was shouting but she knew she wasn't.

"God damn you Sheila I will not let you go! Stop fighting me, stop it and listen!"

"I won't listen to you, you slug, I won't listen to another word, let me go you're hurting me!"

They kept wrestling, and Sheila's long-held belief that if you were angry enough, had enough adrenalin going for you, you could do anything, move mountains, died a protesting death.

"Who the hell do you think you are," she panted, flinging her eyes open. "You are no phys-ed teacher you teach math for Christ's sake let me *go*!"

At least he was sweating, she thought as she stared into his grim face. She tried again, pulling up all her strength and flailing out with arms and legs, but he had her arms tight in his hands and he didn't seem to feel her feet kicking him. I should have my goddam shoes on, she thought.

"Don't hate me, Sheila," he said when she subsided, breathing fast. "Please don't hate me. If you can't understand, okay, you can't understand. But don't hate me. I could never, ever, hate you. I could never do anything but love you. I know I hurt you, for God's sake I know it. But that doesn't mean I don't love you."

He let go of her. He dug a handkerchief out of his pocket and handed it to her. She wiped her face. She wanted to disappear.

He got up, wincing, and sat in another chair. He reached over and turned off the television set.

Her arms stung.

He came over to her and took hold of her hands and pulled her to her feet. She let him put his arms around her. She looked bleakly over his shoulder at the wall, the lower half of which was made of cork and covered with children's drawings and things they had cut out of magazines. There was a photograph of a Caterpillar tractor and its driver. Pictures of animals.

"Sheila. Let's start again."

From here? she thought. How can you start from halfway through. Her arms went around his waist, loosely.

"Do you remember the time at the lake, Sheila?" he said softly. "It was the first time we met, remember? I took you out there and you said you wouldn't let me make love to you, not all the way, remember?"

She nodded, staring at a picture of a horse and its colt.

"I wanted you so badly I hurt, but I was a very good boy."

"Yeah, sure," she said, remembering.

He was stroking her back. She remembered the moonlight silver on his skin and the shudders in her as she looked at him naked above his jeans, jeans hanging on his hips, jeans swollen in the front, silver skin, his hands under her sweater roughly on her breasts.

"I didn't do anything you didn't want me to do. Did I?" His hands were moving down her back, slowly, softly down her back to her buttocks, taking gentle handfuls of her buttocks, squeezing, letting go. . . .

I'm just hungry, that's all, she told herself. A person can starve . . .

"Let's go upstairs, Sheila," he said, and she went with him up to their bedroom.

She began to take off her clothes but he was there, brushing her hands aside. He unbuttoned her sweater and took it off and his lips took the nipples of her breasts, one at a time, into his mouth, through her brassiere. She quivered and closed her eyes and reached out for him, but he brushed her hands away again and undid the button and the zipper on her skirt band and let her skirt drop to the floor. He knelt in front of her and rubbed his mouth across her belly, through her pantihose, and down to her thighs, rubbing his mouth on the inside of one thigh and then the other as she stood beginning to shudder and sway above him. His lips came closer to the centre of her and his tongue darted out and her knees let go. He sat her on the side of the bed and stripped the pantihose from her body and pulled them from her feet. He unhooked her brassiere and took it off. He knelt in front of her again and with only his mouth touched her shoulders and neck and breasts and belly and she shook inside, her insides turned themselves outward and cried. He stood up and took off his sweatshirt and his jeans. She watched his chest, still broad, still hard, and his belly, slightly round now above a waist that didn't dip inward as much as it had that night at the lake—she watched as these things were revealed to her. He took off his jeans. She heard the belt and saw it being unbuckled as she had that night, and she heard and saw the zipper unzipped as she had that night, but she didn't run away this time, her insides crying at her in anger; she didn't run, she waited, and the jeans came off and the bumpy shorts came off and there was his cock, straight out and swollen. She lay back on the bed and opened her arms and that body laid itself down atop her own and they were like two halves together—except it was different; it was like having a stranger there. They groped at each other in desperation; they sucked and kissed. Sheila felt him gobbling her, moaning, hands raking her body as his mouth buried itself in her breasts, her hair, her ears, her belly, her crotch, and she felt him in her mouth, and she didn't know if all this was happening at the same time or if they were taking turns. Her body was thirsty for his mouth, her mouth couldn't get enough of his body; then she felt him slide into her and she grabbed him. . . .

They lay sweaty and panting in the darkness. After a while she stroked his hair. They lay there longer, until the air was cool on them, and she saw the crumpled heaps of their clothing on the floor and the disordered bed and arms and legs flung out upon it.

"Hot damn," said Ed, the words muffled, his face pressed into the bedspread and against her side. "Hot damn."

She kissed him on the neck. His skin smelled like popcorn.

Sheila looked up at the ceiling and thought about things.

Chapter
12

She opened the door and there he was.

He hadn't returned through all those months and now, in autumn, there he was. She was very glad to see him.

"Come in, come in," she said, and in the kitchen she gave him some water.

He had to walk all around the house again, to reorient himself. He explored the rooms he liked and looked cautiously into the others. Then he went to the basement door and stared at the knob until she opened it, and he padded down the stairs.

She didn't go with him. She didn't like the basement. It was filled with things she did not like.

Soon he came back up, and there was dust on his whiskers and on the fur on the top of his head. Betty was frightened at the sly look in his eyes. She was shocked, to feel even a second's fear at a small, harmless cat. But he had gone down there, alone and curious, and he knew why she had not followed.

But then that look was gone, and he sat down and licked his paw, and with the paw he cleaned the dust from his whiskers and the top of his head. She had been going to do that for him, until she saw the look in his eyes.

She followed him into the living room, where he sat down and began cleaning himself all over. She sat on the carpet and watched him. He looked at her sometimes, with his steady green look, and she felt that they were friends. A cat was as good a friend as any other, she thought; better than some.

She had tried to tell Heather about the cat but

Heather just looked bored, which was strange because she had always liked animals. She had always wanted a pet, but Jack wouldn't have it. Betty had always said she didn't want one, either. She didn't know anything about animals, how to feed them or care for them. And they would meow and yowl, cats; and dogs would bark and jump about, which she did not like either.

This cat was different because he did not live there, he only visited. Someone else fed him and cared for him. He just came to visit.

She talked to the cat. She sat on the floor while he had his water and she had her tea, and she talked to him about many things.

I drink so clumsily, she thought, lifting the cup to my mouth and slurping and putting the cup back down on the saucer. All he has to do is flick his tongue in and out of the water, sometimes raising his great green eyes to stare at me. She tried to drink her tea from a bowl, as he drank his water, but her tongue wasn't made properly. The tea dribbled down her chin and splashed out of the bowl, and the cat looked at her and smiled.

Of course, she thought, I can do things which he cannot do, too—with my hands.

She stretched out her hand towards him and felt his electricity again. He was filled with it. She wondered what would happen if she plugged the toaster into his mouth and pushed down the little bar that made the bread descend between the red coils. She took her hand away and the electricity spilled out of him; but when she put her hand near him again, again the electricity filled him. She admired that. He is a lucky cat, she thought.

She tried to play with the cat. She found an old ball of Heather's and rolled it towards him, thinking he would roll it back with his paw. He just watched it as it rolled, a small blue rubber ball travelling across the mustard-coloured carpet in the living room, and when it got to him it bumped into his front paws and stopped. He looked at it, and at Betty, and frowned. He got up and walked around it and lay down again. She did this several times, and each time he refused to push it back to her.

Finally she rolled it towards him quite hard, and when it hit him it hurt him slightly. Still he would not roll it back. This time he didn't even move, except to lay his ears back and pull the skin away from his teeth and then, with all his sharp white teeth showing, he made a hissing, growling noise in his throat. His mouth and eyes became enormous and angry. She laughed. This was how he liked to play.

She crawled towards him, hissing between her teeth and growling. She went closer and closer to him. He stopped snarling and his eyes slitted in his head and his ears stayed back. When she was very close to him, just inches from him, she reached up her hand like a paw and poked at him, playfully. His paw came out so quickly she didn't see it move, and she felt a sharp pain in her nose.

She jerked upright. He ran across the room and crouched down, watching her. She put her fingers to the top of her nose and felt sticky blood there. It wasn't very much blood. She went upstairs and looked in the mirror in the bathroom and saw it, a crimson smudge on the top of her nose. She cleaned it off and watched the blood well slowly up again; cleaned it off; watched it well up still more slowly; cleaned it off; finally there was no more blood, just four red pricks on the top of her nose, as though she had been stabbed lightly there with a fork.

When she went downstairs the cat was sitting at the front door, staring fixedly at the doorknob.

She opened the door and pushed him outside, hard, with her foot. He landed on the grass. She closed the door quickly on the cool grey day and didn't watch him leave her front yard.

It's lucky that they are such tiny marks, she thought. Nobody will notice them—nobody at all.

Chapter
13

Sheila's desk was piled with student records. Behind her, file drawers in the wall bulged with hundreds of pieces of paper, some of which stuck out above the tops of the drawers, gasping for breath. Across the office and opposite her sat the desk of the senior department secretary. It was also littered. If I worked here full time, thought Sheila, this place would be shipshape. Through the window on her left seeped the bleakness of a winter day.

Part of her job was covering for everyone else's lunch hours. At this time of the day, therefore, she was the only one in the office. Usually she was busy; today, though, it was as though classes had been called off and everyone sent home.

There's been a nuclear holocaust, she thought, and everybody's gone home to die with their loved ones, but somebody's forgotten to tell me. I'll die here, on the job, doing my duty.

She listened. She could hear sounds from the hall, and she saw people pass by the frosted glass window in the office door. The university hadn't been deserted after all.

Sheila sat back in her chair and wondered what she was doing there. Earning money. Why? To buy extra things for the house, and for the kids, and occasionally for herself. Was this women's liberation? This was no career. It was just a job.

But lots of men didn't have real careers, either; just jobs. Ed did, though. He had a career. She seethed with resentment. I want a career, she pouted. Then laughed out loud. Doing what? Maybe I could be a hooker. I wonder how people go about becoming hookers. Is there a placement agency for hookers? Do you have to fill in forms? take tests? or what? You probably just go down to Seventh Avenue and stand around. But you'd have to be careful you didn't stand around in somebody else's territory. Probably you have to get yourself a pimp. Yeah. So that's no career, either. Unless you get to be a high-class call girl. Somehow I don't think I'd ever make it as a high-class call girl.

She sighed hugely and stretched her arms above her head. That damned woman, thought Sheila. She's twenty minutes late. Again!

She scribbled a note for the senior secretary, grabbed her coat and purse, and hurried out.

Goddam wind, she thought, walking home from the bus stop. I hate it, it makes me so *angry*. She clutched her collar up around her face, trying to hold her coat closed around her legs. Her handbag bumped against her knees and the wind kept grabbing the ends of her coat and snapping them away from her body. Goddam wind . . . never mind, I'll be home soon. Maybe I'll make myself some cocoa and curl up in front of the TV and watch a soap opera. The wind gusted from behind her and she staggered. *Damn* wind!

She slitted her eyes to see down the block. Four more houses to go. Thank God I don't have anything to do when I get home except make dinner—Ed's being very considerate these days, vacuumed up a storm over the weekend, he did. Three more houses. Lots of time to get warm and calmed down before the kids come home. God this wind makes me so *mad*, two more houses . . .

She glanced left and saw that Betty's curtains were closed again. That ridiculous woman, she thought, fuming, that useless woman. I'll bet she still hasn't done a thing in that house. I'll bet she didn't do a single thing I told her. I'm damn sure she never called those Servicemaster people. . . .

Sheila stood on the sidewalk, buffeted by the wind. She walked slowly towards her house, then suddenly wheeled around and marched straight up Betty's walk and rang her doorbell.

She shivered as she waited. Stupid woman, she's probably peering out from some damn window to see who it is while I stand out here bloody freezing. . . .

The door opened. Betty whisked out onto the porch and closed the door quickly behind her.

"Hello!" she said. "I've been meaning to go to visit you again for such a long time, weeks now, maybe even months I've been meaning to go, but I haven't, I haven't, do forgive me, won't you? And now here you are, here you are at my house and I haven't even invited you!"

"Look, Betty, I'm damn near freezing standing here in my coat and you've got just a sweater on. This is idiotic, are you going to ask me in or not?" She pushed towards the door, but Betty blocked it and raised her hands, palms outward.

"You're not disturbing me, you understand, not a bit, but my house is a wee bit messy again, just a wee bit. Why don't we go to your house to chat? May we? Would that be all right?"

"Oh for God's sake," said Sheila, grabbing at her coat collar—the wind was flicking the ends hard against her cheeks. "I don't care where we go. Let's just get inside."

"Yes yes, I know," said Betty, grabbing Sheila's arm and charging down the walk with her. "It is cold, isn't it, so cold, I should have worn my coat but then I didn't know I would be going anywhere, did I? I'm very busy these days, very busy, lots of plans, but I do think that friends should continue to see one another now and then, just now and then, so as not to intrude upon one another. But if we don't see each other occasionally why then we can't continue to be friends, can we?" She deposited Sheila, flustered and seething, upon her own front porch and waited for Sheila to unlock the door. "My, I do like your porch," she said, shivering.

"You didn't go away this summer, did you?" said Betty

as Sheila grimly put her things away in the closet and stalked off towards the living room, turning up the thermostat on the way. "I noticed that you didn't go away for a holiday. Neither did I," said Betty, plopping down upon the sofa. "What a pleasant room," she said with a smile. "Yes, somehow I knew this room would be pleasant. I'm sure the rest of your house is just as pleasant, too, just as pleasant." She looked at Sheila expectantly, her head cocked to one side.

Sheila said nothing. She watched her visitor with indignation. Finally, "No, we didn't go away this year. Did you?"

"No! No, I said I didn't," said Betty. "Didn't you hear me?"

"I guess I missed that."

"I do talk a lot, I know. Jack—that's my husband, Jack —Jack is always telling me that I either talk far too much or I sit there without saying a word and he can't tell what I'm thinking and he says he doesn't know which is worse!" She chuckled and looked around the room. "Such a pleasant room," she murmured, with a sly look at Sheila.

"I went to see you," said Sheila, "because I wondered how you'd made out with your cleaning. Did you get Servicemaster to come in? Or what?"

"Did I . . . oh. Oh no. No, I didn't get anyone to come in. I decided to do it by myself," said Betty, smiling.

"How did it turn out?"

"Oh, I haven't done it yet," said Betty cheerily. "I wanted to wait until the hot weather had passed. Cleaning is such a difficult thing to do, I certainly didn't want to do it in the summertime, in the hot summertime. I will do it . . . next week, I think. And your advice," she added politely, "will be most helpful, I am sure."

"I didn't have much to say, as I remember. I really think it's too big a job for you to tackle by yourself. That's all I remember telling you."

"No no, you had many suggestions, many very useful suggestions." Betty laughed. "When I get it all finished, all shined up, perhaps I'll invite you in for tea."

"That would be very nice," said Sheila. She looked at her watch.

"When does your husband come home?"

"Oh, about four-thirty or so."

"My husband sells things which have to do with oil wells. Bits and things. What does your husband do for a living? What's his job?" She rested her chin in her hands and looked at Sheila seriously.

"He's a teacher. A high-school teacher. He teaches math and science." When he isn't doing other things, she thought, to hurt herself. Then she remembered that that was all over.

"How very interesting," said Betty, her head bobbing up and down. She stared at Sheila for a moment and then leaned back in the sofa, a dreamy expression on her face.

"How did you meet him, your husband—what's his name?"

"Ed."

"How did you meet Ed, then?"

"I met him at a party."

"A party?" Betty exclaimed. "You met him at a party?" She laughed heartily, and when she stopped Sheila saw that she had tears of laughter in her eyes. It looks like her eyes are running, Sheila thought with distaste.

"That's amazing, positively amazing." Betty stared at Sheila, beaming. "You see," she said confidentially, "that's how I met my husband, Jack, too—at a party."

"I'm sure it happens to a lot of people," said Sheila dryly.

"May I tell you about it?" Betty pleaded, clasping her hands. "May I tell you about it? How I met my husband? Would you like that?"

Oh Christ, thought Sheila, the woman probably has nobody to talk to at all except her kid. "Sure," she said.

Betty settled back happily on the sofa and her eyes wandered to the ceiling.

"It was when I had my job, of course. In Vancouver. The party was in an apartment building in the West End. It was given by a girl named Cherry, whose name I had forgotten until recently." She laughed. "I had forgotten her name, even though she is Jack's cousin and we worked in the same office in Vancouver and she invited me to a party where I met my husband, isn't that dreadful? Isn't it?" Sheila nodded.

"When I arrived for the party there were already a few people there. Cherry wore a long red dress, I remember; most unsuitable it was." She clucked disapprovingly. "She led me into the bright bright kitchen and introduced me to the people. The men wore shiny suits and their hair was short and their ties were skinny. The suits didn't seem to fit properly; I couldn't tell what was wrong with them." She looked suddenly towards Sheila and added, hastily, "Jack had not arrived yet. This is before Jack arrived." Sheila nodded again. Betty resumed staring at the ceiling.

"There were two men there, and two women. One of the men was tall and gangly and he was a typewriter repair person. The other was shorter, stockier, altogether sandy-looking he was. He wore a green suit, and there was dandruff on his shoulders. His eyelashes were so fair his eyes looked naked. He sold things at The Bay."

"You certainly remember all this remarkably well," said Sheila.

Betty looked at her severely. "I remember it as long as I'm *looking* at it, of *course* I remember it well. But then you can't sit about all day long looking at old things, can you?" She glared at Sheila, who shrugged and motioned her to go on. Betty's eyes returned to the ceiling and the lights went on in them again. She was very good at remembering. She cast herself upon the past with blind confidence, and it enveloped her.

The two girls worked as stenographers somewhere—wherever it was, they told Betty that it was a terrible place; they had to work so hard and couldn't talk to one another except at coffee breaks and the days were endless, they said.

She wondered why they stayed, then. Stenographers' jobs must be easy enough to find, she thought. She knew she would find a good one if she were a stenographer. Then she began to think again about taking typing and shorthand classes at night, and suddenly she resolved to do just that. She would phone around Monday morning and decide which school to go to.

Betty lowered her head slowly until she was looking at Sheila. Her eyes were bleak. "I never did, of course. . . ."

Cherry gave her a drink, a gin and tonic it was, and Betty continued to listen to the stenographers, carefully and sympathetically. They were like two little birds who had escaped from their flock for the evening, gleaming and slightly ruffled with excitement, eyes darting brightly to the door, waiting for new arrivals. She was listening to them chirp away about their jobs and at the same time she was thinking of how her life would change when she had learned typing and shorthand. She would work in a big office with carpets and music and windows. She would make appropriate friends. She would earn more money. She felt very excited.

"What about your husband?" said Sheila.

"I am coming to that," said Betty with dignity. "Right now, as a matter of fact."

She wondered who else was coming to this party. And, just as she was wondering that, the doorbell rang and Cherry flew to open it. The other girls fell silent, their gazes fixed on the door, eyes narrowed to peer through the brightness and the cigarette smoke in the kitchen to see who was arriving into the shadowed hallway. Then they began chortling and chirping away again, with the two men this time, and for the first time Betty felt alone.

She hadn't really wanted to come. She didn't do too well at parties, and had to be alert all the time so as to know just when to leave. It made her uncomfortable that people said they went to parties to have fun and talk to other people, whereas really what they

96

were all doing was looking for a man, or a woman. When other people began to look brazenly around them, about three-quarters of the way through a party, Betty would want to leave. She would not want to be around, because as soon as they thought they had found each other a man and a woman would sprawl together in a chair or on a sofa or even on the floor behind some piece of furniture, and they would rub against each other until their clothes were rumpled and the woman's lipstick was all over her face and all over the man's, too, and it would be all greasy and unpleasant and embarrassing.

Sheila was feeling embarrassed herself, as she watched Betty's hands rubbing against her fat thighs. She cleared her throat as though to interrupt, politely, but it was too late.

Betty couldn't imagine what pleasure they found in it. She had been to several parties by then, and once or twice she had stayed too long and had seen all this.

Once a man even tried to rub up against her like that. It was dreadful. He felt bumpy in all the wrong places. She could smell his perspiration and his greasy hair and, through it all, the smell of something he had dabbed all over himself before going to that party. He had stood there in his tiny bathroom somewhere and looked at himself critically in the mirror and straightened his tie and smoothed his hair with some cream. Then he had smiled in satisfaction and, as the finishing touch, he had taken out a little bottle of something and dabbed it all over his face where he had shaved.

She didn't remember much about that man, except that he was fat. There was a roll of fat just above his belt. She knew that, because she grabbed him there in shock when he took hold of her by her shoulders and started to try to kiss her. She pushed him away, and told him as nicely as she could that she didn't like that, she wanted him to stop. She said she had to go home. He wanted to take her home but she said no, and she got her coat and walked out the door. But she heard him say, "Who the hell does she think she is?" as she left, and she just smiled to herself. She knew who she was, all right; he didn't, that was all.

So at Cherry's party she knew what would happen. It was just a question of time. But there was some delicious-looking food, and probably the guests would get to that before the rubbing and moaning began. Still, she would have to keep her eyes open, stay alert, because sometimes these things happened early.

The newcomers were in the kitchen now. There were four of them. Three wore shiny suits, like the men who were already there. The fourth was very big—tall and big, not quite fat. Thin, even. He had ordinary brown hair, short, like all the rest. But he wore not a suit but a sweater with a V-shaped neck, and a shirt and tie peeked out from underneath. The sweater was beige. His name was Jack Coutts.

She liked the look of him and he must have liked the look of her, too. She was very thin, then, very thin, and also quite young, and her hair was long and hung down her back.

When the food was served they sat beside each other and ate some of Cherry's ravioli and some French bread and drank coffee.

He was pleasant to Betty. Remote and polite, just like she was. His eyes were brown; he had a sharp nose, and beneath it was his mouth, which she kept looking at because it was full and covered straight white teeth. She watched his lips move as he ate and talked. They moved with great authority, saying just what he wanted them to say, gathering themselves tidily around bits of food, never allowing them to become spotted with bread crumbs or tomato sauce. They were full and fleshy—but neat, tidy, controlled.

When they finished eating she glanced towards the rest of the people there. They were becoming more quiet. There was quieter music on the record player. Cherry had cuddled up against the typewriter repair man. The two girls who were stenographers had separated. Each was sitting with a different man, each against a different wall. Betty said to Jack, "I must leave, now," and he said, "Let me drive you home," with such civility and politeness that she agreed.

She stopped talking.

"What happened then?" said Sheila.

"What do you mean, what happened then? Nothing happened then. He took me home."

"But, you married him. . . . "

"Yes, yes I did."

"How much later?"

"Oh, a year or so later, a year or so, yes," said Betty vaguely, poking around in the sofa, eyes peering where her hands poked.

"How come you moved here?"

Betty stopped poking and looked up. "We moved here because he worked here."

"But I thought . . . I mean, you said that party was in Vancouver. . . ."

"Yes, yes, it was in Vancouver," said Betty impatiently. "I lived in Vancouver; he did not. He had once lived there, and when he went back he sometimes visited his cousin, and this time I met him when he visited her because she was having a party." Betty stood up. "I've got to go home now."

"Sorry," said Sheila. "I didn't mean to pry."

"No, you weren't prying. It was my idea to tell you about how I met Jack, after all. But now I must go home. Thank you so much for inviting me."

Betty trotted home through the windy cold.

Sheila got dinner ready; and later she tried to tell Ed about her neighbour.

"She's wingy," he said bluntly.

"Don't be mean, Ed. She's not quite normal, maybe, but she isn't wingy, whatever that's supposed to mean. She's lonely, that's all."

"Yeah, I know. Why doesn't she get a job, I wonder? Or join something, or something."

"Oh for Christ's sake, is that all you can think of? Joining something? God. Joining something. Her husband's practically never home; I wouldn't believe that crap about trips out of town, by God. And meanwhile there she sits in that absolutely filthy house without even a radio let alone a television set, no wonder she's wingy!" Sheila was breathless, and flushed.

"Sheila. Hey. I love you," said Ed softly. "Let me help you with the dishes."

She let him.

Chapter 14

He was through for the week, and it was only Wednesday. On Monday he was supposed to show up at a drilling site a few hours' drive from Calgary. He could have four days at home.

Goddam, I wish I'd done better this trip, he thought, packing his suitcase, throwing things in and punching them down. I know I used to be a better salesman, I know I did—what the hell's gone wrong? Flutters of fear; he beat them down with the dirty shirts and underwear.

He checked drawers and countertops and the closet by the door to make sure he hadn't forgotten anything. He looked around the room. It was oppressive, but no worse than hundreds of others. They all buy their furniture from the same wholesaler, he thought. They all have the same tastes in wallpaper and cheap prints or photographs to hang on the walls; the rooms all smell the same.

They smelled of absence, at best. At worst, Jack thought they smelled of cat pee. At least his house didn't smell of cat pee. Dirt, old food—but not cat pee. He thought about his own room—the single place in the world where he could close the door, look around, and feel that nothing was in there except himself.

He put on his overcoat and boots, picked up the room key, and wrestled suitcase, briefcase, and boxlike sample case out the door. He put his things in the station wagon, checked out of the motel, got in the wagon, and started the motor.

He let it idle while he unplugged the car and scraped frost from the windows. The wind howled, and he stopped scraping to dig his gloves out of his pockets and put them on.

The station wagon rattled worriedly as he pulled out of the motel parking-lot. The roads he travelled aged cars quickly. He'd have to think about replacing the wagon soon.

He checked the time. Half an hour to get to the highway, still no snow, so three hours to Calgary. He'd get out of Edmonton by going along the Stony Plain Road to 170th Street and over the Whitemud freeway, which led straight to the Calgary Trail.

At least his Christmas shopping was done. It was something he dreaded every year. He was ashamed of the paucity of his list. Betty and Heather; that was it. No parents, no aunts and uncles, no brothers or sisters. It was at Christmas that he felt most alien to the people he worked with, shared the highways and the sidewalks and the workaday world with.

He turned onto the Whitemud and was soon speeding across the North Saskatchewan. The leafless trees shivered in the river valley, their autumn glory forgotten, winter's white blanket not yet spread.

Jack lit a cigarette. He wished he could give Betty a clean house for Christmas. Not your normal gift, he thought wryly. He'd offered to get her a cleaning lady, of course; he'd suggested that a long time ago, when he couldn't even afford it, when Heather was born, and the place began to fall apart. Betty wouldn't hear of it.

She was pretty then, Betty was. She was still slim, and her yellow hair was long and soft.

"Come on, baby," he'd said. "You've got enough on your hands with the kid. Let's get somebody in to clean once a week. What do you say?"

"I don't want to," she said. He remembered the way she looked—pale, her hair unkempt, exhausted; and frightened, too. Betty didn't know much about babies.

"I'm not used to this!" she had cried out, her white fingers stiff and spread apart against her skirt. "I just need to get used to it!"

He had put his arms around her. "Okay, okay. Look. If it doesn't bother you, it doesn't bother me. One thing at a time, right?" He held her by the shoulders and beamed into her pale face, and hugged her close again.

Now Jack was on the Calgary Trail, through the lights at 23rd Avenue, heading down the open highway. He settled himself more comfortably in his seat and lit another cigarette.

He thought about how he had raised the subject again and again, as the house deteriorated around Betty. Finally, ashamed but desperate, he rented another place, and they moved.

"Let me find you some help now, so you can keep this place just like it is."

"No, Jack, no, don't you see? This can be a new start!" she said with bright eyes and a smile for him. "The problem with the other house was that I simply let things go too far. You'll see," she said confidently. "Things are going to be much better. You'll see."

She kept it clean for a couple of months. He admired it every time he came home. "The place looks great, Betty, just great." He had seen her trying.

But that house, too, had defeated her. And eventually they had moved again. The new place got dirtier, and Betty got fatter; but Heather grew up just right, and became Jack's reason for going home. That was another thing he didn't like to think about. I did *not* reject her, he thought angrily. I have *still* not rejected her, he thought grimly.

When they moved the next time, into a house near a school, because Heather was six, he tried again.

"Betty, for Christ's sake," he pleaded, "let me hire a cleaning woman. Look, you could even go back to work if you want, part time."

"What kind of job could I get, do you think," she said contemptuously.

"The kind you had before, in Vancouver. You did it well, remember?"

She was not plump now, or even pudgy. She was fat. That, he found, did not particularly appeal to him.

She combed her long, greasy hair with her fingers and shook it back over her shoulders. She folded her hands in her lap. "You don't find a good class of people in places like that." She glared at him. "I do not want to work again. Not any more."

One day a couple of years later he came home, and the dust that was there had been there the last time he entered the house, and other layers had fallen to rest upon it. Newspapers had piled up on the coffee table, unread. There were dishes in the sink from several meals ago. She had not done the grocery shopping.

He found her lying on the sofa, a box of chocolates shoved against the pile of newspapers within her reach, and there was some chocolate smeared on her face, and on her fingers, and on the pages of the magazine she was reading. *Photoplay*. He had never seen her reading that before.

Heather was sitting on the floor beside her mother, doing a jigsaw puzzle. Her hair was uncombed; the shirt and pants she wore were dirty. That was the first time Jack got angry.

"What the hell's going on around here?" he said.

"What do you mean?" Betty said. "I didn't expect you. You said you wouldn't be home until next week. You can hardly expect the house to be prepared for you if you come home a week early."

"What about Heather? Have you been sending her to school looking like that, her clothes filthy, her hair all tangled? My God, Betty!"

That weekend he taught eight-year-old Heather to wash and comb her own hair, to choose clothes that were clean, to hang up her clothes when she took them off, to keep her own room tidy. That weekend he told her her mother was a little bit unwell and couldn't do things like keep the house clean and that she was not to worry, but to be cheerful and helpful. He watched Heather as he spoke to her, and tiny movements of her eyes, her face, her body, told him that she'd already figured out most of this by herself.

Jack shook his head angrily. He wished he could stop thinking about it. He always thought too much about things as Christmas approached.

He slowed outside Red Deer and pulled into the parking lot of a take-out restaurant.

He sat there for a few minutes, the car motor running, the heater on.

Her mother had died just a few months before they decided to get married. Oh Christ, he thought, if only it had been her father who had died! The old bastard never even wrote to her. Betty's mother had loved her, that seemed clear enough, and by Christ, he thought, I could do with someone else to take on some of the worrying.

He remembered the worst day of all, when he'd come home and found that she had cut her hair. His mouth fell open when he saw her. She had laughed and laughed, covering her teeth with her fat hands. Her hair got kind of wavy, cut that short. It made her head look much smaller, and her body much larger. He didn't like it at all. He was horrified. He demanded that she let it grow. She'd just simpered at him. That was more than a year ago, just before they'd moved the last time, and still it wasn't any longer. It was the day he found Betty with her hair cut that he made a decision. He called their family doctor, stammering, and tried to explain the situation. The doctor had referred him to Dr. Jessup.

It hadn't been difficult at all, Jack remembered, as he got out of the car and went into the restaurant for some coffee to go. It had been almost easy to persuade Betty to see Dr. Jessup. He had been deeply afraid that she would refuse. She was suspicious at first.

"What kind of a doctor? There's nothing wrong with me, for heaven's sake, nothing at all. I couldn't be healthier."

But he told her, "It's a kind of doctor you talk to about things, Betty." She had looked at him thoughtfully, and agreed to see the doctor.

And she's been seeing him every goddam week for a year, thought Jack, as he found a pay phone and put in his call. Thank Christ it's free, anyway.

"Well, how're things?" he said when Jessup came on the line.

"I was hoping you'd call soon. As a matter of fact, we seem to be getting somewhere," said the doctor.

"What do you mean?" said Jack stupidly. A slim and laughing, long-haired Betty flashed into his mind, and he gazed at the vision with little hope.

"Betty has made a couple of friends. I don't know who they are, but I assume they live in your neighbourhood. It's encouraging."

He sounds bloody enthusiastic, thought Jack, astounded, and it occurred to him that the doctor might even spend time thinking about Betty when she wasn't sitting in front of him and Jack wasn't on the phone to him.

"Yeah, that sounds good," he said cautiously.

"She's getting out, seeing people. We're starting to make some real progress."

"Yeah. It's been a long time." Jack wondered if she'd brought them in for tea, or whatever, and winced at the thought. But maybe she'd even cleaned the place up a bit for them.

She might get normal, Jack thought dazedly. She might get thinner, and grow her hair; I might want to sleep with her again, he thought, and felt the blood rush across his face.

"We can't expect everything to happen overnight, of course," said the doctor, but Jack could tell that he was pleased.

The snow had almost stopped when he came out of the phone booth and crossed the parking lot to his car. If the sky had been clear he would have been able to see the mountains soon. He pulled back onto the highway, heading south.

New friends, he thought. In the neighbourhood. They all looked like normal enough people—those he'd noticed. What the hell do they talk about? What the hell do they think of her? Christ, what do you know. You just never know.

He watched the highway slide beneath him. He tried to prepare himself for the same house, the same Betty. But it isn't going to be the same Betty, he thought, and couldn't control his quick eagerness. Even if she looks exactly the same, and of course she will; even if the house is just as filthy as ever, and it probably will be; still, something has started to change. And maybe the next time I go home, or the time after that, I'll be able to see it.

The highway rolled on, the cloud-shrouded mountains in the west moved invisibly closer, and ahead of him, less than an hour away, was Calgary. He drove on, nibbling at the inside of his mouth.

Chapter
15

They were sitting in Bertha's kitchen, and through the glass doors they watched a back yard swept by cold wind, bare trees shivering, the lane spewing dust, the world not yet covered by the snow that hovered in the mountains. It howled faintly somewhere, the wind, and niggled around the glass door. Bertha shivered, as though the wind had breathed down her neck.

"I'm sure I can't figure why anybody ever came to live here in the first place," she said.

Betty was startled. "I came because this is where Jack works, but I did prefer it in Vancouver," she said.

They looked out upon the yard, upon the ghosts of last winter's snows. Bertha wondered glumly how deep the snow would fall this year. She wondered, too, how many chinooks would come to blow away the nightmare of winter for a few days or hours and then flee, leaving ice to choke the sidewalks, leaving behind people like Bertha, who knew the chinook winds were only an illusion of spring but who still believed in them when they were there, and so suffered bitterly when they left.

"Anybody with a grain of sense prefers Vancouver," she said.

"You've been there!" said Betty. "You've been to Vancouver!"

"You'd be hard pressed to find anybody in Calgary who hasn't," said Bertha.

"People complain about the rain in Vancouver," said Betty excitedly. "But I never minded it, never never. It was like being in a shower, or a bath. It was . . . personal."

"That probably wouldn't be too good for my hip, either," Bertha said. "But at least I'd be able to get around. Winter's a bad time for me. It's hard to keep your footing in the snow and ice when your old hip keeps coming apart on you," she said.

"What do you mean, coming apart?"

Bertha said impatiently, "Not coming apart, exactly. Just feels like it." She slapped her right side lightly. "Damn thing's less dependable every day. Hurts, too." Betty made no response.

Bertha made up her mind to get Heather coming over regularly again, as she had when she was younger. Poor mite must need somebody to talk to, under the circumstances, she thought.

"Yes," she said, "I'd sure be better off in a place where the winter doesn't take itself so seriously."

"If you think it's so dreadful here, why do you stay?" said Betty.

"Why does anybody stay anywhere? I don't have anyplace else to go. Lived in this house for twenty years." Bertha struggled to her feet and hobbled slowly to the stove. She refilled their coffee cups and limped painfully back to the table with them. "Next time we need more, you get it," she said to Betty.

"I haven't lived anywhere for that long since I was a child," said Betty. "I've lived in . . . let me see . . . five houses in Calgary, five different houses."

"I see your husband was home this weekend," said Bertha after a moment.

"Yes. He's gone again, now. He went away again this morning." Betty crossed her ankles.

"Why do you stay in your house all day?" asked Bertha suddenly. "You don't have to worry about the snow or the ice. Why don't you get a job, like the one you had before you were married?"

"Why did you do that? Why did you say that? You know that I can't get a job!" Betty's hands were shaking. "Not any more! It's too late for that, much too late, even if I went back to Vancouver it wouldn't be the same, never again!"

Bertha watched, astounded. She pulled herself to her feet and hobbled around the table with a sigh. She patted Betty on the back.

"I'm sorry, Betty. Really. Didn't mean to upset you." She stroked Betty's hair. "There. Better?"

Betty looked up into the battered chipmunk face.

"My happiest times weren't in my job," she said loudly, her heart thudding, as Bertha struggled back into her chair.

"No?" said Bertha, panting. "What, then?"

"When I was a little girl," said Betty, her heart thudding so hard, like a drum, that her own words were blurry in her ears. "In Victoria. With my mother. You never knew I lived in Victoria, did you?"

"No, I didn't. I've been there. Butchart Gardens and all. Pretty." Bertha's voice was muffled. Betty's heartbeats came faster and faster louder and louder until they made a single low-pitched moan in her chest and she swung her heart around and stared straight backwards as far as she could see . . . and like a sweet dream it curled around her, that good time, a good time, a very good time, surrounded by colours and life, she was, and a warmth that does not exist, that has no name . . .

"I came first," she said as Bertha watched her curiously. "Not only born first, I came first with her. My mother had yellow hair and sometimes she took afternoon naps and I would say, 'I don't want to sleep, Mommy,' I would say, 'I don't feel sleepy,' and she would say, 'Lie down with me Betty-love, Mommy's sleepy, lie down here with me,' and the light lay softly upon the bed, warm, it was. We would cuddle up on the soft bed; she smelled like spring, then, always like spring, and sometimes I would sing to her. . . ."

Betty began to croon. Her face was slack and her pudgy fingers played with themselves and her voice had changed—high for the child, low for the mother. Bertha thought worriedly of getting her an aspirin. . . .

"And Daddy one morning—a Christmas morning, I'd already had some presents—but he came in with a cardboard box, not heavy, but delicate? breakable? He carried it so carefully, and I said, 'What's inside?' and they said it was for me. . . . "

Way back Betty saw it and looked hard with all of her mind and it came sharp and large, enveloping her. He had put the box upon the table. It had sounds inside it, tiny sounds. Betty's hand were wet and cold.

"What's that?" she said. "What's the sounds?"

He opened the top of the box carefully, carefully, and whispered to her, "Look," lifting her up. On a green towel, an old green towel from their own kitchen, there on a corner of that old, green, white-striped towel lay a thing like a sticky-looking caramel with eyes—a puppy.

"A puppy," she said. His eyes were full of fright; noises like dollhouse bedsprings squeaking came from his throat; fear-filled eyes watched her as her hand came near, eyes watching, not flinching— he was never to flinch, no matter what; head not moving, eyes going from her small hand to her small face as her hand touched the top of his head. It was sticky, like a caramel.

"What's his name?" she asked them, and her father said, "Whatever you like. He's yours—yours to keep and yours to name."

She touched his head with her fingers; it felt knobbly and weak, like a walnut that didn't know about nutcrackers. She decided to call him Candy. . . . Candy, lying snuggled into the summer earth like he was his own teddy bear, his soft eyes closed.

"Now, that's real nice," stammered Bertha. "I've got an idea. Why don't we have some soup? What do you think, eh? Some nice hot soup. . . . "

Betty looked back, back, and she saw ladies come for tea, a room filled with them. *There was a blue carpet with flowers throwing itself beneath the feet of the ladies in swishy dresses, silly shoes, hair in curls or buns; the smell of perfume was heavy, making Betty cough—perfumes and powders mixed like the wrong flowers put together, a throat-burning witches' brew. And voices clashing, too, like teeth grinding or scissors slashing.*

110

But her mother was drifting through, not caring, skirt swaying, red lips moving, blue eyes watching—no smile there, only attached to her mouth. The cups and saucers were so pretty, roses on them, tea glowing like autumn through thin white china, dying pink roses. Plates were buried under piles of tiny sandwiches, cookies, cakes for dolls.

And Betty was there—looking, smelling, listening; made of blotting paper. Her hair was in yellow curls, there was a lacy collar on her dress, she wore white kneesocks, her white patent shoes were gleaming. And all of her was made of blotting paper.

"Such a sweet dress," said a lady, a knife through the cloud of the ladies' selves mixing there. Everyone stopped munching, talking, shrieking, laughing, moving about the room, trampling the flowers on the carpet.

"Come closer. Let me see," she said, and Betty's eyes caught her mother's in midair. Her mother made a real smile, nodded, and Betty stumbled across the carpet, trying to step only on the blue, not on the flowers. She didn't know if she was too big or too small, only that she did not feel right, as though she were the stranger there; and through the forest of crossed legs she stumbled to the lady sitting and waving to her, dark red dress, dark red lipstick, funny hat mostly veil perched on rolls of dark hair, eyes small and questioning, holding out her hand. Betty tripped over a silken ankle, fell against the table. Cups shrilled at her as they wobbled drunkenly in their saucers. Three pieces of cake and a sandwich toppled from plates onto the floor.

She ran from the room, bumping slithery things, shaking off fluttery hands, and in the hall closet she stood still, listening to her face burn, hearing her eyes gush.

In a minute her mother was there, kneeling in the closet, pulling Betty towards her—warm, silken, one scent, a single murmur, "It's all right, it's all right, my darling, it's all right," and Betty opened her arms and put them around her. She was fragile.

"Betty!" Bertha called out desperately. "Do you want me to play the piano for you? I've been practising. Do you want to hear something? Betty! . . ."

She was slim and yielding and then she was fat and ugly, Betty

111

remembered; and she remembered the anger, too. Her mother carried a huge burden on her stomach. He told Betty it was a baby.

"Why?"

"We love you so much, we want another one—a baby who will become another child."

"Why?"

"You'll love it, too—like you loved Candy."

"Will it be mine?"

"It will be your brother or sister."

"Will it be yours?"

"It will be our son or daughter."

"Why?"

"Because we love you so much."

It came and lived in the house.

"Shut that door, Betty!"

"Why?"

"Shut it! You can't come in here!"

Betty saw a crinkled red thing, no eyes, big mouth screaming, legs and arms short and fat, all jerking, funny red sausage down there, between its fat jerky legs. Her mother came out holding a blanket filled with it.

"I'm sorry, dear, but you can't come in while I'm bathing him."

"Why?"

"Because of privacy."

In school it was good to have a baby brother.

"What's he look like?" Giggles. "Has he got a thing?" More giggles.

"A what?"

Lots of giggles. "You know, a thing. Between his legs."

"Oh yes, he's got one. . . . "

Bertha was becoming frantic. Betty's voice continued steadily, with changes in pitch but hardly a pause. Would she ever run out of words? Bertha found it hard to make much sense of what she was saying.

The baby got bigger, finally learned to do things, and turned into a boy. Sometimes he made them angry, when he got bigger. Betty nodded with satisfaction as she remembered. *He*

112

made them angry by throwing stones or falling down on his tricycle. His father got angry when he fell down. His mother got angry when he threw stones.

Betty watched. Their mother still liked her better; Betty wasn't sure about their father.

It was not good to have a brother. He rumpled up the family. Betty was not sure where any of them fit, any more. She didn't do much to him. Usually they caught her. But still he would follow her. He was stupid stupid stupid.

"Where ya goin'?"

"To play."

"Take me."

"No."

"Why?"

"You're too little. Too stupid."

"Where ya goin' to play?"

"In the woods."

"I can come."

"No."

"I can come if I want."

"Then come."

"Wait for me!" She was running; he couldn't keep up; she could hear him start to cry.

She would go into the woods and climb a tree, a cherry tree. She would look up—sky filled with green leaves, purple cherries, leaves shuddering in summer breezes, light breezes, just letting the leaves know they could be moved. Cherries hanging from sturdy stems, not falling until past ripe—hanging there, moving like breathing. She was reaching up, picking cherries, eating, purple juice on hands, on face, on tongue. Looking back up, she couldn't see where they'd been taken; more sprouted where she had picked. Sitting there, stuffing cherries into her purple mouth with purple fingers.

"Now I certainly wouldn't have thought of you as a tree-climber, no sirree," said Bertha loudly. "Betty. Betty, I do think it's time we had a bite of lunch. Some soup and toast. What do you say? Wouldn't that be nice?"

She forgot him when he was gone, from house, from school, from friends. He didn't exist.

113

And then he didn't. He was taken right away. Disappeared, just like that—first to a hospital, then to a small hole in the ground. She wanted to play a trumpet as she watched the small box fall slowly into the small hole, but she didn't have one. She skittered about up and down on her two feet, watching. Her father's hand clamped down on her shoulder, digging five small holes there.

Standing still. Waiting.

Going away. Waiting. The hardest time of all.

Then going home; back to school; waiting.

The tricycle was gone. Still waiting, waiting.

Boxes of clothes and toys were gone; the room was repainted; desk, chair in there, office for her father.

"I waited and waited," said Betty, "but the heaviness stayed. It never did go away." She touched her shoulder. "I think I still have those five holes there, yes I think I do. . . ."

The air in the kitchen was filled with her words. Bertha wasn't sure at first that Betty had stopped talking, the words filled the kitchen and bounced and clattered against one another. Betty's face was white and blank, there was nothing written upon it, it was all inside that head, nothing outside at all to read.

"Betty. Betty." No one outside to talk to, either.

Bertha got up from her chair, slowly, slowly. The hip was very stiff and the pain was great, but she hardly felt it. She limped badly, but she got around the table and put her arm around Betty's shoulders.

"Come now, Betty. Come on, Betty, I think it's time I took you home. We'll have some lunch next time, and next time I'll play for you, too. Come on now, come on. . . ."

Betty stood up, docile, and with Bertha hobbling beside her she walked slowly down the hall and out the door and over to her own house, and she smiled at Bertha and closed the door in her face.

Bertha stood on the porch. She felt the wind taking swipes at her, and saw the sullen sky. Snow was beginning to fall, offhandedly—small cold flakes that hoped to take the city by surprise.

Bertha looked around for Heather but didn't see her. She wondered if Heather were inside the house. She shivered, standing there in the cold.

"My goodness my goodness my goodness," she whispered, and she hobbled home, shivering and shaking her head.

Chapter 16

Shelley met Heather in the drugstore. She was buying some jelly beans with her allowance. Heather was buying comic books.

They stood at the counter together, waiting to pay for their purchases. Neither of them looked at the other, or said anything, until the woman in front of Shelley stepped back to let the woman ahead of her turn around and leave. This pushed Shelley back, too, and she bumped into Heather.

"Sorry! Hi, Heather!"

"Hi."

They continued to wait in silence. Shelley paid for her candy and stood near the door, shy and awkward, until Heather was finished.

"How about we walk together?" said Shelley brightly.

"Okay."

They went out into the winter day. A crowd of little kids ran past them, deliberately bumping them, and ran on, shouting things back over their shoulders and laughing. Shelley hollered at them and ran a couple of steps, just to scare them.

"You're sure lucky you don't have a brother or a sister, boy," she said, waiting for Heather to catch up.

"Why?"

"Nobody to fight with all the time, for one thing."

They went around the stores and across an empty lot.

"I fight with my mother," said Heather, long blonde hair falling from beneath her blue tuque, hiding her face as she shuffled her boots with precision through the new snow.

"Yeah, well so do I, sometimes," said Shelley, casually.

She tried to imagine it. Her mother had a very loud voice when she got angry. "But with Peter I fight a whole lot."

She opened her mouth wide and blew warm air out slowly, making a cloud of steam to push her head through as she walked.

"Wanna read comics?" she said hopefully, with an eye on the bag Heather was carrying. Heather had bought ten of them, all at one time.

"You don't have any to trade."

"I've got some. A few."

"I've probably got them, too. Or at least read them."

"I'll trade you some comics for a book," said Shelley.

"You don't have any books I want to read, probably. They'd be too easy for me."

"What kinds of books do you like? I bet I have some."

"I don't like books, much. I like comics."

"Well, what should we do, then?"

"Dunno." Heather reached down for a mittful of snow. She put down her bag and began shaping a snowball.

"My dad's coming home again soon," she said.

"That's good. Where's he been?" Shelley wondered whether she should shove her jelly beans into her pocket and make a snowball too.

"Dunno. He goes all over the place." Heather reared back her arm and heaved the snowball at a fence. "This time he might take me with him when he goes away again."

"What do you mean? In the middle of school? For a holiday? Where to?"

"Not in the middle of school, I guess. After the Christmas holidays. For good. Some place far away."

From behind the hedge across the street a small grey cat ran. Heather stood still, watching it.

"Kitty-kitty-kitty."

Heather squatted in the snow and the cat slowed its pace and turned to walk towards her. It rubbed against her knee. Heather put down her bag and picked up the cat. She rested her cold cheek against its head, and snuggled its body into her arms.

"Is that your cat?" said Shelley.

"Nope," said Heather, turning her back.

Shelley watched her, the blue tuque bent, pale blonde hair fanning across the back of the red ski jacket. "It should be your cat. It likes you," she said.

Heather turned around. The cat gazed out at Shelley from Heather's arms.

"It's going to happen, I'm positive," said Heather. "He's going to take me away." She kissed the top of the cat's head and put him gently on the ground. He rubbed himself against her knee.

"You mean without your mother?" said Shelley. "Just you? Just the two of you?"

"Yeah."

"But why? I mean, why would you leave your mother at home? By herself? How long would you be gone?"

"I told you," said Heather impatiently. "For good."

"But why not your mother, too—if you're moving, actually moving."

The cat was crouched in the snow. Suddenly it ran away and disappeared behind the fence.

Heather kicked a snowdrift; white grains flew upward in a half-hearted attempt to reach the sun.

"That sounds awful, Heather. I mean, you'd miss her. You'd get awful lonely for your mother if you just went off and left her behind."

"I miss my father, too, when he goes away."

"Yeah, but you know he'll come back. When he goes away you know he's coming back. Don't you? Heather?"

Shelley peered at Heather intently, but Heather just stared into the glare of winter.

"Do you want to go skating?" said Shelley.

"Nah."

"Heather? Is he coming soon? I mean, any day now?"

"Yeah. But we won't go now. Not until after Christmas."

118

"But you will then? You're going with him? For good?"

"That's what I told you, didn't I?" She shook her head and tramped her feet; stood there planted solid, impatient, uncertain.

"But that means I wouldn't see you any more. If you went away."

Heather looked at her, eyes glinting in their sun-squint.

"We don't play together anyway. I'm too old for you."

"Yeah," said Shelley. "I guess." They went on slowly. "Whose cat is that, anyway?" she asked.

"Nobody's."

"Who looks after it, then?" said Shelley, worried.

"He looks after himself."

Chapter
17

She had resolved not to be caught by surprise this time. She ticked off on sausage fingers what she had to do to be prepared. "Grass, food, house," she mumbled.

But it was winter, and she didn't need to worry about the grass. It lay beneath the snow, waiting for spring, sleeping, not growing.

The snow, however, brought its own problems. She had watched her neighbours from behind her curtains. Some wrestled the snow with plain shovels; others used machines that blew it into high waves which piled higher and higher and stayed alongside the sidewalk, not receding like the waves of the sea.

Betty had a plain shovel, but she didn't use it. She just tramped doggedly up and down the walk in her high rubber boots, trampling down the snow.

She waited for one of her large days, and then she went out to the supermarket and bought many things.

The large days had been a nuisance, at first. She became huge, enormous, striking parts of her body against doorways and tables. She banged herself about no matter how carefully she proceeded along the halls, through doorways, or down the stairs. The only place she still seemed to fit, then, was upon her bed.

But she had discovered another thing about these days. On her large days at least she was without fear. She could go anywhere, without fear. So she waited for one of these days, and put it to good use by going to the supermarket and buying many things.

She didn't use all of her money. She carefully kept back enough for the things she would still need before he came—things like bread and magazines and chocolates.

But with the rest of her money she bought food to save for when he next arrived, and new bottles for the bathroom.

It seemed to Betty strange that people should fuss and mess around in their kitchens with various kinds of foods —juggling them, cooking them, tossing them around, causing them to appear on tables with steam coming from them and strange odours and sauces drowning them—so that other people would murmur and praise and eat with eyes rolled towards the sky.

She bought some cans of vegetables—peas and corn and beans. And many cans of stew and spaghetti. And she put them all away in the cupboard.

And six jars of jam, she bought—six different kinds, six colours glowing through glass. And four big boxes of cereal, to be added to the two already there—one for Heather and one for Betty.

She found it satisfying to open the cupboard doors and see the vegetables and meats and jams and cereals there. Everything waiting for him. He would be surprised, she knew; he would be delighted; it would be like coming home to a restaurant.

Then she tidied the house. She didn't bother with her own room. She kept that room the way she liked it, because it had nothing to do with anyone else. She didn't do Heather's room, either, because the child had to learn to keep her own room tidy. She had to learn these things.

She wiped the bathroom. She took an old grocery bag and filled it with bottles and sponges and toothpaste tubes and things, and she put the bag outside in the garbage. It did look better in there, much better; Jack would hardly recognize it, she thought.

Downstairs she put all the newspapers into piles. She didn't understand how there came to be so many. She only got one newspaper each day, delivered to the door, and still they piled up and up, like snowdrifts inside her house.

In the kitchen she washed all the dishes. She did not enjoy that. Some of the food would not come off. It stayed on the plates in speckled patterns, like a bird's egg. It stayed in the cups, shadows of tea and coffee stuffed down in there. It stayed in glasses, ghosts of Heather's milk. Still, she thought, every plate and cup and glass and knife and fork and spoon has been in hot soapy water, and so it is clean.

She washed the counters, too, and the table, which still had many white rings all over its surface. She decided to buy a cloth the next time she went downtown on the bus. It would be bright and cheerful in her kitchen.

When she had finished all this work she was exhausted. Her head was spinning; her mind was numb. She went up to her room and lay down upon her bedspread, to rest and collect herself.

Later she got up and walked around the house.

She could scarcely recognize it. She could hardly believe it. And it had taken her only one day, just one day.

It was disappointing when Heather came home, because at first she didn't notice anything different. So Betty took her around the house, showing her.

"Look in here, look in the kitchen," she said, and Heather followed her in there, and when she saw it, she smiled.

"It looks good," she said.

Betty told her she would have to do her own room, and Heather made a face.

"I'll do it on Saturday," she said.

"But what if he comes home before that? What if he comes home on Friday?"

"Today is Friday. He won't come today. It's too soon. Not until next week."

She was guessing, Betty knew. She was just too lazy to clean her room that day. But Betty didn't argue. Heather had spoken quietly and politely. Betty just nodded and said, "All right. Saturday. Saturday will be fine."

If he were to come home before that it would be too bad, she thought grimly, but it would be her own fault.

He didn't though.

Heather had forgotten by Saturday, and Betty had to remind her. She was exasperated, but she did make her bed and pick up her clothes, and Betty was pleased.

But when she went back to school after the weekend Betty walked around the house, looking at its cleanness; and suddenly she realized that she had not done the floors.

She knew it didn't matter that she had cleaned the bathroom and piled up newspapers and washed all the dishes last week. If she didn't do the floors, as well, it would be the floors that he would see.

She was angry with him then, for a minute, as she looked around the house and saw what she still had to do.

I will not use that vacuum cleaner, no, she thought. I do not like that vacuum cleaner; I keep it at the back of a closet where there is no plug-in near by. If I brought it out to use it and then let go of it for even a minute it would get away. It would unwind its cord and plug itself in and turn itself on and start sweeping back and forth, back and forth, inhaling dust and dirt into its great canvas lung, making bigger sweeps, wider sweeps, bumping into the sofa again and again, until finally the sofa would be swallowed up; then it would move towards the windows and catch the curtains in its brushes and chew them down and swallow them; and then it would turn around, humming and whirring, and it would move towards me, sweeping back and forth, back and forth, coming nearer and nearer and catching my red slippers then the hem of my red dressing gown I would feel myself growing smaller and smaller, feel that vacuum cleaner growing larger and larger, its brushes enormous like bristly black teeth dead decaying opening biting me into its mouth. . . .

With the broom she swept the floors and the rugs.

The dust blew up onto the furniture and into her nose and eyes. She kept on sweeping, stronger and stronger, and when she began to sweat she opened the back door and swept all the dust and dirt out into the back yard, onto the patio, where more snow would fall on it and make it disappear.

But the more she swept, the more dust and dirt there was. It kept coming up in clouds and choking her. She waved her hand around in front of her. Her eyes burned with the dust and dirt which had been down there so long.

Finally she stopped and went outside to breathe the cold air.

When she returned to the house the dust had settled back into the carpet, onto the floors. It didn't look as though she had cleaned the floors at all.

She put the broom away and made herself a cup of tea.

He will see that the floors are still dirty, she thought. He will see that before he will see the clean bathroom, the clean kitchen, the neat piles of newspapers.

She was sitting at the kitchen table, crying into her tea, when she had her idea.

She decided to make a large sign, saying WELCOME HOME JACK! He would be so surprised and pleased by that sign, she thought. He would see immediately how hard she had worked to prepare the house for him.

She jumped up from the kitchen table and began to look for a large piece of paper. In a kitchen drawer there were small pieces, but no large ones.

She could find none in Heather's room.

She went into Jack's den, tiptoed in there where it was so neat and tidy and cool and clean. She tried to open his desk drawers, but they were locked. She had forgotten that he locked those drawers. A big piece of anger settled in her chest when they wouldn't open for her. She knew he locked them to keep Heather out of his things. But why can't he leave a key with me, she thought, in case of emergencies? I am not a child.

She pulled and yanked at the drawers, but they would not open.

Then a thought came into her head, bright and shining.

In Heather's room she found a big, fat felt pen, and she ran into Jack's den and stood up on his sofa and in big black letters, every one perfect, she wrote on the wall WELCOME HOME JACK!

It took her quite a while. Every letter was perfect— exactly the size of the one that went before it.

She got down and stood back and looked at the sign on the wall, and it looked just as she had imagined it.

Except that the room was uneven, now. It was tilted heavily towards one end.

So she got the chair from behind the desk and moved it closer to that wall, the one behind his desk, and she wrote the same thing on that wall, blackly on the white wall, WELCOME HOME JACK! Carefully. Carefully.

She stood in the doorway and looked at the two signs.

Black on white. He might not like that, she thought, head cocked to one side, thoughtfully. He might wish she had used many different colours instead of just black.

He might not like it at all, she told herself. He might not like it that I have written on his walls. I know that. I am not a child.

But she had done it, and both the signs looked neat and prim and tidy on those pure white walls.

She wanted to see his face when he looked at them.

She could almost see the first expression that would pop out on his face like a big pimple when he saw them. He would be astonished, bewildered . . . and something else, something she couldn't quite make out in her mind, no matter how much she peered, no matter how hard she strained to see.

She had never been so anxious for him to come home.

125

Chapter 18

It was sobering, this fear she felt contemplating the out-doors.

She realized, squinting indignantly out the window at sun flashing blindingly on snowbanks, just how long it had been since she'd set foot outside the house. Things hadn't been this bad last winter, and that she found depressing, very depressing.

It's pretty out there, she thought gloomily, sitting at her sewing machine: sun so bright in a cold, glittery sky; snow heaped everywhere, because of the storm the day before. It hadn't had time to get dirty, and its whiteness was so pure Bertha could hardly bear to look at it.

There was lots of activity up and down the block. People were busily clearing away the sidewalks in front of their houses, and some were hanging Christmas lights along the eaves and draping them over trees in their front yards.

She could hear shouting and screaming, and she craned her neck to get a look farther down the block to where she figured a group of kids must be having a snow-ball fight or making snow angels. She couldn't see that far though.

She watched boys pass her house, alone or in groups, heading for the community ice rink a couple of blocks away. The smaller ones were as wide as they were tall, and she marvelled, as she did every winter, at these small, serious figures, black hockey skates around their necks, faces muffled in scarves, heads enveloped by tuques, so bundled by anxious mothers that their limbs had no room to bend and they appeared to roll down the sidewalk.

Her hip had started to throb. It hurt whenever she pressed her knee against the lever that made the sewing machine go. She didn't like to think about that.

Bertha limped to the telephone and dialled Bob's number.

"Arlene? It's me. Are you two planning to be home today? I'd like to come over."

There were excited squawks at the other end.

"No, I don't want you to come and get me. I'll take the bus."

She let Arlene babble on for a minute while she pulled up a kitchen chair and painfully let herself down into it.

"Don't be silly, Arlene. It's a fifteen-minute ride. Maybe twenty. And it's only a block to the bus stop. I'm not an old cripple, you know. I'm taking the bus. That's that. What time do you want me?"

She got herself upstairs and swallowed two of her painkillers. She put the bottle in her purse, just in case. Then she went back into the kitchen and called the boy who cut her lawn in the summer and shovelled her walks in the winter. He was at hockey practice, but his mother said he'd be over later in the day.

She dressed for her adventure with great care. The radio said it was cold—twenty below. She could see that just looking outside at the shiny, snow-packed streets, the children's breath that made clouds of fog, the men who stopped their shovelling to stamp their feet. There was brilliance in the sun, but no warmth.

She sat down to put on her boots, high ones with crepe soles that were supposed to grip the snow with confidence and fling it aside contemptuously. Putting on the boots was difficult, a struggle, and it caused her a lot of pain. Bertha looked at them dubiously. They're heavy enough, God knows, she thought, and if I should get myself stuck in a snowbank, they'd probably come in handy . . . but I'm sure I don't know how they'll work on the icy

127

stuff. They were new, a gift from Arlene, who had taken her shopping in September, which Bertha had thought was rushing things.

The ache in her hip was subsiding. It had just needed a rest.

She got to her feet and went to the closet for the rest of her gear. A heavy black coat—Arlene had wanted to buy her a leather one, for heaven's sake, with a big fur collar, ridiculous, she'd felt like a fool just trying it on. She wrestled into the coat, holding the ends of her sweater sleeves to keep them from wrinkling up around her elbows and leaving a space for cold breezes to whisk up her arms. She wrapped a scarf carefully around her neck and the lower half of her face. There wasn't much wind; the scarf would probably stay in place, at least until she got on the bus. She put on a pair of fleece-lined mittens, pulled a woollen hat over her head and forehead, took hold of her handbag, opened the door, and went out onto her porch.

Sounds of winter struck her with the cold. There *were* children gambolling around, two houses down. She heard their shrieks clear in the crystal air. She grinned. The old houses looked snug and settled, tucked all around with snowdrifts. She liked the uneven look of the street—roofs at different heights, houses close to the sidewalk or far back on their lots. There were no garages to spoil the look of the street. They were built around the back, leading into alleys. If she were a driver she might not like that much; but she wasn't, and she did. She didn't like houses that sprouted an extra room, obviously bigger than any of the others, in which slept the one or two family automobiles. She'd never liked dogs in the house, and she didn't like cars there, either.

Can't stand here on the porch all day, she thought. She shuffled through the snow, down the steps, and along her walk to the sidewalk; and like a child she took mingled delight and dismay in disturbing the woolly white

128

blanket that covered her front yard, faultlessly smooth and sparkling until her footsteps dragged holes in it.

At the sidewalk she stopped. She saw that she had only twenty-five feet or so to walk on snow already packed by passersby into the smooth, gleaming hardness she knew was almost ice.

She stepped out with her right foot, then her left, and as her left foot landed, the right one slipped a tiny bit and shot pain into her hip. She decided to walk in the snow along the edge of her lawn and lifted her right foot cautiously, aimed it at the snow; her left foot slipped, and the right one hit the snow, but with such pain that, startled, she half pulled it back and the left foot slipped out from under her and she lost her balance.

As she fell, she cursed her hip blackly and bitterly; she knew that any person with both legs working properly could have prevented this, but not her. Three steps out onto the sidewalk and down she was coming.

She sprawled in a heap upon the sidewalk, and as she struck, pain lanced through her hip. But she thanked her stars for the heavy coat and the woollen hat upon her head, and she wished she had had the foresight to wear pants instead of a dress: snow flew up as she landed, half on the sidewalk and half in the brittle lilac hedge, and some of it fell back down onto her legs, which she was upset to realize were generously displayed as she lay there, coat up around her thighs.

"Mrs. Perkins! Mrs. Perkins! Did you hurt yourself?"

Bertha looked up, and between her eyes and the blinding sun a head appeared, sunlight gilding its outline, yellow hair hanging below a sky-blue tuque. She couldn't make out the face clearly, the sun was too bright, but she saw that it was Heather.

"Well now, Heather, I'm not just sure yet. Do you want to help me up?"

By this time two men who had been shovelling snow across the street had run over. They pushed Heather gently aside and set Bertha upon her feet.

"You okay, Mrs. Perkins?" said one. She was mildly surprised to hear him use her name, since she didn't remember ever laying eyes upon the man.

"Yes, I think so, thanks. Heather will help me into the house. Thank you, both of you. It was silly of me."

She turned away their offers to clear her walk. They went back to their houses, and as Bertha hobbled inside, leaning on Heather's shoulder, she heard the muted clanging of shovels on snow-packed concrete begin again.

"Just bring me that chair there, Heather, that's a girl," panted Bertha, waving towards the kitchen chair she'd sat upon to put on her boots.

"There," she said, sitting down. "Now let me see what the damage is."

Her mind probed her body. Her backside was complaining, but she knew that wasn't serious. Her hands stung a bit; the palms of her suede mittens were scraped. But it was the hip that was really howling.

"Oh my goodness," she muttered. "Heather, I think I better get me into the living room and set me down in my own chair."

She reached out for Heather, who came forward and took her arm. Together they got Bertha into the living room and into her chair.

"Never mind your boots," she said, as Heather started back towards the hall. "Come sit down here."

Heather sat on the loveseat opposite Bertha.

"Could you do one more thing for me, do you think?" said Bertha.

"Sure. I can do anything you want."

"I want a glass of water."

Heather went to get it, and when she came back Bertha took another pill.

"These are for my hip."

"Yeah, I figured that," said Heather. "You hurt it when you fell, eh?"

"Yes, I did, a bit."

"Where were you trying to go?"

130

"I was going to the bus stop. I'm going to my son's place for dinner."

"I guess you better not, now."

"Well now, that's what I'm sitting here trying to decide," said Bertha, cautiously half lifting herself to put more weight on her good hip. "Not whether I'm going—I'm going, all right—but whether I ought to go by bus or maybe take a cab."

"I think you better take a cab," said Heather, blue eyes serious in her pale face.

"How come you haven't been around to visit me for so long?" said Bertha.

Heather's eyes dropped and she began taking off one glove and putting it on again. "Oh I don't know." She looked at Bertha. "You're friends with my mom now."

"Well for heaven's sake, can't I be friends with both of you? Your mom and I, we have an interesting time talking, but she doesn't help me feed the birds."

"No. She probably doesn't like birds, much."

"Now she's interested in some of the same things I'm interested in, and you're interested in some of the other things I'm interested in. So any fool can see that I can be friends with both of you."

"What's she interested in that you are?"

"Well let's see. My piano. She likes to hear me play the piano. And she likes to have a cup of tea or coffee and sit and talk. But she doesn't like to feed the birds, and she doesn't like to water the plants, and I need somebody to help me with those things now and then."

Bertha's face was getting pink, from sitting inside with her coat and boots and scarf and hat still on. Little bits of her gray hair were coming out around the edges of her hat. Heather thought she could see pain in Bertha's face, although she wasn't talking about it.

"I guess it's hard for you to get out in the back yard and fix up the thing for the birds, eh?"

Bertha nodded.

131

"I guess it's hard for you to get the plants down to water them, too. Or to climb up to them, to water them."

"Pretty hard."

"I guess your leg hurts you more than it used to."

"It does, it does indeed."

Heather sighed. "Maybe I better come around sometimes to help," she said, worried.

"Well now, that would be very nice. I have a little boy who comes to shovel the sidewalk . . . humph. Anyway, I have him. And my son and daughter-in-law come around, too.

"But you know," she said seriously, "I don't really like them to know that I need them. I'd sooner just have *some* things for them to do, and let them think that everything else I manage by myself. You know?"

Heather nodded. "You want them to think you're independent."

"That's exactly right."

"That's what my father calls me. Independent."

"Are you?"

Heather shrugged. "Oh I don't know. I guess." She stood up. "Is there anything else I can do for you right now? Do you want to feed the birds or water the plants?"

"Not today, I think. I've got to get to Bob and Arlene's. You come back tomorrow, and we'll do it then."

"Can I call a taxicab for you?"

"No thank you, Heather. I believe I'll just sit here and rest for another few minutes. I can call one for myself when I'm ready to go."

"Okay. I'll go now, then." Heather went to the door.

"Heather. Thank you very much."

"That's okay. I'll be back tomorrow. 'Bye."

Bertha groaned out loud a few times when the door had closed behind Heather. Her hip had stopped shooting daggers up into her back and down into her legs and had settled down to throb, the pain pounding in dull thuds. She sat there, rocking back and forth on her good side and moaning, and she wondered how Arlene and Bob would react if they could see her. She chuckled through her groans.

It had almost been worth it, though, to have got Heather back again. The child needed a sharp eye on her, and a good ear to hear her.

Bertha took a deep breath and hoisted herself to her feet to go call a cab.

"I thought you were coming by bus! Oh I'm so glad you didn't, Mother; really, the streets are treacherous." Arlene pulled Bertha inside and helped her take off her things.

"I see you're wearing your new boots. How did they work?"

She must buy those dresses by the dozen, thought Bertha. Same style, different colours. This one was dark blue.

"Oh fine, just fine, Arlene. They're excellent boots."

"Hi, Ma!" said Bob, coming into the hall. "I wish you'd let me come and get you. You shouldn't be spending your money on cabs when we have a perfectly good car to take you places."

"You're not my chauffeur, Bob." She took his arm. "Help me to a chair. But I'll be pleased if you'll take me home."

"Of course I will, Ma, you know that."

He took her, slowly, to the straightest-backed chair in the living room, and she sat, carefully, stretching her left leg out in front of her with a huge sigh.

"Is it bothering you, Ma?"

"Well now, it pretty well always bothers me some, Bob."

"Yeah, but you look a little pale, a little drawn. Doesn't she, Arlene?"

"You do, Mother. How about a nice hot cup of tea?"

"How about some sherry? You got any?"

Bertha preferred her own old, comfortable house to

133

this one, but she didn't mind visiting here now and then. Modern houses didn't have a great deal to recommend them, but at least this one had a fireplace. It was a big house, too.

That's about the only thing I don't like about mine, thought Bertha. The rooms are poky, downright poky.

Bertha had assumed that since Bob and Arlene had bought such a large house—a bedroom on the main floor, in addition to a living room and a dining room, plus two more upstairs, along with a den for Bob—they must be planning a large family. But she'd been waiting eagerly for two years, now, ever since they moved from the apartment, and still there was no sign of a grandchild.

After dinner they sat in the living room again. Bob and Arlene kept looking at one another, sneakily; there were holes in the conversation, filled only by Bertha's chatter.

"What's the matter with you two?" she said finally.

"Nothing!"

"Oh for heaven's sake, Bob. You're peering at each other every two seconds; you don't know what to talk about—what's on your minds?"

"Well, Ma. We got you a present."

"What for? It's still a month, almost, till Christmas. And my birthday."

"This isn't really a present, Mother," said Arlene. "It's just something we want you to have, and we don't want to wait until Christmas for you to have it."

"Well then, let's see it," said Bertha.

They brought out a long, skinny box. It looked like the kind of box people send out flowers in, except it was too long even for that. Bertha undid the wrapping paper.

"It's from Birks, for heaven's sake," she said, and took off the lid.

It was a cane. An elegant cane, covered with black leather, with a large black rubber tip at the end.

Bertha took it out. She didn't know what to think of it.

She swung it around in the air, looking at it critically. Bob and Arlene couldn't think of anything to say, so they sat quietly watching her. She was pretty sure they were nervous.

She poked it at the carpet. It felt very strong. She put it straight down beside her, rubber tip on the carpet. She leaned on it and stood up.

"My goodness me," she said, astonished. Her hip was astonished, too; here was her body, standing straight up, and her hip had done hardly anything at all. "My goodness me."

She flung out the cane in a clumsy arc and pounded it down into the carpet again and leaned on it instead of on her right leg. It was a strange feeling. Be hard to learn to really trust the thing, she thought. But if it comes from Birks, it must be all right.

She circled the room, the jerky thrusts of the cane becoming more controlled. She listed to the right, and could feel that she moved clumsily. But that cane gripped the carpet the way her crepe soles should have gripped the snow. She wondered how the cane would do on ice, and decided despondently that it would do not one whit better than her own feet. Still, it was certainly easier to get around inside with the cane; it was a great deal easier.

She limped back to her chair, sat down, leaned her right arm atop the cane, and announced, "I like it. I like the thing."

Bob and Arlene laughed out loud, and Arlene got up and jumped around.

"You're going to bore holes in the rug, doing that with those shoes on," said Bertha, but even that didn't stop Arlene from smiling behind her rhinestone glasses.

"That's what I call a present," said Bertha, inspecting it again.

It wasn't at all what she would have expected from them. She knew, pushing herself up on her new cane, that she'd be able to manage just the way she was for a good long time yet.

Chapter
19

He drove up to the house, took a deep breath, and got out, suitcase in one hand and briefcase in the other. He walked up the sidewalk, figuring he'd shovel it the next morning, and onto the porch and through the door.

"I'm home," he called, and he smelled the sour smell of the place and saw the sofa sitting lopsided on the living-room floor and saw the newspapers piled up along the wall and an immense depression fell upon him. She's not getting better fast enough for me, he thought, friends or no friends.

Heather ran down the stairs, her fair hair hanging in the air behind her, pale, thin arms outstretched, a grin upon her face, her blue eyes gleaming. She flung her arms around his neck and he dropped his cases and hugged her, smiling.

"How's my girl?"

"Fine, Daddy."

He heard Betty clumping quickly along the upstairs hall and saw her coming down the stairs, hair frizzly atop her head, face grimy, purple dress bunched around her bust and hips, huge fat knees twinkling below as she thumped down the stairs, legs pumping, fat feet thrust into red slippers. He let go of Heather and put an arm around Betty's shoulder and kissed her on the cheek.

"I'm home," he said again, and she beamed at him.

She can't be glad to see me, he thought. I don't care about that big smile and all the excitement; she can't be glad to see me or she would have washed her face, for Christ's sake, and changed her dress, that thing is filthy. He wondered, despairingly, where all his hope had gone.

She looked at him, wonderingly, her head cocked in

that irritating way—so posed, so deliberate, as if she were trying to be a cute little girl for him. Then her face was split by an enormous grin and her eyes lit up and he couldn't imagine what had caused this. Had she just realized it was him, for God's sake? Did she meet everyone who came through the door that way? He looked at her, incredulous. Be patient, he told himself angrily. Be patient.

She sobered, and said, "I'll start dinner, Jack. Why don't you and Heather go into the living room; you can read the paper or talk and I'll get dinner. Go along now, go along." She pushed him through the archway into the living room. Heather ran ahead and snuggled into the couch. He sat beside her and put an arm around her and asked her to tell him about school.

From the kitchen he heard nothing for a while. Then cupboard doors opened and banged shut and he could hear her shuffling around in a drawer and grabbing handfuls of silverware, and she began to sing—a clear, tremulous voice rising triumphantly from the kitchen. He stopped looking at Heather and glanced towards the kitchen.

"She's in a good mood," said Heather. "She always sings when she's in a good mood."

The singing continued, getting louder and louder. "The Wedding of the Painted Doll" was the song she sang. Jack wanted to ask her to stop, but she was in a good mood, she was singing, and he didn't want to hurt her feelings. For Christ's sake, I've only been in the house for five minutes—but it went on and on, and finally he yelled.

"Hey!"

The singing stopped. All sounds from the kitchen stopped.

"When's dinner?" he called, trying to sound pleasant. The silence in the kitchen continued.

"Soon!" Betty's voice boomed out. "Soon!" She appeared around the doorway into the dining room, flushed, quivering with energy. "Why don't you put your things away first, Jack, put your things away upstairs."

"Come and help me, kitten," he said to Heather, and they went into the hall.

He took his suitcase and Heather took the briefcase and they went upstairs and down the upstairs hall to his den. He opened the door and turned on the lights. He started to walk into the room, but his eyes snagged on the wall behind his desk and he forgot to move his feet. He couldn't figure it out. What was going on? He heard Heather gasp.

And suddenly Betty's voice, right behind him, right in his ear, hollered, "Surprise!" and she darted around him and into the den and into the middle of the room; smiling and smiling, she danced up and down, face red, chest moving up and down. "Surprise!"

He stared, sick, at the wall, where WELCOME HOME JACK! appeared to be written in large, black letters, the words weaving drunkenly downwards from one side of the wall to the other. Betty stared at his face and laughed. Jack looked thoughtfully at the wall, then at Betty, then he glanced around the room and saw that the same message had been printed on the wall at the opposite end of the room. He felt himself gathering anger.

"See? Welcome home! Welcome home Jack!" Betty laughed. "It took me ages, simply ages. What do you think? What do you think?" She came close to him and peered into his face. He could smell her breath, which was stale.

"Why didn't you use some paper?"

Betty gave him more peals of laughter.

"Of course I would have used paper, of course I would have, but I couldn't find any. Isn't that amazing? In this whole house, this whole big house, there wasn't one piece of paper big enough to write welcome home Jack on it, not one, isn't that funny?"

"You could have used a brown bag from the Safeway store," said Heather, shocked. Betty's face became redder, and cloudy.

"Why didn't you go out and buy some?" said Jack, still staring at the walls, still holding his suitcase.

"Well I would have, of course," said Betty, impatient, glaring at Heather, "except that I wanted to do it right away. I might have forgotten to do it at all if I hadn't done it right away."

"But Mom, you've ruined his walls!"

"*His* walls? *His* walls? What do you mean, *his* walls?" Betty's voice grew loud and shrill. "This is *our* house, *ours*. These walls are as much mine as anybody else's, aren't they, Jack? Jack?"

He looked at her. "Yes, Betty, of course. Of course they're your walls. You've ruined *your* walls, do you like that better?" He was breathing fast now, and he felt prickly all over. He was angry, and he felt strange, as though he'd come to the wrong place.

Betty leapt in front of him and grabbed his face between her hands. She stared hard into his eyes, and Jack stared back at her; her face was wrinkled up with effort, and he wondered what the hell she was looking at, what she was looking for. He heard her breathing, heavy, and saw her pale eyes and her pudgy face. In her eyes was coldness and a tremendous effort to see. Shock hit him through the strength of her hands, and he felt himself flinch, felt his mind turn and run; and then she began to smile in her cold eyes and she let go of his head. He trembled when she let go of his head.

Heather watched.

Betty planted her fists on her hips.

"There," she said.

She marched out of the room and down the stairs and through the house and Jack and Heather heard the cupboard doors banging and Betty singing "The Wedding of the Painted Doll", and Heather began to whimper and Jack put down his suitcase to comfort her.

Chapter
20

"Mom, I'm going to be late for school."

"No no no you're not, it's only eight o'clock, you have lots of time. You eat your cereal and talk to me, talk to me about Christmas. I think we'd better make plans for Christmas, don't you? It's not so very far off now and your father will be home and we'll have a real celebration, a family celebration for Christmas, won't that be nice?"

"Oh, Mom."

"I don't understand your attitude," said Betty sharply. "I don't understand it at all. Christmas is a family time; I'm trying to make plans for it and you aren't even interested. I don't understand it. Why aren't you interested?"

"Oh, Mom. You say this every year."

"Do I? Do I really? Do I say this every year? And what do we do, then, every year at Christmastime?"

Heather slumped in her chair and stirred her cereal around in the bowl with her spoon. "Oh, Mom."

"No, I want to know. If I say this every year, and if you remember it so well, then you must also remember what happens every year at Christmas, what we do every year at Christmas, and I want to know what that is, what you remember."

She reached across the table and grabbed Heather's arm. Heather looked at her hand clutching her arm.

"Nothing much. Dad gets a tree. We decorate it. He gets a turkey. He gets presents. That's all."

"*Dad* does all this? *Dad* does it? Not me? Not me?"

"Well sure, Mom, you do things, too. Come on, Mom, I've really gotta go. Come on!" She wrenched her arm free and threw the spoon onto the table.

"Don't go yet, Heather. I have lots of ideas for Christmas this year, honestly I do, I got them from my friends, I'm all excited about Christmas, you'll see, you'll see."

Heather looked at her suspiciously. "What friends?"

"What friends? Why *my* friends! My *new* friends! I've made two of them. Right next door! One on either side!"

"You've made friends with Mrs. Dwyer, too? With Shelley's mother?"

"Sheila. Yes. Isn't that wonderful?"

"I guess."

"And with Bertha, too. She lives on the other side. She's having her son and her son's wife over to her house on Christmas Day. Maybe we'll drop in to say hello!"

"Oh, *Mom*, I don't even *know* those people!"

"You know Bertha, all right, don't tell me you don't know Bertha, she told me the first time I met her that you used to go over there to visit her, so don't tell me you don't know her."

"Not her; her family. I don't know her family."

"Now Sheila, Sheila doesn't have any family near by, and neither does her husband, but Sheila's mother might come from somewhere quite far away, I can't remember where, and then there will be Sheila and her husband and her mother and her two children. And they're going to make a Christmas cake, and each year they make some decorations for the tree, they *make* them, Heather, they don't just *buy* them. . . . "

"Oh Mom!"

" . . . and Bertha makes mulled wine on Christmas! That's hot wine. With cinnamon and . . . other things in it. We could do that, too. That would be very nice, extremely nice, I thought. And I'm going to ask Jack to put up Christmas lights on the outside of the house this year. He has to do that part of it because I can't climb a ladder well. But you and I are going to make the Christmas cake, and maybe some cookies, and some tree decorations, and maybe I'll ask Jack to make the mulled wine, too, that's a good thing for him to do . . . I should write all this down. . . . "

She looked vaguely around the kitchen for a pencil and some paper, her fingers drumming on the top of the table.

"Stop it! Just stop it!" Heather shouted, flinging herself up from her chair. Betty looked at her in amazement. "You'll never do all this, never!" Heather was crying. Betty couldn't understand it. "You'll forget about it even before I get home from school, I know you will, I know it! And Christmas will be the same as ever and I'll *hate* it *hate* it I just wish it was all *over* that's all don't talk about it don't talk about it!"

She rushed from the kitchen, and in a few seconds Betty heard the front door slam. She sighed and shook her head.

"I've got to make a list," she whispered, and began searching. She found paper and pencil in Heather's room, and she took them back down to the kitchen and pushed the dishes to one side of the table.

CHRISTMAS, she printed at the top of a piece of paper, and underneath she printed CAKE, DECORATIONS, WINE, LIGHTS. Beside the first two she printed ME & HEATHER, and beside the last two she printed JACK. She looked at the list. She smiled. She felt very efficient, very organized.

That afternoon when Heather came home Betty was lying on her yellow bedspread. She heard Heather go into the kitchen. In a little while she heard a knock on her door. She thought about ignoring it, as she often did, but she said, "Come in," and Heather came in. She had a piece of paper in her hand.

"I did the dishes."

"Good."

"I found your list."

"What list?"

"Your Christmas list."

"Oh."

Heather came over to the bed and sat on the brown

chair. Betty found it irritating that she had sat down without asking. But she was very quiet sitting there. Betty's irritation faded.

"We could do this," said Heather.

"Do what?"

"The things on this list. We could do them."

Betty sat up slowly and leaned back on her hands. "Could we?"

"Yeah. Sure."

"How?"

"We'd have to get the recipes. For the cake and the wine. You could get them, from your friends. Or I could."

"No. Not you. I could."

"Okay. You could get the recipes. Then I could write out all the things we need to make them and I could go and get it. Except for the wine. I couldn't get that."

"Jack could get that."

"Yeah. He could. So I could get the stuff for the cake and the decorations. You could ask Mrs. Dwyer . . . "

"Who?"

"Mrs. Dwyer. Shelley's mother."

"Oh. Sheila."

"You could ask her what kind of tree decorations they make and get her to write down what things you need to make them. And I could get those, too."

"You think we could do it, then?"

"Yeah. Yeah, I think we could."

Betty sat on the edge of her bed. "You're very sturdy for such a frail child."

"I guess."

"All right then. Let's do it. Let's make them."

"When are you going to go over there? To get the recipes? And find out about the decorations?"

"Tomorrow. I'll go tomorrow."

"Okay. Don't forget."

"I won't forget." She stretched out a hand towards Heather, but Heather was looking down at the list and

143

didn't see it. Betty watched her daughter curiously. She was so nice, sometimes. But such a stranger.

Who was she, anyway? Had Betty ever been like this? No no no no daughters stay the same mothers stay the same you can't be both never never never. . . .

Chapter
21

"Has anyone seen my purse?" yelled Sheila.

"It's in here. On the coffee table," Ed yelled back.

She ran downstairs to get it. "It's got my lipstick in it." She ran back upstairs to the bedroom.

"What's going on?" Ed stood in the doorway.

"It's parent-teacher night and it's my turn, remember?" She brushed her hair, hard. "What's the time, anyway?"

"Seven. You've got lots of time." He came in and sat down. "We could both go, if you like. The kids would be all right by themselves for an hour."

"Too bad you didn't think of that sooner," said Sheila, dabbing her face with a powder puff.

"It'll just take me a minute to change my shirt," he said, standing.

"No, don't," said Sheila. She turned around.

"How come?"

She turned back to the mirror. "I'm taking Betty."

"Betty? Betty who?"

"Betty Coutts. From next door."

"Oh for God's sake." He sat. "You're taking *her*?"

"That's right." Sheila touched up her mascara. "Her daughter goes there. I asked her if she was going tonight and she got all nervous and stammered around, so I said she could come with me if she wanted, and she said she did."

"Oh for God's sake, Sheila."

"Well, what's the matter with that?" she said, whirling around.

"Don't glare at me, for God's sake. I'm just surprised, that's all. I thought the woman bugged you."

"I think about her."

"What do you mean, you think about her? Well, hell, I don't blame you. She's cuckoo."

Sheila stood up. "She's not cuckoo. She's lonely."

"Yeah, but since when were you a good Samaritan? You've always avoided neighbours like the plague. There are probably all kinds of lonely people around here; do you plan to take them all on?"

"Don't be ridiculous," she said. "This one just got forced on me, and I guess I feel sorry for her. She's different."

"Yeah, I think so, too."

"I would greatly disapprove of some of your friends, also, I'm sure," she said, going out the door.

"Now what's that supposed to mean?" Ed called after her, angrily.

"I'll get the door, Mom," said Shelley, and she let Betty in.

"My goodness, my goodness, and here I thought I'd be late!" said Betty loudly, showing her teeth.

"Hi, Mrs. Coutts," said Shelley.

"But you haven't even got your coat on yet, have you!"

Sheila set her handbag down on the hall table and got her coat from the closet.

"It's quite warm outdoors, quite warm," said Betty, her cheeks bright pink. "You won't need scarves and things, not tonight."

" 'Bye all," said Sheila.

They walked into the school together. It was the first time Betty had ever been there. She looked around as though she were a traveller and felt superior, and then she thought about Heather coming here every day—Heather knowing this school as well as Betty knew her house— and she felt afraid again. But Sheila was beside her, and together they walked through the lobby and turned down a wide hall. There were people streaming in the same direction—mothers and fathers, all of them, but more

146

mothers than fathers. Sometimes they greeted one another.

"Hello! How are you! Are you sending Brian to camp?"

"Oh yes, he wouldn't miss it. . . . "

"Isn't it lovely weather? I hope it stays for a while—just long enough to melt some of the snow. . . . "

Into the gymnasium they went. In here the noises were booming. Betty clutched her hands together on the strap of her handbag and was glad that Sheila was there. They went on and on, down an aisle, through rows of chairs, Sheila sailing along as though nothing at all were wrong. But Betty could feel people looking at her and whispering.

She remembered standing in front of her mirror, putting on lipstick and eyeshadow. Such a long time it had taken, because she wanted it to be just right. She was already wearing her coat and hat by then, because she wanted to be ready on time, and she got very very hot putting on her makeup. She got to Sheila's house early—Sheila was rushing around, frantically. Betty had laughed and stood there in the hall feeling poised and relaxed as she watched Sheila rushing about. Now, in the auditorium, *she* was the frantic one and Sheila was poised and relaxed; she couldn't understand how it had happened.

They found two seats and sat down. Betty began looking around, jerkily, at the people there. The noise was very loud: shrill laughs, booming voices hollering greetings, and underneath it all a ribbon of whispered conversation about Betty winding itself around and around her neck. It was very hard to breathe, very hard, so she undid the buttons on her coat; and as she looked down to do this she saw with a shock that she had forgotten to change her dress. She still had on the polka-dotted one with the stains down the front. Hastily she did up the buttons again, looking around furtively to see if anyone had noticed.

"What are you doing?" asked Sheila.

147

"Doing up my coat, it's cold in here, so cold, isn't it? Aren't you cold, too? Aren't you?"

"Not me. I'm not."

Betty saw that Sheila had taken her coat right off. Betty removed her gloves and held them in her hand, trying to look casual.

"What happens?" she asked.

"What, here?"

"Yes."

"After a while the principal comes out and talks for a few minutes, and then he'll probably introduce all the teachers again, and when that's over we go off and find our kids' teachers and talk to them. You have to stand in line for a while, but not long, usually."

"How do you know where to go?"

"The principal tells us. He'll say, 'Miss Jones is in Room So-and-so,' and then you go to Room So-and-so."

"But how do you know which teachers to see, you can't see all of them, you wouldn't want to see all of them."

"Oh God, no. You just go to the ones that teach your kids. Who teaches Heather?"

"Who teaches her? I don't know. She's never said."

Sheila shook her head sceptically. "Then we'll go up and ask the principal or somebody. Don't worry about it."

Betty looked nervously around the gymnasium. Stuck to the high high walls were big black cut-outs of human figures doing gymnastic exercises and throwing balls. The big room was almost filled with people now, all laughing and chattering. She continued to hear shreds of conversation about her—comments about her good coat and the blue woollen hat she wore, about her gloves and her handbag, and about her size. She knew they were talking about her, she could hear them, and she began shaking her head gently from side to side, distorting the voices before they reached her ears, so that they faded out and abruptly in again. She shook her head harder and harder

148

so the fading in and out happened faster and faster and then she couldn't distinguish any of the words at all.

Sheila was shaking her arm. "Betty! What's the matter? Does your head hurt?"

She stopped, warily. Just a hum in her ears, no voices. "No, no I'm fine, fine."

The principal came onto the stage. She knew it was the principal because he said he was. He had a soft voice, so it was good that he had a microphone. He didn't seem to know how to use it properly. He would adjust it with his hands and let go of it, and it would fall back down its metal stand. So his voice started out loud, filled with sharp whistles which hurt the ears, and when he let go of the microphone and it dropped, his voice faded out, just like when she shook her head. But he seemed not to be doing it on purpose; he seemed quite agitated that it was happening. Betty laughed. He finally got it to stay where he wanted it, but the whole time he spoke his hands hovered near the microphone as though he wanted to grab it, or at least be ready to grab it when it fell again— but it never did.

Betty didn't hear much of what the principal said.

Next he introduced the teachers. From throughout the audience they popped to their feet and bobbed their heads and sat quickly back down again. Betty tried to get a good look at them, but couldn't; they popped up and down too fast, like jackrabbits. Why don't they want me to see them, she wondered urgently. Then the principal said some more things—ah yes, he's saying in what rooms which teachers would see the parents, thought Betty. She began to feel panicky, not knowing what teacher she wanted to see. Then she remembered that Sheila was there.

The principal stopped talking, and the audience got up and began moving towards the doors. They talked and laughed and there was a buzz that became a roar, and again the undercurrent was there, the thorny undercurrent which spoke of Betty in rasping whispers.

149

"Listen, what room's your daughter in?" Sheila was pulling at her arm.

"She's—she's—I don't know, she's in Grade Five."

Sheila looked exasperated. "Okay. Wait here."

Sheila vanished up the aisle, struggling against the current, heading for the stage where the principal squatted at the edge, talking to some parents and laughing with them. Betty remained in her seat, pretending that if she did not move nobody could see her.

"Excuse me," said a woman standing above her. She wanted to get past. Betty couldn't think what to do. "Excuse me," said the woman again, irritated.

Betty moved her legs out into the aisle so the woman could get by. Other people coming down the aisle were stopped by Betty's legs and by the woman trying to thrust herself out into the stream of people. Betty stared at her knees, with the good dark blue coat over them. The people edged past. The woman struggled around Betty's legs. Betty was sweating. She felt as though she'd been placed in a cage.

She looked at all the people coming down the aisle towards her, the features of their faces swollen and ugly, teeth huge in ugly smiles as they threw laughter over their shoulders at other ugly-faced people. She could not see Sheila. She wondered how long it would take the gymnasium to empty itself of people. Then she would be sitting there alone, in silence, and could figure out what to do. But it was taking such a long time, such a very long time, and still the people streamed on and on. . . .

"Come on," said Sheila, and she hoisted Betty to her feet and propelled her out into the current.

They were swept down the aisle, around the back of the gymnasium, out the door, and into the hall, where Sheila shoved Betty against a wall and looked intently at a piece of paper crumpled in her hand.

"You go to Room Ten, Miss Jorgenson, and I'm in Room Three and Room Five. I'll take you to Room Ten, okay? You just wait there when you're finished, and I'll come back and get you." She clutched Betty's arm again and launched them out into the hallway. "Christ, I hate these things."

Betty said nothing. Sweat was pouring down her scalp and she wished she could take off her coat. Her feet hurt in her rubber boots, which were too small for her and which she seldom wore for this long a time. She lurched along next to Sheila, around and around the school in a dreadful kind of waltz, and then Sheila pushed her into a classroom.

"There you are. Just stand in that lineup. I'll be back as soon as I can."

Betty knew immediately that this was not a room in which Heather spent much time.

There were maps all over the walls, and some mathematics equations were written on the blackboard in chalk. There were no school desks, she was surprised to see. Just tables and chairs. She wondered where the students kept their books and their treasures. There was carpeting all over the floor—brown. The room had no windows. Against one of the longer walls was a long table, like the others, and behind it sat a young woman, and in front of it a man and a woman sat talking earnestly with her. The line stretched from that couple to the doorway through which Betty had just come. There were several women alone in the lineup, and three women who were with men.

Betty felt not quite so strange. She was not the only person here alone to talk with the teacher about her child. And she had not come by herself, either; a friend of hers was somewhere else in the school, talking to another teacher—or waiting to talk to one. The couple laughed at something the teacher had said, and pushed back their chairs and stood up to leave. Standing, they continued their conversation with the teacher for another couple of minutes. Betty began to feel impatient. Then they said

151

goodbye and left, smiles plastered upon their faces. A woman took their place and sat down.

Other parents joined the lineup behind Betty. She thought about turning to talk to them; then she heard their breathing and her skin prickled and she stood tensely, unmoving, until they had lost interest in her.

Betty knew that if Heather had really spent a great deal of time in this room, she would have been able to smell her. She began to wonder just where Heather did go every morning; just how she did spend her days. She wished Jack were there.

There was just one couple ahead of Betty in the lineup now. She realized that she had no idea what to say to this teacher. She looked at her carefully. Pug nose, freckles, long hair in a ponytail, no makeup. "Miss Jorgenson" the sign said. This was Heather's teacher? Why had she not called Betty to tell her that Heather was not coming to school? She had probably craftily waited, not saying anything about Heather's absences, until Betty showed up for this, the parent-teacher conference, so that she could confront her with it face to face.

But it isn't my fault that she doesn't come, thought Betty. I give her breakfast and I send her off to school every morning. She played with the clasp on her handbag. She was agitated, worried. Could they blame her? Could they?

"Hello," smiled Miss Jorgenson.

"Hello!" said Betty jovially, and smiled widely at her.

"Won't you sit down?"

"Why yes," said Betty, surprised. "Of course, I'd like to, thank you, my boots are too tight and I had forgotten that my feet were hurting, thank you!"

Miss Jorgenson continued to smile. "I teach one of your children, do I?" she said.

Betty looked at her in astonishment. She laughed, slapping her handbag on her knee. "One of my children! You teach all of my children! All one of them!" She laughed again.

"Ah. And who is that?"

"Who is . . . Oh! Heather! Her name is Heather!"

"Oh yes, Heather. She's a lovely child, Mrs. Coutts."

"How did you know my name?"

"Well, I know Heather's name. And so I know yours. Your last name, that is."

"My first name is Betty."

"Ah. Well," said Miss Jorgenson, shuffling through some papers on the table. "Well, Heather is doing just fine, Mrs. Coutts. She's a bright little girl, a hard worker. About the only comment I have to make other than that is that she's very quiet."

"That's good!" Betty was enormously relieved. The teacher hadn't even noticed that Heather wasn't often here! Because she was so quiet!

"Well, yes, it is. But perhaps Heather is *too* quiet, do you know what I mean?" said Miss Jorgenson, seriously. "She doesn't spend much time talking to the other children. She keeps to herself, you know? Is she like that at home? Does she have friends in the neighbourhood?"

"Oh yes, yes, she has many friends, many." Betty was very tense. She hadn't known what it would be like to meet a teacher. She didn't like it, she decided. There were too many other people around. This teacher seemed a pleasant enough person, but stupid. Oh, there were so few clever people in the world!

"But you don't teach her about making friends, do you?" said Betty. "You teach her about reading and books and figures and history and things like that. Why should it matter if she's quiet? There are a lot of quiet people in the world. They are quiet so that other people can be heard. There is nothing wrong with that."

She was sweating profusely. She could feel drops on her forehead and knew that in a minute they would begin to fall down the front of her head and be seen. She was confused and angry. There were murmurings in the line of parents behind her; she could feel their breath again. She reached behind her and made swatting motions.

153

"Oh no," said Miss Jorgenson, her smile gone for good. "Of course there's nothing wrong with that. Mrs. Coutts . . . "

But Betty had gotten up from the chair and was working her way back through the lineup towards the doorway. There were a lot of people in the lineup. They had big chins and small eyes. She reached the door and went through it into the hall, and tried to remember what to do next. She was supposed to wait for Sheila, that was it.

She leaned against the wall and stood on one foot and then on the other, easing the pain in first one and then the other. The noise was much less out here. Occasionally a parent or two parents together would scuttle out of a classroom and head for the front door of the school, talking busily together. As parents came out of the classroom she'd been in, they looked at her strangely as they passed, and she knew they were talking about her. A man in a pair of overalls, carrying a big mop and a pail with a wringer thing on it, sauntered down the hall, whistling. He was short and bent over, and he had grey hair and a lined face. He nodded to Betty as he passed, which startled her.

Sheila rushed down the halls while struggling into her coat. She'd been thinking more about Betty than about her children while she talked to their teachers. Betty had seemed extremely nervous—and she didn't even know Heather's teacher's name, for God's sake, thought Sheila, worried. I don't think she's ever *been* in this place before.

She hurried along, greeting people she vaguely remembered, wondering whether Betty would still be in the building. My God, I hope she didn't try to leave before she even saw the teacher, she thought.

She turned a corner and saw Betty leaning against the wall, handbag clutched in front of her, standing on one foot.

"Sorry I was so long, it's hell to have two of them; you

have to do the whole bit twice," she said breathlessly. Betty's face was flushed. She didn't say anything as Sheila pushed her along, down the hall, around the corner, and out the big doors into the mild, whispering night.

Snow was melting. Sheila heard it dripping from the roof of the school in its new form. The sidewalks and streets were clear of snow, gritty with gravel and salt. Patches of darkness had appeared in the school grounds where the snow had disappeared and left the brown grass exposed.

They walked along slowly, through the strong, warm wind. It feels like spring, thought Sheila. But she knew it would soon be cold again, and snowy.

"How's she doing?" she said to Betty.

"Who?"

"Heather. How's she doing at school?"

"Oh. Fine. Fine." Betty walked with her head bent, studying the sidewalk.

"So are mine. Thank God. At least I don't have *that* to worry about." Damn, she thought. But Betty made no response. Sheila looked at her curiously.

"You're awfully quiet," she said.

"Yes, well, I'm feeling quiet, at the moment."

"Is anything wrong?"

"Oh no, nothing is wrong, nothing at all. I'm only thinking." She watched her feet walk, in their high rubber boots.

They turned the corner onto their block. When they got to Sheila's house, she said, "You asked me for a recipe. For Christmas cake."

"Oh? Oh yes, I did." Betty had stopped when Sheila did.

"Do you want to come in and get it now? It'll just take me a minute to write it out for you."

Betty raised her eyes from the sidewalk. "I don't think so, thank you. Not just now." She waited.

"Okay," said Sheila. "But you better get it soon. It's

155

supposed to age for a while. Before you eat it." Betty didn't say anything.

"Well, I'll go in, I guess." Sheila started up her walk. "Goodnight," she called.

Betty was lumbering along the sidewalk towards her house. She didn't answer.

Chapter
22

"Now I came here for a reason today, I know I did," said Betty several days later, as she struggled with her high rubber boots. "Isn't it dreadful to have to put these things on just to come over here from next door. I do hate them, they hurt my feet."

She yanked the first one off and Bertha took it from her and put it on a boot tray in the corner.

"They don't hurt them right now, of course, because I've come such a short distance, but the other night at the school—oh yes!" She straightened up with the second boot in her hand. "I wanted to tell you about that."

"Come on in, then, for heaven's sake, and tell me about it."

"But that wasn't all. I know that wasn't all. I wanted to ask you something else, too, I know I did. . . . " She looked hopelessly at Bertha. "I can't remember."

"Don't worry about it," said Bertha. "If it's important, you'll remember it. If it isn't, well then it doesn't matter, does it?" She took the second boot from Betty's hand and dropped it next to the first. "Did you bring any slippers?"

"Slippers? Slippers?" Betty looked down at her bare feet. "Oh no, I never thought to bring slippers, I didn't think." She cringed, and her toes curled under, trying to hide. "How silly of me! Oh how silly! I didn't expect to go barefoot in your house, really I didn't!" She looked at Bertha in horror.

"Do you think I care? I don't care. Now for goodness' sake, come in, come into the living room, where your feet will be on the carpet." Bertha flicked out her cane, plopped it down in front of her, turned herself around, and limped towards her chair. I'm getting downright professional with this thing, she thought proudly.

Betty skittered to the loveseat and sat down, putting one square, flabby foot over the other.

"Now," said Bertha. "Tell me about the school. That Heather's such a bright little thing, I'll bet her teachers love her. What did they say?" She got out her knitting. It was a lot easier than sewing.

Betty was wearing slacks which appeared to be dark brown, and tucked into them was a white blouse with large buttons. She also wore a black cardigan buttoned almost up to her chest. She sat, twitching her feet so that first one, then the other, was covered by its mate. Her hands played with her slacks, fingers trying to find a non-existent crease or pulling off bits of fluff and dropping them on the floor.

"There was only one of them. One teacher." Her face churned itself into many creases. "I wouldn't have gone, only Sheila asked me to go with her—Sheila who lives on the other side of me."

Bertha nodded, knitting briskly. "The Dryers. Or Dyers. The busy one."

"She has children who go there too. It was called a parent-teacher conference. There were hundreds and thousands of parents there, and I got very hot because I could not remove my coat. I went because Jack has been telling me and telling me to go."

"And so he should," said Bertha.

"He doesn't get many opportunities to go to the school and talk to Heather's teacher, and he wanted me to go this time."

"A good idea."

"But I couldn't have gone, except for Sheila, you see," she said desperately.

"That's all right, then," said Bertha, knitting. "You went. That's the important thing. I bet she'll take you next time, too." Thank goodness I'm not the only one she knows, she thought.

Betty shivered, an unpleasant sight. "I didn't like it

158

there," she said, staring at her twitching feet. "I didn't like the people." She looked up, wonderingly. "And . . . and . . . I knew as soon as I got into that classroom that Heather does not go there every day!"

The click-click of Bertha's knitting needles stopped. "What are you talking about?" she said. "Did the teacher say Heather's been playing hookey?"

"No no no no. That woman is not clever. She said that Heather is quiet in school. She didn't even realize that Heather is not there every day!"

"Then how do you know she isn't? Did Heather tell you?"

"Of course not! She doesn't want me to know!" She leaned towards Bertha. "But I didn't smell her in there!" She sat back and watched Bertha shrewdly.

"In the classroom? You didn't . . . smell her in the classroom?"

"That's right! So you see, she can't have been going there every day. And I don't know what to do about it."

Bertha put her knitting away in the bag. Her heart was speeding up. She crossed her arms. "Well now. I'm not sure you should do anything about it. What did the teacher say about Heather's schoolwork?"

"Oh, she said what you said. She said she was bright. Which of course I knew. And a hard worker. That I did not know."

"Well then," said Bertha, her heart still racing. "If she can do well at school without even being there," she said, "then there is nothing for you to worry about."

Betty looked at her suspiciously. "Shall I not tell her that I know, then?"

"No," said Bertha firmly. "No, I wouldn't do that. But maybe you should tell your husband about all this, next time he comes home. I think that might be a good idea."

A smile spread across Betty's face, like syrup over a pancake. "That's an excellent idea," she said softly. "Truly an excellent idea. I shall do it. And meanwhile," she said, slapping her hands upon her knees, "I shall not worry."

She looked brightly around the room. "Well then," she said. "What shall we do now? Will you play for me?" She cocked her head and smiled.

"Not today, Betty. Not today." Betty looked disappointed, so she added, "I'm working on my Christmas carols. I'll play one of them for you, soon as I have it all polished up."

"That's it!" Betty shouted, and Bertha's heart stumbled. "Christmas! I remember now. I wanted to know if you would tell me how to make hot wine!"

"Oh sure," said Bertha, and she gave her chest a bang. "I'll write out the recipe for you before you leave. Come on now," she said, reaching for her cane. "Let's go to the kitchen and get ourselves some tea."

"I was wondering," said Betty as they sat at the table with their tea, "I was wondering if perhaps we might drop in on Christmas Day. Just for a few moments. To exchange greetings."

"Sure," said Bertha.

"I told Heather you wouldn't mind! I told her!"

"How could Heather think I'd mind that, for heaven's sake. I would be very very happy to see her on Christmas Day."

"I was a very pretty little child, did you know that?" Betty said brightly. "I have a picture . . . sitting on my mother's knee. She had her hair done up in a shiny yellow bun and she wore her eyeglasses. Her dress had flowers on it and she was slim and she smiles in that picture. That was before he came along. Her arms were around me. I had lots of yellow curls on my head and . . . I am wearing a sweater which she knitted for me. A pink one, it was."

"You loved your mother very much, didn't you," said Bertha. "And now you're a mother yourself, and have a daughter to love *you* that way. . . . "

160

"She died, you know," said Betty abruptly. She drank some more tea. "Died," she said, and put the cup back in the saucer. "He sent me a telegram." Her voice was much lighter, softer. "After the funeral he sent it. I picked up the black telephone in my small apartment and a strange person read it to me. I was in Vancouver. She died in Victoria. I didn't go to her funeral." She looked surprised.

"My goodness," said Bertha, shocked.

"He didn't like me. At first he liked me, but not later. And still not, when she died."

"You mean your father? He didn't *like* you?"

Betty looked around the kitchen, as though from a great distance. "Your house is quite clean," she said. "Quite clean," she repeated, sharply.

"I have a woman come in once a week, you know. I can't do it by myself any more."

"One would have to do it every day, over and over again, the same things, just to keep the house looking the same way, tidy. Like running and running and never actually moving, as happens in dreams." She was holding the teaspoon in both hands and clanging it gently against the saucer.

"I have that dream often," she said. "I am running away from someone; or perhaps it's some thing, I'm not sure. I must escape from it, and I'm running along the tops of cliffs overlooking the sea." Her eyes were empty. The clanging of spoon against saucer became louder, more insistent. "Things are not dark, but the sky is not full of light. I think I am escaping and I take a quick look over my shoulder, but I see the something or someone drawing steadily closer."

"Betty . . ." Bertha reached across the table and removed the spoon from her fingers. Here she goes, she thought, and wished the phone would ring.

"Then I see that there is a string tied to the middle of my back, and the person has hold of the other end and is pulling me gently towards him. He runs and pulls me towards him, while I am running and standing still."

161

"Betty. A lot of people have dreams like that. I have them myself, sometimes."

"Then there is a pair of sharp scissors in my hand, from my tools, I think, and I reach back and cut the string and run ahead again; I am always slim and tireless in this dream. For a while I feel the ground whipping past beneath my feet and the sea is a blur on my right, and then I look behind me again and the string is there, again held by the man chasing me, who is even closer now. And this goes on and on. I cut the string and run and it's there again and I cut it . . . I always wake up before the dream ends."

Bertha reached out to touch Betty's hand, which turned over and clasped Bertha's hand strongly. She looked at Bertha, glassy-eyed.

"It almost doesn't frighten me any more. I start to dream it somewhere inside my head and I already know the pattern it will take, and that I will wake up."

"Now, now, my goodness me . . . "

"But some day it's going to trick me," Betty whispered, "and I won't wake up. The thing will get closer and closer and I won't wake up, it will catch me, grab me by my shoulders . . . "

"No no it won't, Betty, it's only a dream. . . . "

" . . . but then I will become enormous, like an enormous balloon, and I will float up into the air with the thing clinging to me, and I will float over the cliffs, over the sea, and hover there until he loses his strength and falls down into the sea and as he falls I will hear him scream and I will laugh again."

They looked at one another. Bertha could smell sweat and she didn't know whose it was.

"Again?" she said softly. "Again?"

"Once someone fell near where I was and I heard the scream." Betty's face was slick and shiny. "I laughed then, because I was very young. That's why. Because I was very young."

162

Bertha disengaged her hand and sat back. "It must have been very upsetting for you," she said carefully.

"I can't remember," said Betty, and got to her feet. "I have to go now." She started towards the front door.

Bertha called her. She didn't answer. Bertha got up and went through the living room and into the hall. It was a long trip; she'd forgotten her cane. She leaned against the wall and watched Betty put on her rubber boots.

"Betty . . . "

"Thank you for the tea," said Betty with a brilliant smile. "Thank you."

She left.

Bertha sat down in her chair and thought. She thought for a long time.

Chapter
23

"Mr. Coutts! Mr. Coutts!"

Jack stopped and looked around. He saw a woman waving from behind the half-open door at the house next to his.

"Yes?" He couldn't see her clearly, although the porch light was on. Just half of her face.

"Could you possibly come over here? For a minute?"

"Well, I'm just on my way in. . . . "

"I'll only keep you a minute," she said from behind the door. "Please?"

Holding on to his suitcase and his briefcase, he went around to her front door. He stopped at the bottom of the steps. She was familiar; he had seen her outdoors a few times, in the summer. He couldn't remember if he was supposed to know her name. He knew she lived alone. My God, he thought, maybe she's got a frozen water-pipe.

"What can I do for you?"

"My name's Perkins," said the woman, and stuck out her hand. Jack went onto the porch to shake it.

"How do you do. Coutts. Jack Coutts. But you already know my name."

"Yes, I know your wife. Could you come inside?"

One of her new friends, he thought, and felt a sense of relief that surprised him.

"Is something wrong?" He glanced at his house and saw a white face peering out from between the curtains in Betty's room. The window was crisscrossed by the branches of the tree outside, and he told himself he couldn't really tell whether it was Betty or Heather. He wondered what he would find this time. Jessup had called it "hostility". He'd said it was probably "healthy". It had taken four coats of paint to cover those words on his walls.

"No no," said the woman. He turned back to her. "I just want to talk to you," she said. "It's pretty cold out there, Mr. Coutts, and the cold's coming in here, too. Could you come in? Just for a minute?"

"Well, I'm just coming home. . . . "

"Now I wouldn't ask you to come in, a perfect stranger and all, unless I thought it was pretty important. Please." She held the door open. He saw a short, grey-haired woman in a dress, with a shawl over her shoulders. He glanced at his house again; the curtain was back in place. He went in out of the cold.

"Come on into the living room," said Bertha, waving her cane. "Sit down here for a minute. Come on," she said.

"Can't we just talk here in the hall? My boots . . . " He held up one foot.

"It's a little hard for me to stand, what with my arthritis. I'd very much appreciate it if you could sit down in here. It will really take only a minute or so. Don't bother about your boots. Please."

He set down his cases and followed her. He was annoyed, but my God, he thought, how can I keep a crippled old woman standing in the hall. And she knows that, too, he realized, and became more annoyed.

Bertha scrutinized him from her chair. Tall, big, with a flimsy moustache and thinning hair. Good eyes, though, she thought hopefully.

"This is difficult for me, Mr. Coutts. Very difficult, me not being either a busybody or a gossip." She noticed that she was holding her cane across her lap and turning it around and around in her hands. She put it down beside her. "I know you're getting impatient, Mr. Coutts. Want to get home to your family. Don't blame you. You probably think I'm a crazy old woman."

165

"No, I don't think that. But you're right; I do want to get home."

"Naturally. I understand that." She fumbled through her mind as though it were a drawer full of words, but she couldn't find any that seemed right.

"I better just plunge right in," she muttered.

"Why don't you do that," said Jack.

She looked behind him at her sewing machine. It was closed up. The table beside it was bare.

"It's like this," she began. Her heart, which had begun to rat-tat-tat away inside her chest when she peeked out her window and saw his car drive up, had not slowed down. "It's like this," she said again. "Your daughter Heather helps me out around here. Watering the plants, things like that. We've been friends, off and on, almost since you first moved here."

Jack clasped his hands between his knees. He thought about the gold chain he had bought Heather for Christmas.

"She's a lovely child, Mr. Coutts. I've become very fond of her." Bertha took a deep breath. "Recently . . . well, not so recently, I guess it was back last spring . . . anyway, your wife and I, we became friends, too."

Jack tried to imagine Betty and this woman together. "That's very nice, Mrs. Perkins," he said. He couldn't understand how it had happened, but he liked the idea.

"It's very hard for me, you see. Now you're right here in front of me—in the flesh, so to speak—I find I don't know what to say or how to say it."

"I can come back," said Jack. "I'll be home for a couple of days."

"No no!" she said, waving her hand in the air. "I've got to get it out right now." She looked him straight in the face. "I'm worried about your wife, Mr. Coutts, and I'm worried about your daughter, too. Your wife doesn't seem to me to be quite right in the head, Mr. Coutts, and I don't know how well she's looking after your daughter and that's the long and the short of it."

166

Bertha's heart was pounding harder than ever, and the room was so silent she thought he must be able to hear it.

Jack sat unmoving. I must have known this would happen, he thought. "What's she done?" he asked quietly. He wanted badly to get up and leave. He felt urgently that he had to get home. "What has Betty done?"

"Well, it's not that she's *done* anything, Mr. Coutts. It's more what she *says*, if you follow me."

"What does she say?"

"Well, she doesn't seem to be in the same place in her mind all the time. Do you know what I mean? No. Well. Sometimes she'll talk on and on about her childhood. It's hard to follow her, but one thing's clear: she's not just telling me what her life used to be like, she's actually going through it again, right here in front of me, and I don't mind telling you, that shakes a person up."

"I'm sorry that she's been . . . annoying you," said Jack with dignity.

"Oh, for heaven's sake," said Bertha. "She's not annoying me. My goodness, I like the woman, Mr. Coutts. I like your wife. It's just that . . . she doesn't seem . . . very fond of your daughter. That worries me."

"What do you mean?"

"It's hard, Mr. Coutts. She . . . she doesn't like to talk about Heather. And I know she doesn't like it that Heather comes over here."

"That doesn't sound too serious," Jack said hopefully, but he wanted badly to get to a phone.

"But there is more," said Bertha desperately. "Betty went to the school a while ago . . . "

"She did?"

"Yes, she did. With the woman who lives on the other side of her—Sheila Dryer, or Dyer, or something. Nice family. But the point is, Mr. Coutts," she said, shaking her finger, "the point is that Betty now thinks that Heather is playing hookey." She put her hand back in her lap.

"Why?" said Jack.

"Now that's a reasonable question. Heather gets good marks, I'm told. Her teacher has good things to say about her. But Betty . . . well, Betty told me that she didn't *smell* Heather in the *classroom*, and that therefore she *can't* be going to school every day. Now what do you think of that?" She looked at Jack with her chin stuck out.

Jack was tired, all of a sudden. He looked down at his feet. The snow from his boots had melted on the carpet.

"She has a doctor, you know," he said softly. He had never told that to anyone before.

"A doctor? What kind of a doctor? A head doctor?"

Jack flinched. "Not exactly. Not a psychiatrist. A psychologist."

"What does she do, call him up when she feels peculiar, or what?"

Jack looked up. There was worry on her face, but nothing more that he could see. "No, she goes to see him every week," he said wearily. "And I call him now and then, just to see how she's doing." He rubbed his forehead.

"Do you want an aspirin?"

"What? Oh no, thanks; I'm fine."

"Well," said Bertha. "Does he know about the thing I told you about? That she went to the school, and that because she can't smell Heather there, she thinks the child's been playing hookey?"

"I don't know," said Jack slowly.

"He should."

"Yeah. I think he should."

"I told her to tell you about it."

"Maybe she will," said Jack, but he didn't sound as though he meant it.

"I told Heather her mother thinks she's been playing hookey." Jack looked at her. "She just smiled, and asked me where she would go if she didn't go to school."

Jack nodded. He stood up, slowly, and looked around him with intense concentration, as though trying to remember where he was.

"It must be a worry to you," said Bertha.

Jack looked at her quizzically. "You mean Betty. Yeah, she's a bit of a worry all right. Sometimes."

"The child's pretty independent, though," said Bertha.

Independent, he thought. Eleven years old, and she's independent. Christ.

Bertha began to struggle to her feet.

"Here, let me help you."

"No, I'm better off shoving myself up with this thing," said Bertha, waving the cane at him and then stabbing it at the carpet. She leaned on it heavily, tottered, then stood upright. "See?"

"I've got to go," said Jack. "I'm sure she's seen the car."

"That reminds me," said Bertha. She got a piece of paper from the top of the piano. "Here. I've written out a recipe for her. She asked for it. Tell her I called you over and asked you to give it to her."

Jack took the recipe card. "She said she wanted this?"

"Yup. She's got all sorts of plans for Christmas."

As Bertha closed the door behind him, she discovered that she was exhausted. The pain in her hip had grown huge.

I've never been one to meddle, she thought. Is that what I did just now? Meddle? But somebody had to.

The stairs leading to her bedroom looked formidably steep.

"I'm home!" Jack called, and stamped his feet on the mat inside the door. The house was very quiet. He could hear his heart beating.

"I'm home!" he called again, taking off his coat and hanging it in the closet.

"Hey!"

He stood still and listened, but could hear nothing. He forced himself not to put his coat back on and run to the phone booth at the shopping centre. He took off his boots, put his cases at the bottom of the stairs, and went into the kitchen, calling. No answer. No sounds. He turned on lights. He went back to the bottom of the stairs.

"Heather? Betty? Where is everybody?" Silence.

He started up the stairs. Betty appeared at the top, in the gloom. She stood there quietly. He stopped. "Betty? Didn't you hear me calling?" She stood silent. "Where's Heather? What's the matter?"

"What were you doing there?"

"Next door?"

"What were you doing there?"

He reached into his pocket and pulled out the recipe card. "Mrs. Perkins asked me to give you this." He held it out to her. She didn't move. He still didn't want to advance farther up the stairs. "Here." Betty stirred and began coming down towards him. As she emerged from the shadows he saw that her face was drooped and sullen. She took the card reluctantly.

"What is it?"

"It's a recipe. She said you'd asked for it."

Betty didn't look at it. She stared into Jack's face. He turned and went down the stairs; jauntily, he hoped. "Are we having that for Christmas? That wine?" He glanced back over his shoulder. She was still halfway down the stairs, looking at the card. "Where's Heather?"

"She has gone to the store. To get some bread." Betty came slowly down the stairs and into the living room.

"Hey! I'll go meet her," said Jack, but Betty put out her hand and he stopped.

"How do you know her name?" she said.

"Whose name?"

"Bertha's. Bertha Perkins's."

"She told me. She called me over to her porch and said she was Mrs. Perkins and asked me to come in and get something she'd promised you."

"What did she tell you?"

"She didn't tell me anything, Betty, what's the matter with you?" He sat on the sofa. "She just told me she was a friend of yours and she had something for you. That's all. Stop staring at me, will you?"

"I don't like it that you went there."

"What was I supposed to do? Did you want me to be rude to her? Say, 'No, take it to her yourself,' or something?"

Betty sighed. "I forgot this. The other day, when I was there."

"I think it's a terrific idea—to have hot wine for Christmas."

"Will you get it?"

"Sure I will."

"We're going to make a cake, too. And decorations. For the tree."

Jack got up and went over to her. He put his hand on her shoulder. "It sounds good. We're going to have a good Christmas."

Betty sighed again. "I don't know." She went into the kitchen. He decided to wait until evening to call the doctor.

At dinner he asked Heather about school.

"It's okay, I guess."

"That school has no desks," said Betty.

"Did you go there?" said Jack quickly.

"Yes, I went, I went to the school," said Betty, forking some spaghetti smugly into her mouth.

"When? Why didn't you tell me?"

"Oh, a while ago. You didn't ask!" She laughed. Spaghetti pieces stuck to her teeth.

"What did the teacher say?"

"Oh, she said Heather was bright, and hard-working—and very, very quiet."

"What do you mean by that?" said Heather defiantly.

"It means you're *quiet*! that she doesn't know you're *there*!" shouted Betty, and laughed.

"Come on, of course she knows she's there," said Jack sharply. "Otherwise why would she say the kid's bright, and hard-working?"

Betty looked from one to the other, slyly.

"Heather, I hear you and your mother are going to make a cake for Christmas," said Jack heartily.

"What's the matter with you?" said Heather.

"Why—nothing's the matter with me. I just said, I hear you're going to make a cake for Christmas."

"You're loud, or something."

"Well for God's sake," said Jack, pushing his chair away from the table. "For God's sake. I'm just being cheerful, that's all! I'm just glad to hear about the plans for Christmas, that's all! If that's being 'loud', well excuse me!" He went into the living room.

"Hey, Daddy!" said Heather, and followed him.

"I want some help with these dishes," said Betty, muttering. "I want some help with these dishes!" she yelled.

Chapter 24

The phone booth protected him from the wind, but not from the cold. Jack took off his gloves to flip, shivering, through the phone book and burrow in his pocket for coins.

"Listen, I'm sorry to call you at home, but I got a problem here." He had to wait while Jessup moved to another phone. It's in a study, I bet, thought Jack, with bookshelves all over one goddam wall, or maybe two.

"There. Sorry. What's happened?"

"This old lady next door," said Jack, wrestling cold-stiff fingers into his gloves. "She calls me over and tells me she's worried that Betty isn't right in the head, dammit, and then she tells me Betty can't smell Heather in the school or some damn thing!"

"Take it easy, Mr. Coutts. I don't think I got that. Tell me again."

Jessup leaned forward in the swivel chair behind his desk and pulled a notepad towards him.

"I'm kind of shaken up," said Jack. "She acted pretty queer at home, too. Betty. Listen, this woman says—well, first she said Betty doesn't seem quite right in the head. Jesus. She's not a gossip, or anything like that. She's a nice woman. She's a friend of Betty's, she says. And Heather's." Jack stamped his feet, trying to warm them. Not quite right in the head, he thought. Christ. "Then she tells me," he said to the doctor, "that Betty went to the kid's school and says she knows Heather isn't there much because she couldn't smell her there, or some goddam thing. What is all this, anyway? What does it mean?"

Jessup printed HEATHER on his notepad, in medium-sized letters. Then he made three question marks next to the name.

"My first reaction, believe it or not, is a positive one," he said. "She actually went to the school. I think that's very encouraging, in itself."

Jack stared incredulously at the frost-clouded glass of the phone booth.

Jessup went on, "Of course I'll get her to tell me about it. Her perceptions aren't clear." He heard muffled music coming from the stereo in the living room. He thought about Betty. He put her into one of the easy chairs that faced him across the desk, looked at her sitting there in her grey coat, clutching her big beige handbag, watched her lean forward to confide something to him, heard the clear sound of her laughter as she sank back into the chair.

What they know, he thought, but won't tell us; what they don't know, and we can't find out. . . .

"Yeah," said Jack finally. "Somebody's perceptions are sure mixed up, that's for sure."

"You said she acted strangely at home," said the doctor. "How?"

"She was kind of suspicious, I guess. Depressed. In a bad mood. I don't know." Christ, he thought, what the hell do I know. He saw a little crack in the earth, and it began to widen, and he was on one side and Betty was on the other. Something, he thought, has got to be done.

"It's Christmastime," said the doctor.

"What?" Jack shook his head impatiently.

"People who are troubled are always more troubled at Christmastime. Don't you remember last year? It was just after Betty started seeing me. She was quite depressed. But she improved when the holidays were over."

"Yeah. But it wasn't anything like this."

Jessup printed CHRISTMAS on the notepad.

"She's making plans," said Jack reluctantly, watching his white breath in the phone booth. He shivered. "Wants to make, uh, hot wine, and decorations for the tree."

"Mr. Coutts, you may be bringing me more good news

than bad," said Jessup, smiling. "But I want to see her next week as usual. We should talk about her visit to the school; get that business straightened out."

"Yeah," said Jack, glumly. "Hey! I just remembered something." He pressed his gloved hand against his forehead. "This woman, she said Betty talks in dreams, or some damn thing." He rubbed his forehead, waiting.

"Betty does do that sometimes, it's true," said Jessup after a minute. "She has done it during her visits to me."

"But why haven't I seen any of it? Does she do it around Heather? God!"

"I don't think you need to worry about that. I don't think Betty—well, to be honest, I don't think she'd want to reveal herself to you to that extent. Or to Heather, either. Not yet."

"Yeah. Well. I don't like the sound of it. Not any of it." Jack hunched his head down into the fur collar of his coat. His ears were burning with the cold.

Jessup printed HUSBAND on his notepad. He hoped Betty would feel like talking at her next appointment. They had a lot of ground to cover. There was no point in trying to go too fast, but . . . He sighed.

"Remember, Mr. Coutts, she's gone to the school, and she's made some friends, and she's taking a real interest in Christmas. Those are all very positive steps. Encourage her. Support her. Let her know you're proud of her." He hesitated. "And Mr. Coutts, if you'd just change your mind about looking for another job . . . "

"I know, I know!" Jack said loudly. "Sorry. Yeah. I know." He hung up.

He pushed his hands into his pockets and started home. It was snowing, and the wind flapped open his coat and struck at his thighs.

I've got to be organized about this, he said to himself as he trudged out of the shopping centre. I could do three things.

I could move into a desk job, or quit, if I had to—he

175

shivered in the cold—and get a desk job somewhere else; and then I'd be home every day, keep an eye on things. Get a goddam cleaning woman.

He stamped his feet at the corner, waiting for a car to pass, then crossed the street through the falling snow.

Or, he thought, I could do all that and then just bloody leave; get an apartment somewhere, with Heather. That wouldn't be any harder on her than living with her mother.

He thought about that as he turned the corner onto his street. He squinted up the block at his house. He'd forgotten to leave the porch light on.

Or, he thought, we can just go on the way we are.

The wind zipped through tree branches like cold fingers across the strings of an untuned harp.

She's been to the school, he thought, and made friends, and she's got plans for Christmas.

He remembered WELCOME HOME JACK! and how the letters had lurched across his white walls so shockingly. But that was nearly a month ago, he thought.

He hurried up the street and down the walk to his house.

He felt the light from Betty's window. It was shining upon the snow beside the darkened porch. He reached for the doorknob and got inside quickly, into the dark hallway, before the light could creep across the snow and fall upon his shoulder. He closed the door and turned around quickly and called, "It's me. I'm home."

He felt foolish.

Chapter
25

Christmas came quiet and gentle into the morning, the wind skidding loose snow across icy streets, making a sound like autumn leaves blowing.

Green, blue, red, and yellow lights strung garish messages across the eaves of houses. A small pine tree in one front yard bloomed all in white; it shone timidly in the darkness, pure and brilliant amid the colours of the neighbouring houses.

Some living-room curtains had been swept back to display the Christmas trees inside, on the tops of which swam angels or stars or Rudolph the Red-nosed Reindeers, and whose branches were swathed, more or less evenly, in aluminum tinsel.

Inside the houses, lights popped on in upstairs bedroom windows and in back kitchens.

And outside the wind played indolently with the snow, and the leafless trees shuddered in the cold, and in the eastern sky faint light would soon begin to glow.

Upstairs in their bed Sheila and Ed heard squeals and snorts and muffled laughter and they knew that soon they would have to get up. Sheila looked at the luminous face of the clock radio.

"Seven!" She giggled.

"What's wrong?" said Ed, who hadn't yet remembered what day it was.

"It's seven o'clock," said Sheila. "This is the latest yet. Next year Peter will be asking for an alarm clock."

She tried to guess how much time they had. The stockings and Santa's presents might keep the kids occupied for half an hour. No, less. Peter would want to run upstairs and show them what he'd gotten. And on Christmas, parents couldn't tell kids to buzz off and play for another hour.

Ed reached behind him and fumbled for Sheila.

"Quit it!" she said, slapping the hand away. "They'll be up here any minute." She turned on her side and hugged him, cuddling in to his back. "I hope it's a nice day. Let's make it a really nice day, Ed."

He grunted comfortably. "Let's make it a terrific day," he said into the pillow. "Let's you and me stay right here all day."

"Who's going to cook the turkey?"

"Shelley?"

"No. Not yet."

"Then let's leave the poor bugger uncooked. Let's fast all day. The kids can eat nuts and oranges and candy. That's all they want anyway." He turned over and pulled her close to him. "We can eat each other," he mumbled, his face in her neck.

"What about my mother?" said Sheila, holding him.

"She can eat nuts with the kids."

The door opened and the overhead light blazed down on them.

"Oh for Christ's sake!" Ed yelled. They covered their heads with the bedspread. Shelley and Peter ran shrieking across the room and hopped on top of them.

"Merry Christmas! Merry Christmas!" they shouted.

Two doors away and two hours later Bertha awoke to sparkles of sunshine seeping through her bedroom drapes. She lay still and, cautiously, her mind sought out her hip. It hurt, but not badly. Then she remembered what day it was, and grinned, and felt abashed that after almost seventy years she still got excited about Christmas.

She struggled up and put on a robe and some warm slippers. It was a special day, after all, and nobody said a person had to get dressed right away on Christmas. But if I don't, she thought, I'll have to come up the stairs to get dressed later. She stood in her room, undecided. Then she flung off her robe and got dressed, resentfully.

She had wanted to poke through the morning in her robe and slippers, sipping coffee and listening to Christmas music and maybe even watching some daytime television, an activity she usually deplored. Then, in lots of time, before Bob and Arlene came, she had wanted to have a bath and do her hair and dress herself carefully in her best clothes. But she couldn't do all this, because she was afraid of the stairs and went up and down them as little as possible now—even with her cane to help her.

I am awful close to feeling sorry for myself, she thought. She told herself that she could poke about and sip coffee and listen to Christmas music and watch television just as well with clothes on.

She picked a blue wool dress and put it on. She brushed out her long hair and carefully wound it into a bun, which she pinned to the back of her head. She put on a little lipstick, frowned into the mirror, wiped most of it off with a Kleenex. With difficulty, she made her bed.

She looked around her room and tried to think what she might need later in the day. The presents were all downstairs, under the tree. She put her hairbrush in a handbag, looped the bag's handle over her wrist, took her cane, and went down the stairs. She was relieved when she got to the bottom.

Then she remembered that she had left her pain pills upstairs. She knew she would need them today; today she would be on her feet more than usual. She looked back up the stairs. They were just too steep. She would wait until the children arrived and ask Arlene to get the pills for her. Maybe Bob. Which would make the least out of it, she wondered, irritated.

She put her bag down and went into the kitchen to make coffee. She put on her favourite Christmas record—

Bing Crosby. Arlene had bought it for her. Bertha listened as music filled the empty house. She thought about Bing Crosby being dead; and then she thought he probably didn't mind at all dying that way, on a golf course in Spain. She thought she wouldn't mind that, either.

The smooth familiar voice sang carols to her and the coffee threw out its scent and through the window the back yard glittered in the winter sun. Bertha was happy, and looking forward to two o'clock, when the children would come.

She wondered what kind of a Christmas Heather was having. She wondered if Heather and Betty had done all those things—made a cake, and decorations for the tree. She was glad Heather's father was home. She shut her eyes tight and locked Bing Crosby out of her head and prayed violently that Jack Coutts would never go away again. If you can't pray on Christmas, she thought, then when can you pray. . . .

Inside Betty's house lay stillness.

There were no lights outside, as there were on Sheila's house. There was no wreath, as there was on Bertha's door. But there was a tree—a small but pretty tree—set upon the card table, which had been moved in front of the living-room window. It blinked its colours in rhythm, there being a gadget on the string of lights which permitted it to do so.

Upstairs Heather stirred in her bed but did not yet awaken. Jack lay heavily still, sleeping deeply. And in her bed Betty opened her eyes and looked at the yellow sun coming through her curtains and at the china girl holding the umbrella under which was the bulb of her bedside lamp and at the big brown chair sitting lumpishly beneath the window. She sat bolt upright. It was Christmas.

She listened carefully, so hard that soon she knew she was manufacturing sounds for her ears to hear. She shook her head and listened again, not so hard this time, but carefully. There were no sounds within her house. Nobody, then, was awake this Christmas morning but her. She got out of bed and wrapped her body in her red robe and stuck her square feet into her red slippers. She tiptoed across the room and opened her door. Still no sounds. She went downstairs, avoiding the squeaky stairs, and into the living room.

She smiled broadly at the Christmas tree. She hurriedly went to the wall and unplugged its lights. Sunlight streamed through the window and cast itself golden over the tree and splashed upon the carpet. Betty sat on the blue-and-white hassock, elbows on knees, head in hands, and stared at the tree. She could find nothing wrong with it. It was perfect. Heather had strung cranberries in long ropes and flung the ropes across the branches. She had popped popcorn and strung that, too. Jack had put on the lights. Betty herself had placed the angel on the topmost branch, standing on a kitchen chair to reach it, since it was very tall, the tree, sitting on the table. It was perfect, she thought, and gave it a child's smile.

She was glad she had not gone to see that doctor last week. He would have spoiled her Christmas, she knew it. He didn't like it that she hadn't gone, but she had explained briskly that she was very busy, getting ready for Christmas; and what could he do?

Under the tree were six presents. And tacked with a pin to the back of the chesterfield was a long sock of Heather's, bulging. Betty frowned. She had not liked that. It was Jack's idea.

"I know she doesn't believe in Santa Claus," he had said. "I know she's too old for it. But I want her to have a stocking anyway." He was quite stubborn about it.

He had gone off to the drugstore or somewhere late in the afternoon to get some things to put into the stocking. Betty had flounced loudly upstairs to her room later that night, as he filled it. Now she looked at it angrily and wondered what was in it. She wanted to look, but she didn't dare. Not daring to put her in a bad mood. She tried to push it aside; she did so want this day to be a nice one. She sat up and clasped her hands together. She got up abruptly and went to the kitchen and began preparing breakfast.

A few minutes later, as she put plates and bowls on the kitchen table, she heard Heather coming down the stairs. She heard a small gasp. Heather appeared in the kitchen doorway.

"There's a stocking there. With my name on it." Her name was on a piece of paper which Jack had pinned to the stocking.

"I know," said Betty.

Heather disappeared. Then she appeared at the doorway again. "Merry Christmas," she said shyly.

"And a Merry Christmas to you, too," said Betty, looking at her. Heather went into the living room. Betty heard paper crunching.

"Don't open any of those presents!" Betty shouted, and hurried into the living room.

Heather looked up from the stocking. "I'm not. I'm just opening my stocking. I can do that before breakfast, can't I?'

Betty sniffed and went back to the kitchen. She put the kettle on for instant coffee. She ran back into the living room.

"What's in it?" she said eagerly, sitting on the hassock.

Heather held up a small bottle of toilet water. "There's this," she said, "and this," pointing to a rubber ball and a cellophane envelope full of jacks, "and this," indicating a package of felt pens, in all colours. She smiled. "I know it wasn't Santa Claus. I don't know who to thank."

Jack came into the room. "Merry Christmas!" Heather jumped up and ran over to hug him. He kissed Betty on the cheek. "Merry Christmas!"

Betty felt uncomfortable and embarrassed. She didn't know what to say.

"I've made breakfast."

"Good!"

They went to the kitchen, Heather staying behind for a minute to gather up her stocking gifts. She took them into the kitchen with her and arranged them on the table beside her plate. Jack patted her knee and smiled.

"This is going to be a good day," he said.

Betty sniffed. She was very large and cumbersome.

Sheila's children had opened stockings, gulped their breakfasts, hollered impatiently while the dishes got done, and then run to sit in front of the tree for the best part of Christmas.

Why should it be the best part? thought Sheila, as she did every year. Why are the goddam presents always the best part?

She wished they were a church-going family. She thought church-going people had an edge over everyone else at Christmas. But you've gotta really believe, she thought, and go every week all year long, or it doesn't count; you'd just feel guilty, sitting there once a year for the carols and the Christmas stories from the Bible.

The presents had been torn open and the carpet was littered with scraps of wrapping paper and frayed ribbon.

"Okay, come on, let's clean up this mess," said Sheila, gathering the discarded wrapping paper and ribbon.

"Oh, don't throw those away, Mommy. Don't throw away the bows!" said Shelley. "I can use them for something."

"Pick them up then, dear," said Mrs. Pennington, helping Sheila, "and put them away in your room, there's a girl."

"Come on, you two," said Sheila. Peter and Ed got up and started shoving things into the garbage bag.

They spent the early afternoon playing Monopoly, and when it was time to put the turkey in the oven, Sheila asked her mother to make the stuffing.

"Of course, dear. I'll make some gravy, too, if you like." Sheila didn't usually bother with gravy. When she did, it turned out lumpy.

Ed had made a fire with some logs he'd bought from someone at school. Sheila liked them better than the compressed-paper kind, which didn't smell and didn't crackle.

"Mom used to smoke," said Shelley, when the turkey was cooking. She was lying in front of the fireplace and had watched her grandmother light a cigarette.

"I didn't know that, Sheila."

"Just for a while."

"Hey Mom, isn't it nice to be all together like this for Christmas? I really like it, being together."

"Where else would you be, Shelley, except together?" said Mrs. Pennington, carefully.

"Oh, no place. But Heather . . . " Shelley turned over to stare into the fire.

"What about Heather?" said Sheila.

"This is probably the last time her family will be together at Christmas," said Shelley.

"What on earth do you mean? Shelley, look at me. What are you talking about?"

"Heather told me once—a while ago, I don't know when—she told me that her father was going to take her away. Not like her parents are getting a divorce," she said to Sheila. "Sort of like Heather and her father were getting a divorce from her mother, I guess. Anyway," she said, turning over to watch the fire again, "she said they were just going to go off and leave her mother there, just like that. After Christmas."

"She was probably just telling you a story," said Sheila. She wanted to leap up and vacuum the rug. But you can't do that on Christmas for God's sake, she thought.

"I don't know," said Shelley, shaking her head. "Look at those flames, Mom. There are almost as many colours as when you burn the other stuff."

"Who is she talking about, Sheila?"

184

"The people who live next door. I'm sure there's nothing to it."

"Do you know them?"

"I know Betty, the mother. And Heather, a bit. I don't know Betty's husband. He's away a lot. She's very lonely."

"Is she the one Ed calls your project?" Mrs. Pennington smiled.

Sheila glanced at her mother. "Yeah. She's the one. She's not my project, for God's sake."

"Oh Sheila, I knew some day you'd start taking up people."

"Now what kind of a thing is that to say!"

"Oh, dear, you know."

She's the most elegant-looking widow I've ever seen, thought Sheila. "No, I don't know."

"It's your enthusiasms. Your energy."

"Mom's got a lot of energy, all right. She yells pretty loud."

Mrs. Pennington laughed, and Sheila reached down to muss Shelley's hair.

"That's enough out of you, squirt. Go do something."

"I think I'll phone Katey and ask her what she got for Christmas," said Shelley. She went into the kitchen.

Mrs. Pennington waited a decent interval.

"And how is everything with you, Sheila?"

"I told you, Mom. Fine. I wrote you that. Everything's fine."

"You seem tense, though, dear. Are you sure?"

"Oh hell, I don't know. Sure. Sure, I'm sure. I've just been working too hard. Taking on too many *projects*," she said with a grin.

Goddam him, she thought. If it's true, goddam him. Goddam them all.

Bertha had the turkey cooking when Bob and Arlene arrived. The house smelled like Christmas; and it sounded

185

like Christmas, with the Bing Crosby record playing; and it looked like Christmas—the tree stood in the living room, the sewing machine was pushed into a corner, there were candles on the piano, and holly sprouted from several vases.

Bertha went eagerly to the door, leaning heavily on her cane, glad that they had come and relieved that they were not late, because she really did need someone to get her pills.

"Merry Christmas!" they called. "Happy Birthday!"

"Merry Christmas!" she laughed, and exclaimed over the presents they held in their arms.

"You're playing my record!" said Arlene.

"I certainly am. It's the third time today," said Bertha.

Bob started the wine heating. They gathered in the living room and looked at the tree and the presents under it. Three of us and three of them, thought Bertha. I wish I could believe they'll have as nice a day as we will.

"Are you sure we have to wait until after dinner?" asked Arlene, whose dress was red today, in honour of Christmas. Bertha didn't like it much. But there you are, she sighed to herself, maybe she's colour-blind and doesn't know what it looks like with that hair.

"That's the way we always do it," said Bob. "As you know," he added, poking her with his elbow. Arlene giggled.

"Yup," said Bertha. "That's the way we always do it." She had decided to wait a bit before asking someone to get her pills. No point in stirring them up. She hummed along with Bing Crosby.

"It's not the way we did it at home," said Arlene. She removed her glasses and rubbed them, hard, with a handkerchief.

"And how did you do it at home?" asked Bertha.

"We each opened one present on Christmas Eve," said Arlene, putting her glasses back on. She looked at the tree. "Then in the morning we opened all the rest, even before breakfast."

Bob laughed. "How did your mother ever get you to the table to eat anything?"

Bertha said, "My goodness, what did you do with the rest of the day?"

"We may not have eaten much breakfast," said Arlene to Bob, "but we were sure ready for the turkey. I admit, though," she added thoughtfully, "that the rest of the day was just a little boring."

"Of course!" said Bertha.

"Now what's left to do?" asked Arlene. "I know the turkey's cooking, but what else is there to do, and who do you want to do what?"

"We'll put Bob in charge of the wine," said Bertha. "Later you can help me with the vegetables. When the turkey's done we'll make the gravy. And of course there's the table to be set."

I'd forgotten what a production this is, she thought, suddenly very tired.

"We'll have dinner about five o'clock, and then we can open the presents."

I really do want a pill. My hip does hurt. And it will hurt a lot more once I start doing things.

"What's for dessert?" said Bob.

"Mince pie. Bought it at the bakery."

"Oh, Ma," Bob laughed. "It'll be great." He went to the kitchen. "The wine's hot," he called. "I'll bring it in."

They stirred it with cinnamon sticks. Bob turned over the record.

"Well, Ma," he said, looking out the window. "It's winter."

"That it is, that it is."

"Is this place warm enough?"

"Of course it's warm enough. If the furnace was acting up again I'd tell you, wouldn't I?" She looked from Bob to Arlene and back again. "Ah," she said softly. "That again."

"Oh Mother," said Arlene, putting down her wine.

"Oh Mother. He can't help it. I'm sorry. I don't want us to spoil Christmas. Your birthday." She tried to laugh. "He worries a lot."

"Of course I worry," said Bob. "What do you expect? She's my mother!" He went over to stand beside Bertha.

Arlene rummaged around in her handbag. She closed it without taking anything out; opened it again; closed it.

"I have my cane," said Bertha. "I'm doing real good."

"Ma, even your cane isn't enough now," said Bob. She felt him looming over her.

"Sit down, for goodness' sake, so I don't have to crane my neck."

"It hurts you," he said doggedly, sitting down. "We can see that."

"It's not going to hurt me any less in your house than it does in my own," said Bertha. "You know how I feel about this. I said no the last time and I'm saying no again. I'm staying on my own, in this house, as long as I can. And that's that."

That does it, she thought. How on earth can I ask them to go get me my pills now, for heaven's sake.

"Well, bottoms up," she said, and took a swig of her wine. "Good, Bob. That's very good stuff."

They raised their mugs to her. "Merry Christmas," they said.

"Merry Christmas," she replied grimly.

Betty opened the oven door and lifted the aluminum foil covering the turkey to see how brown the thing was getting. It looked almost done. She wanted to call Jack and ask him if it was time to take it out, but she didn't. She'd keep looking at it herself until it was just the right colour, and then she'd take it out herself. But she'd have him carve it, of course. The man should carve. Besides, she didn't know where the knife was.

She looked at the small table and wished she'd managed to go downtown and buy a tablecloth. But it

188

wouldn't matter, not with a delicious meal on it. The table wouldn't even show.

She went into the living room, where Heather was playing a game with Jack. She wanted to play, too, for a minute. Then she decided she didn't, after all, and she went upstairs to her room.

She looked at her presents. Jack had given her a new robe and slippers, yellow, to match her room, he said. They were very nice. Heather had given her some perfume. She took off all her clothes and dabbed on some perfume and put on her new robe and slippers, her Christmas present—from Jack. They felt scratchy, like strangers grabbing at her body and her feet. She took them off. She didn't want to get dressed again, so she put on her old red robe and her old red slippers and felt very comfortable. She decided to lie down on her bed for a while.

There was no sunshine coming in through the window, and things in her room looked dingy. She got up again and closed the drapes and turned on the lamp.

She lay quietly on her bed, thinking. She thought a lot at Christmas. That was one reason why Christmas was a difficult time. The thoughts were shadows which lived in her head. Their edges kept changing, and the more she thought, the bigger they became. She lay upon her bed, trapped by the shadows, and there was one larger than the rest, with sharper edges. She was glad she didn't have to worry about that any more; but if it would never happen again—and she knew it wouldn't—then why did that shadow stay there? She watched, enraged but helpless, as it grew bigger and bigger. She couldn't move from her bed and it became so enormous it filled the whole space inside her.

She had told him Christmas Day was not the right day for that sort of thing, but he had said Christmas was a day for joy and this was joy. But it was not joy for Betty. She could not even comprehend how the word had become linked with that activity. And this time it was more horrible than ever, far more horrible, because she had known all along, while it was happening, what it was going to do to her. And she knew she had to let it happen, because that was what she was supposed to do.

He took off all his clothes and laid himself beside her on the bed they shared, interrupting her afternoon nap, and put an arm around her and kissed her hair. She felt his breath in her ear, hot, like breath always is. At least she didn't have to feel her own. She tried to get up, but he pulled her back.

"You have such beautiful hair," he whispered in her ear, and stroked her hair with his heavy hand, away from her forehead, where the skin was cool and sleeping. He woke up her skin, moved his hand down her arm and the side of her body to the bottom of her dress, and up, up along her thigh, beneath the dress, and everywhere his fingers touched her, the skin awoke and cried out. But there was nothing she could do for it except lie there and wait, crush her teeth together and wait. Her hand sprang to his, where it kneaded her thigh, sneaking closer to that part of her. She clutched his hand, wanting a rest, wanting more time.

"You have such a pretty body," he whispered, "not fat and not too skinny, like those models."

It humiliated her. What did she have to do with models? She didn't understand him, and she jerked upon the bed, jerked away from his hands.

"Lie still, Betty, you should enjoy it, too. I know you don't want me to know, but I think you do enjoy it, don't you?"

She wished he would stop talking. She didn't like to hear him talk. She could feel her face becoming red from having to listen to him. He had raised himself on one elbow, and was stroking her hair with one hand while burying the other gently in that part of her.

She squeezed shut her eyes and thought about the puppy. She'd forgotten his name, but she remembered him, all right; but she didn't want to, pushed him out of her mind, what to think of, then? Not her mother, oh her mother would scream and rip Jack from the bed and cuddle Betty against her body and croon to her oh where are you where are you Betty screamed inside her head as Jack murmured, kissed her forehead, stroked her hair. "It's long," he said to

190

her, "just like a little girl's; when we have a baby I hope it's a little girl; we'll let her hair grow long like yours. . . . "

Betty's eyes snapped open. She reached for him with both her hands. She took big handfuls of his hair and pulled. Jack's hair was yanked back from her still-clothed breasts; he grabbed her hands.

"Oh Betty Betty," he said and pushed her hands down hard upon the bed on either side of her head. She struggled, and noises came from between her teeth. His face was too close; she saw the moustache, the hot brown eyes, his mouth, and then his large lips pushed against hers. She felt her lips part, felt him kissing her teeth. She kept her teeth tightly together.

One of his hands let go of her wrist and fumbled at her panties, pulling them down. He lay on top of her and pushed her legs apart, and she let him push her legs apart because it was what she was supposed to do, and now she knew it was almost over, so she could let them spread, shutting her eyes tight and not thinking. He pushed his thing inside her. She did not want him in there, but let him come. He put himself in there and then he pumped and pumped himself, his buttocks quivering, shining through the hairs that covered them, and soon he made a high sound into the pillow beside her face and lay still.

She felt the wetness in her and on her. When he finally pulled himself out of her she would have to clean it up, all sticky and gluey. The thought of it made her want to vomit. She turned to look at Jack's head still buried in the pillow and thought again of the puppy.

That was the last time she had let him stay inside her while he finished himself. But it was already too late. And now, of course, it never happened at all any more. Never. She thought, lying on her bed in the Christmas sunshine, chuckling to herself, that if he ever crept into her room and tried to do that again she would hit him with the lamp.

Downstairs Jack and Heather were playing a game which Heather had given him. He was smoking the cigar which Betty had given him; she could smell it all the way upstairs. And there was a Christmas tree in the living room, already dropping needles upon the rug. That tree would eventually drop every single one of its needles upon the rug. She decided to make sure Jack took it down and cleaned the rug before he left again.

The shadows were gone from her head. She had found that they needed to show themselves to her, every now and then, and if she agreed to look at them they went away again, and didn't come back for a long time.

She took down her box of tools and spread them out and looked at them.

She wondered why she was collecting these things; what she thought she would ever do with them. It didn't worry her, though. She knew there was a reason. She just hadn't discovered it yet. But she would, in time; when it was time. She put them back in the box and put the box back on the shelf in the closet and lay down again.

She would be glad when Jack had to go back to work. Then the house would be fully hers and she could get on with her own life: the magazines, the chocolates, taking the pills when she had to, visiting her new friends. . . .

Betty sat up. Bertha! She'd promised to go over and see Bertha today.

She got out of bed and dressed herself. She went downstairs.

"Come on, come on, we've got to go out!"

Jack and Heather looked up from their game in amazement.

"Go where?" said Jack.

"To Bertha's house! I told her we would, I told her we would go over there today to say hello to Bertha and her family, to say Merry Christmas. Come on! Come on!" She rushed to the closet and fumbled around inside for her coat. "We've got to get our things on, even if it is just next door, it's very cold out there, very cold."

"I think we should wait until after supper," said Jack.

Betty turned to look at him. "Why?"

"Why? Well, we don't want to disturb them while

192

they're eating. And, if we went over there now, our turkey might burn and then we wouldn't have a nice dinner. Let's have supper first."

"She's my friend, not yours," said Betty furiously. "I guess I should know when it's all right to go over there." She opened the front door and peered outside. "There's that car parked in front of her house." She frowned at Jack. "What time is it?"

"It's only four o'clock," said Jack.

Betty thought. "All right," she said finally, with conviction. "This time I believe you may be right. We'll eat our turkey first, then we'll go over there. They will probably suggest that we have some dessert with them. And since we don't have any dessert here, that would be pleasant."

"We could have had dessert," muttered Heather.

"Heather," said Jack.

"What? What was that?" said Betty. "What did you say?"

"I said we could have had dessert! We could have had a Christmas cake!"

"Heather!" said Jack.

"We could have! We could have!" said Betty. "But we didn't! A Christmas cake is a very big thing to make! Very big!"

"Yes it is," said Jack. "And we've got a turkey, and some wine, and look at the beautiful tree we have this year."

They all turned to look at the tree.

"Its needles are falling off," said Betty. "I would like you to fix that up before you go away again." She stalked into the kitchen. "Heather! Come and help me make the vegetables."

"Go on, Heather," said Jack. She got up and went to the kitchen.

The phone rang.

"I'll get it," Ed shouted from upstairs.

Sheila and Mrs. Pennington were setting the table. "The white candles, Sheila? And maybe this holly in the middle?"

Sheila went to the dining room. "That's good, Mom. Very pretty."

She got a stool to stand on and hauled the good china out of the top cupboard.

"How long's dinner?" said Ed, coming into the kitchen.

"About an hour. We're just getting the table ready ahead of time."

"I think I'll go out for a few minutes. Forgot to get ice yesterday."

"Where are you going to get ice on Christmas Day?" said Sheila.

Peter came in. "Boy, it sure smells good."

"At a gas station. You can always find a gas station open. Even on Christmas," said Ed.

"You going to a gas station? You going out?" said Peter. "Let me come!"

Ed hesitated. "No, I don't think so, buddy. Maybe you'd better stay home. Play with your new toys."

Peter looked dismayed. His eyelashes started to quiver. "Aw, Daddy. It's Christmas. Let me go with you. Please?"

Ed looked at him impatiently, then at Sheila. "No. Not this time. Be a good boy—set up that new train, okay? We'll play with it when I get back." Peter left the room, sniffling. Ed got his jacket from the closet.

"It's not worth it to wander around the city on Christmas Day looking for ice, for God's sake," said Sheila.

"I won't be long. I'll try two or three places, and if I don't have any luck I'll come right back." He kissed her forehead and swatted her rump lightly.

"What do we need ice for, anyway?" demanded Sheila suddenly. "We've got egg nog—what else do you want to drink?"

"You never know, somebody might drop in. I won't be long."

Sheila and her mother peeled potatoes, wrapped the mince pie in aluminum foil to be heated later, prepared the brussels sprouts. Shelley sat at her place at the table, reading a new book and waiting for dinner.

"I think that's about it, don't you?" said Mrs. Pennington.

"Yeah. Now we just wait till the turkey's done. And Ed gets back." She got the egg nog out of the refrigerator and slammed the door. She poured two glasses, added rum, and sprinkled nutmeg on top.

"Where did he go?"

"To get some ice." Sheila carried the glasses into the living room. The fire was almost out. "You know. For the egg nog."

"Sheila," said Mrs. Pennington softly. "He was restless. There isn't much for him to do, once he's built a fire."

"There's conversation," Sheila snapped. That stuff, she thought with disgust, looks like a lot of tiny bugs floating around in my egg nog.

"But you were busy. With the dinner. He just wanted a breath of fresh air. That's all. Sheila? That's all."

"Yeah," said Sheila. "I know." She shut her eyes and took a drink. At least it doesn't taste like bugs, she thought.

I forgot to ask him who was on the phone.

Bertha sat at the head of the table and watched them, one on either side of her. Their plates were heaped with turkey, mashed potatoes, gravy, vegetables, cranberry jelly, pickles and olives, and each had a roll and a splotch of butter on the side plate. They ate, took a drink of white wine, ate again, drank again.

Bertha's plate was full, too, but she wasn't eating much. It was hard to think about eating. There was too much pain in her hip. Funny how tired it makes me feel, she thought. It's using up all my energy.

"Something wrong, Ma?"

"Nope. Just taking a breather. How's the turkey?"

"Delicious!" said Arlene, forking another bite into her mouth. "Everything's just delicious."

"Don't talk with your mouth full," said Bertha. Arlene's head bent over her plate. My goodness, thought Bertha, just what do you think you're doing. She patted the girl's hand. "Sorry, Arlene. I'm feeling snappish."

Bertha picked up her fork and tried to eat. She thought about getting up to serve the mince pie. She thought about getting up to start the dishes. They'd help, she knew that; but she didn't think she ought to let them do the dishes all by themselves. After all, it was her house. Yes, dammit, it's my house.

It's a shame to waste this meal, she thought angrily. I'll be damned if I will. Christmas dinner comes exactly once a year, and I can't afford to waste any of them. The pills work fast; I'll go and get me one before this plateful turns stone cold.

She got up from the table, using her cane. "I'll just be a minute," she said. She hobbled through the living room and limped slowly upstairs. Not bad, she thought. Not bad at all. I'm doing just fine.

She got her pills from the bathroom medicine chest. I ought to keep them in my pocket from now on, she thought. She took two of them, to make sure they'd work fast.

She hobbled into the hall. She could hear Arlene and Bob murmuring to each other. She knew they were probably talking about her, and she felt like a child who's been sent out of the room. She knew they were concerned about her and wanted only to help; but it still made her angry to have anybody else trying to plan out her life.

She grasped the banister. "Stop whispering down there, you two," she yelled. That'll shake them up, she thought with satisfaction. She threw out her bad leg to the side and placed it on the next step, followed it down with her good leg. "I can hear you, plotting away." She grinned.

196

"We're not plotting, Ma. My God," said Bob loudly.

"Oh, I can hear you all right," she said breathlessly, and threw out the bad leg again, too vigorously. Pain shot through her hip and she gasped, slipped, and fell, and as she pounded down the stairs she was almost glad, through her terrible pain, that it had finally happened; now she would know just how bad it could be, falling down the stairs, which she had been afraid of for such a long time. In a heap at the bottom she knew it was very bad indeed. She tried to call for help but nothing existed, not even her voice, nothing except the pain which bit at her so ravenously that she knew it must have been waiting for a long time for this to happen. Helplessly she let it gnaw at her, and she wondered if it would devour her whole body, or stop with just one side of it.

The children came running and she felt such a fool again, as she had lying outside in the snow. They gawked at her in horror. She knew she lay in a graceless pile with her skirt up above her knees. At least it isn't outdoors this time, she thought dimly, through the agony in her right side; at least I'm spared that this time.

Bob knelt beside her and asked her where it hurt. Arlene had run to the telephone, and Bertha could hear her calling for an ambulance. She shook her head weakly at Bob and tried to wink at him. She couldn't talk; the ambulance was the best thing. Arlene was crying, she saw, and not worrying at all about her eye makeup, which was running blackly down her cheeks.

The doorbell rang.

"My God," said Bob, "that was quick." He ran to answer it, and Arlene took his place beside Bertha.

"Don't worry, Mother, they're here now, you'll be all right, oh Mother Mother I'm so sorry."

"Helloo! Merry Christmas!" said Betty, pushing her way past Bob and hurrying over to where Bertha lay upon the carpet. "What are you doing down there?" she said, and laughed gleefully. Behind her lurked Heather and Jack. Jack spied Bertha.

"My God," he said. "Did she fall?"

"Yes," said Bob. "There's an ambulance coming."

"I'm so sorry, Mrs. Perkins," said Jack. "Betty. Come on. Let's go."

Betty cocked her head and looked at Bertha. She shook her finger at her. "Now you shouldn't be lying on the floor like that. It's Christmas!" She laughed again, and looked around with interest at the others. "What's happened here? Have you had dinner? Have you had your dessert yet?"

"We've had an accident," said Arlene. "Mother fell."

"Fell?" said Betty. She looked up the stairs. "Ah yes. Down the stairs. Stairs can be very dangerous. Well I'm sure she'll be all right. You'll be all right!" she hollered down at Bertha.

"Betty," said Jack, taking her arm. "Let's go home. We're just in the way here."

Betty pulled loose indignantly. "In the way? In the way? How could I possibly be in the way? I'm her friend!" She beamed at Bob and Arlene. "What can I do?"

"You can go," said Arlene, dangerously.

"Now now," said Betty. "It's . . . Arlene, isn't it? Yes, Arlene. I can be of much use, I'm sure. Here, let me pick her up. I'm very strong." She squatted down and shoved one arm under Bertha's shoulder. Bertha yelped with pain.

Arlene hit Betty on the side of her head. "Get out! Get out!" she screamed. "Leave her alone! Get your hands off her, you crazy old bat! Get out of here!"

Betty's face looked like a punctured balloon, skin rubbery and flabby and crinkled. Jack took her arm and thrust her out the door. He reached back and took hold of Heather, who was crying. He muttered something and closed the door.

Bob brought a blanket and tucked it in around his mother. Her face was white and her eyes were closed. Arlene huddled beside her, whimpering.

198

The bell rang again. Bob went quickly to the door, wrenched it open, and this time it was the ambulance.

How funny, thought Bertha. I thought they were supposed to drive up with sirens blaring.

She told the ambulance men she wanted the pain to go away. She felt cowardly; but nobody can be brave, she told herself, when pain really decides to show you what it can do.

Oh God, she thought, I promised myself I'd keep an eye on her. I promised myself I'd keep an eye on her. . . .

Jack knocked at the door.

"Betty? Betty?"

He knocked again. Still no answer. He opened the door. He could see a shape on the bed.

"Betty?" he called softly. "May I come in?"

It was late. Heather was asleep. He walked in and sat down on the chair under the window. He could see in the light from the street lamp coming through the window that her eyes were not closed.

"Don't be upset, Betty," he said quietly.

"I'm not upset," she said in a normal tone.

He was startled. "Well that's good. They had a bad thing happen over there."

"I know. I know all about bad things happening," she said clearly.

"When Bertha gets home, maybe you'll go over and see her again."

"I might. Gets home from where?"

"From the hospital."

"Why is she in the hospital?"

"She broke her hip when she fell."

There was silence for a few minutes.

"How do you know that?"

"I went over when her son came back to the house. Just wanted to be able to tell you how she is."

"He doesn't live there."

"Who? Her son? No. But he had to come back to turn off the lights and lock up. And get some things she'll need in the hospital."

"Lock up?"

"Lock the doors. So nobody can get in while she's away."

"How long will she be away?"

"Quite a while. I'm not sure. You can call the hospital if you like."

"Why would I do that?"

"To ask how she is, for God's sake!" He got up and started out of the room. "Betty . . . maybe we'll go and visit her there, next time I come home. Both of us. Together. Betty?"

There was no answer.

"Good night," he said. No answer. He went out and closed the door.

Betty thought about the house next door. Bertha had put a wreath on the door. Betty wondered if it was still there, or if she'd taken it to the hospital with her. She thought about the house, about how the dust would thicken. The dishes from the Christmas dinner would stay on the table and become so dirty they'd never come clean.

But that woman might come and do them. That Arlene. That dreadful person. She was practically Bertha's daughter. Daughters . . .

Betty closed her eyes. She was glad Christmas was over. Christmas was dreadful. Always. Why hadn't she remembered that in time?

Downstairs, Jack turned off all the lights except the ones on the Christmas tree and sat on the sagging sofa. We ought to be able to help each other, he thought, as he lit a cigarette. We ought to be in the same bed, hugging, comforting.

He sat, smoking. He couldn't remember the last time he'd hugged Betty with both arms. Probably couldn't get them around her anyway, he thought, and desolation hit him as he remembered that long silky hair. It was a very long time ago, he thought. . . .

He had always come to her quietly, so as not to startle her. She was like a bird, like a child. Her modesty was great, and he loved it, but he also loved it when her modesty began to melt; though he was never certain that this had happened, he liked to think it had, at least sometimes.

He was gentle with her, and loving, and he talked to her, and told her how pretty she was. He was proud of himself for this; for not hurrying, for never—well, seldom —forgetting her shyness, even in the midst of lovemaking. It was one of the things that came with marrying a girl who was a lady, he used to tell himself solemnly. Just one of her little . . . eccentricities; one of the things that made her childishly different from the other girls he'd known.

He shook his head, disbelievingly, and put out his cigarette. He had been thinking about that Betty as someone who was dead.

Jack was extremely tired.

He went up to his den and closed the door softly behind him. He left the Christmas-tree lights on, and they sparkled through the window towards the snowy street.

Chapter
26

The stubborn cat came back soon after Christmas, and she finally had to admit that he did not like to play. He was too serious. This cat did not find anything amusing. No matter what she told him, he would not laugh.

He was serious, and he was also conceited, she thought coldly after he had been in the house for a while. He did not seem to know that she could do things which he could not, and that the things she could do were more important than the things he could do. He did not realize that it was she who put the water in his bowl; that it was she who opened the door so that he could come in or go out. He thought that because he willed these things, they happened.

Betty knew that Heather would not come home from school because she was sleeping over with a friend. Jack was still away. So when the cat sat in the hall in front of the door and stared at the handle, she did not open it for him. She did not open the door, but just sat on the stairs and watched, because it was so funny, watching him stare at the doorknob.

She decided to pretend she thought he had gone, and she went about the house singing and tidying up. Every once in a while she would sneak a glance at him, and still he sat there, stubborn, eyes raised to the doorknob. Then she ran into the bathroom and closed the door and turned on the taps so he could not hear her, and she laughed and laughed.

After a while he turned around and stared at her, and began to follow her about the house. She ignored him and went on singing, and she rubbed tables with a cloth and put newspapers into piles.

She went upstairs. She made her bed and pulled the curtains and shut her door. She took out her tools and touched them and watched them gleam in the light from her bedside lamp. She sat on her bed with her tools for quite a long time, and she forgot about the cat. Then she heard a scratching sound at her door, and she felt a headache begin.

She opened the door and pushed past the cat, closing the door quickly behind her so he couldn't get into her room, and she went into the bathroom and found her pills and took two of them, as she was supposed to.

She went to the kitchen to make some soup, and while she heated up the soup in a pot on the stove and found a clean bowl to put it in, she knew the cat was sitting on the floor watching her. He had not made any sounds.

I wonder how he feels, she thought. Does he think I cannot see him? Does he think he is dreaming? Does he wonder why he is not outside? Why this time the door has not opened for him? She laughed under her breath.

Her headache was hurting badly. She knew it would get better when the pills began to work, when she had eaten her soup. She decided to have some bread, too, and she took a loaf from the cupboard. She looked at the loaf of bread in dismay; Heather had not gotten the sliced kind! I am so angry, she thought, so angry, she is supposed to *always* buy the *sliced* kind!

She opened many drawers. They were filled with bottle openers and eggbeaters and egg lifters and wooden spoons and sieves, everything all in a hodgepodge. No wonder I never open these drawers, she thought, only that one, the one with the table knives and forks and spoons, only that one is tidy—everything is just thrown into it but there are only three kinds of things so it is easy to find what you want.

She looked and looked, and poked through all the things, and tried to close the drawers but couldn't. Her hands were trembling. Things pushed themselves up from the mess and she couldn't cram them back down inside, so the drawers wouldn't close. She left them open. Her hands shook, still. She was so hungry for some bread, so hungry, so frightened, the soup was boiling on the stove and she had to find it, had to, and finally there it was, the bread knife, right at the bottom of the drawer, all dusty with bits of grit and salt and dust.

She looked at it lying there. The edges of her mouth twitched down in small, deafening convulsions. She reached for it softly—heard the soup hiss, turned around, grabbed the pot, it was a cheap pot *why doesn't Jack buy better things the handle burns* she dropped the pot and the soup splashed out all over the floor. The cat vaulted out of the way, out of the room. Tomato soup steaming in a spreading slick surface all over the kitchen floor going wherever it liked, hot, red . . . she went out of the kitchen and upstairs and threw her tools off the bed and climbed in under the covers. . . .

It was morning. The light came through the curtains, all green, like rocks under water. It is slimy light, she thought, opening her eyes to it. I will close my eyes again and wait until the light is yellow. But then she saw the cat.

He was lying on her chair, her big stuffed brown chair. She had not said he could lie there *what is he doing in my house* I have not opened the door for him. . . .

He lay staring at her with green eyes like the light, and scattered over the carpet between her and the chair with the cat lying on it were all her tools. Her tools.

She got out of bed slowly, looking at him all the time, and as he watched her she slowly picked up all her tools and put them in their box; the box was lying on the floor, too; how had he done this, how had he found her tools and opened the box and thrown them all out upon the floor? He had left them there, too, so that she would see them, and know what he had done.

She picked them up slowly, keeping her eyes on the cat. She picked up the big kilt pin, all gold and shiny; the long hat pin with the pearl knob on the top; the jackknife with the leather handle and the leather pouch to hold it; the long-handled two-pronged fork—she usually laughed whenever she looked at that one, remembering how angry Jack was when he couldn't find it once; the screwdriver with the bright orange handle she had found in the lane one day; her sewing scissors; her pliers; her eyeglasses with no glass in them because her eyesight was perfect; the tweezers she had gotten from Sheila's house —she picked them all up and put them back into the box and put the box on the top shelf in her closet behind her hats which she never wore. Then she turned slowly around and she looked at the cat.

He was still lying there, staring at her, and the light was still green coming in through the curtains. His electricity was gone. She walked over to the cat and reached out and picked him up by the tail.

The electricity was in her; she could feel it slamming into him through her hand, as though he had stuck his paw or his nose in an electric socket. It was very hard to hold on to him. He was much heavier than she had imagined. His fur was not soft—it *was* soft, she corrected herself, but when she held him by the tail she didn't feel the fur, she felt the tail, the bones in the tail, and the weight of his body hanging from those bones.

She walked out of the room and down the stairs. The cat was howling now; it was howling and spitting and hissing and writhing and hitting itself against her arm, her body, her leg. She held her arm away out from her body, but he threw himself around almost in circles, so he still hit himself against her, scratching her, clawing her, making her bleed again.

She opened the door and threw him outside, into the cold.

He picked himself up, quickly but slowly, and ran quickly but slowly across the street between two houses and disappeared.

Chapter
27

Arlene walked quickly down the hospital corridor. I must have been here dozens of times by now, she thought, and still it bothers me. She was irrationally afraid that someone in a white coat, passing her in the hall, would get a whiff of a rare disease she had been carrying about for years, and would whisk her into a room and keep her there, sticking needles in her and taking tests and glowering at her as though the disease, of which she had been happily ignorant, were something she'd created herself, like a baby.

She hurried into the private room. It was a tiny room, stuffed with a hospital bed, two chairs, a nightstand, and a television set hung from the ceiling. The venetian blinds were closed, but scraps of sunlight floated in and dispersed themselves upon Bertha's bed like white confetti.

"You again?" said Bertha. "You've got better things to do than come here."

"Mother!" said Arlene. She stopped just inside the door and thought about turning around and going back out.

"Oh damn," said Bertha. "I didn't mean it that way. Come over here." She waved Arlene towards her with both arms. "Give me a kiss."

Flustered, Arlene leaned down and kissed her forehead.

"There. Now sit yourself down."

"It's a beautiful day," said Arlene. "We're having another chinook." She sat in a chair between the bed and the window. "When are you getting out of here?"

"Next week. I walk around quite a lot now."

"Is it very painful?"

"Some. Some. No more than before. They can't fix that. But the break's healing like it should, so they tell me."

206

"And what are you going to do, Mother?"

"Getting right down to business, are you?" Bertha hoisted herself up in the bed.

"We're worried about you."

"Worried, worried, you two are always worried." Bertha poked at her hair, trying to tidy the bun at the back of her head. "Well, the way I see it, I can do one of two things. I can go back to live in my own house, or I can go and live with Bob and you." She made a face. "Or I could go to one of those nursing homes, or whatever they call them, I guess."

"Mother, why are you so stubborn?"

"What do you mean, stubborn? How am I being stubborn? I thought I was putting that rather well. I thought I'd worked things out pretty carefully."

"Why don't you want to come and live with us?"

"You know why, Arlene. I want to be independent. I've told you that enough times, God knows."

"Mother, you fell down those stairs and broke your hip. What's going to happen if you go back there and you fall down the stairs again? When you're alone there? What will happen then?"

"There's no need for that kind of talk. I've got to be more careful, that's all."

"Let me do that for you."

"No, it's all right." Bertha stuck in the last hairpin.

"It's not just a question of being careful; you know that. Your leg hurts when you put weight on it, and so you're going to lift it up, without even thinking. And then you're going to fall."

"Arlene, I know more about my condition than you do, and I'd thank you very much to just keep quiet about it."

Arlene got up and went over to the bed. She looked down at Bertha. "Mother, you're kind of selfish. Did you know that? You keep thinking about what *you* want. You keep thinking of how *you'd* feel, if you came to live with us." She walked to the window and looked out through the slats in the blinds.

Bertha saw that she'd bought a new spring coat. It looks good on her, she thought, surprised.

"How do you mean, I'm selfish?"

Arlene turned to look at her. "Take me, for instance," she said. "You and Bob are all the family I've got. I know we repeat ourselves but we *do* worry about you, *both* of us, a *lot*."

Bertha watched her. The girl was pretty, despite the makeup; no doubt about it. Not too smart, maybe; but then, neither was Bob. Neither am I, for that matter, she thought.

"I love you, Mother," said Arlene. "That's the thing, you see. We both love you. This isn't something we keep asking you to do because it's our duty. We *want* you to come and live with us."

"So you won't have to worry about me any more," said Bertha, and had to clear her throat to get it out.

"Yes, so we won't worry. Of course, that's part of it." Arlene sat carefully on the edge of the bed. "But there's more. I don't have a mother or a father any more. And my brother's so far away I never see him. I feel like you're just as much my mother as you are Bob's. I know you don't feel that way . . . but I do."

Bertha got her a tissue. "You ought to get the stuff that's waterproof," she said.

"You mean my eye makeup? Yeah, I should."

"Well. That puts another light on things."

"We have all that room, you see. A huge bedroom on the main floor, with its own bathroom; you wouldn't have to go up and down steps at all. And carpeting all over the place, even in the bathroom, so you wouldn't slip. . . . "

Bertha waved her hand impatiently. "I know, I know all that." She stared up at the blank television screen. "What about my stuff? I've got all that stuff there, all fitted in," she said ominously.

"I guess we couldn't get *all* of it in," said Arlene hesitantly. "But you could put your piano in the living room,

208

and there's plenty of room in the bedroom for your sew-ing machine and your television set. It's a huge room, Mother, simply huge."

"I don't sew any more. Why don't you two move in with me?" She laughed at the look on Arlene's face. "I know, I know."

She tried to imagine herself living in their house. The bedroom would be nice enough, she thought. It's got a big window that looks out from the side of the house, and there's a lot of lawn there, and even a lilac bush, if I re-member rightly. Lots of room for my clothes—my good-ness the closet takes up darn near a whole wall, and the rest of it's filled with the door to the bathroom. I'd have my own bathroom, anyway. . . . Could put my television set in there, all right. A couple of plants . . .

"What about my plants?"

"I don't have any plants at all, Mother. I'd love it if you would bring your plants. All of them."

Where would I drink my tea, Bertha thought. In their kitchen, where else. In that Formica-topped kitchen that was full of electrical doo-dads; I'd sit at that slippery table . . . or I could sit in the dining room, on one of those hard chairs . . . and I wouldn't be alone. She'd be there. Same dress every day, only a different colour. Watching me every time I got up or sat down, in case I fell.

And when I wanted to play the piano, sideways, with my right leg stuck out, and sing along as I played, there she'd be, running around to turn off the record player or the radio so as not to disturb me. . . .

"I'd be a handful," she said loudly. "Especially at first. Till this hip . . . "

"It's not going to be the easiest thing in the world, Mother. I know that," said Arlene softly. "But if we love each other, you see . . . "

But do I, thought Bertha. Do I love you? Don't think I've loved many people in my day. Sam. Bob? Yes, I do love Bob, I guess. My goodness, her eyes are all red and she does look nervous. I wonder if she's afraid I'll say no, or afraid I'll say yes. . . .

"All right," said Bertha suddenly. Arlene hugged her. "Now now, that's enough of that." She patted Arlene on the back and pushed her away.

"But there's something I want you to do for me," she added.

"What is it, Mother?"

"Have you been going over there to water my plants, keep an eye on things?" I'll never see that place again, she thought. Not when it's mine. And I know I'll never go inside it again. She had a lot of pain, suddenly, and it wasn't in her hip.

"Of course I have. I told you I would."

"There's a fern hanging in the kitchen. A big, healthy, bushy one. I want you to take it next door and make sure the child gets it. Heather. Betty's little girl."

Arlene nodded. "Okay, Mother. I'll do it."

I wish I could see her, Bertha thought. I wish I could see that child again. My house, and that child . . . oh dear God, what can a person do? . . .

The next day Arlene drove to Bertha's house with a list, a key, and a lot of cardboard boxes. As Arlene dropped the third armload of cartons in the living room and turned to hurry out for the last few still in the car, she jumped to see Betty standing in the doorway.

"What are you doing here?"

"I came to see your mother, where is she?" said Betty eagerly.

"She's not here."

"Then what are you doing here?" Betty came into the hall. "What are all those boxes for?"

"That's none of your business," said Arlene.

"Well of course it is," said Betty. "Of course it is my business. I am her friend."

"She's not coming back."

210

"Not coming? What do you mean, not coming back? Is she dead?"

"No, she's not dead! She's coming to live with us."

Betty went into the living room and looked around. "Why? This is such a pretty house, such a nice house. Why is she going somewhere else, then?" She looked at Arlene strangely. "Does she know that you are inside her house?"

"Of course she knows! She asked me to come and pack her things."

"But why?" said Betty, coming closer, looking at Arlene. "Why is she not coming back here?"

"Because of the stairs. She fell on the stairs. You remember, don't you? On Christmas Day? She broke her hip. Now she's afraid of stairs. Our house doesn't have any—none that she'll have to climb, anyway. So she's going there. All right?"

"No, of course it's not all right. It's not all right at all. She must come back *here*!" said Betty loudly. She looked at Arlene again. "She never fell down the stairs before. Not in all the times I was in her house. Why did she fall when you were here, and never while I was here?" She was very close to Arlene.

"Listen, Mrs. Coutts," said Arlene, not permitting herself to move away. "My mother-in-law has arthritis in her hip. It has been harder and harder for her to get around. We worried about her. I'm glad we *were* here when it happened. But we can't let her live alone any longer. Now would you please leave, so I can start packing her things." She walked to the door and held it open. "Please."

Betty looked around the living room, bewildered. It was very dusty, and the furniture looked tired.

"Mother said to say goodbye to you, and that she'll write you," said Arlene. "Oh, wait." She disappeared down the hall and came back holding the fern from the kitchen. "This is for your daughter. Heather. Mother wants her to have it."

211

Betty took it. "What does she want *me* to have?" she said.

Arlene stood grimly by the door.

Betty trudged outside. She turned around. "Who will come to live here?"

"I don't know. Mother will sell it to somebody."

Betty went home, holding the fern out from her body as though it smelled bad.

Chapter
28

She heard the front door close and stood in the kitchen smiling and breathing and thinking about all the things there were to do and wondering which of them she would do first.

And then she knew that Heather hadn't gone.

The whole house turned to watch her. She felt squashed up inside. She hurried to the front door, and just as she came into the hall she saw a flash of white disappearing into the living room. She saw it from the corner of her right eye, and felt the skin on the right side of her body wrinkle.

She backed towards the closet and felt behind her, among the clothes hanging there, and, hunched down, still watching the living-room doorway, she rummaged with her right hand through the clothes lying on the floor of the closet. She picked something up and brought it around in front of her and quickly glanced at it: Heather's ski jacket.

There was a sound from the kitchen.

She had been wrong. Heather didn't go to school every day now after all. Squatting in her red robe and red slippers she felt like crying. She heard herself begin to whimper. She clapped her hands over her mouth and didn't breathe for a minute.

She tiptoed down the hall, through the living room and dining room, and into the kitchen. Her teacup was sitting on the counter beside the sink. Empty. In the sink she saw amber traces of her tea. The teapot was gone from the top of the stove. There had been a whole pot of tea there for her to drink while she made her plans, and now it was gone, the tea and the pot, both gone. She looked through all the cupboards, but she knew she would not find the teapot, and she didn't.

She could feel Heather in the house, staring at her and laughing in her throat.

"Heather? Heather? Heather, I know you're there, there's no sense in hiding, no sense, I can find you, you know that."

I will never find her, she thought with despair.

If only I could change my size whenever I wanted to, she thought. I can't sneak around the house like she can: my shadows are enormous, she can see me coming; my steps are not soundless, she can hear me coming.

Heather either was in the living room or had gone upstairs; Betty knew she would not have left the house. Not yet.

So she walked into the living room, calling, and there in the middle of the carpet Heather had pushed the vacuum cleaner. It sat there squat and silent.

Betty left that room quickly, while it still sat sullen but mute, still. She knew it wouldn't unwind its cord and plug itself in unless she were there to watch.

There was a muffled sound from above. She ran heavily up the stairs, calling, "Heather, Heather, what are you doing, please don't hide from me, it upsets me."

A quiet giggle, she heard. The bathroom door was open; to the right, down the hall, Heather's door quietly swung closed.

Betty went into the bathroom first.

I knew it, I knew it. She had to move her shoulders up and down fast, jerking them up and down, so as not to cry. There was the little plastic bottle that kept her green headache pills; there it was lying beside the bathroom sink with its top off, and it was empty, empty.

She got down on the floor, muttering, trying not to cry. She looked all over the floor and emptied the wastebasket out on the floor and searched through the garbage piece by piece, carefully looking all through it, but they were not there.

The sink was all wet. She must have put them *all down the drain, all my pills*. She leaned against the counter, arms trembling. Then she saw something flash in the mirror, and she pulled up her head; but there was nothing there, just the memory of a white flash.

She ran down the hall to Heather's room. The door was open a crack now. She hesitated, then threw it open all the way.

It lay in innocence, that room. The bed was not made. Betty saw the hollow in the pillow where the child's head had lain. The covers were thrown back. A giant Raggedy Ann doll lay sprawled there, grinning stupidly, twitching its limbs. Heather's clothes were scattered all over the floor; there was a pile of comic books on the floor beside the bed, pushed over like a deck of cards. The curtains were closed. Over everything in the room a grey light filtered, like the light inside a cave, or a big balloon. Betty yanked open the door to the closet. Nothing there, nothing but empty hangers and piles of clothes on the floor and boxes filled with games and handicrafts on the shelf. I never see her playing those games, thought Betty, never see her making feather flowers or doing beadwork, but the boxes look worn, and they are put up there neatly, not like her clothes.

A scurrying sound came from the hall. She pushed herself out of the room. Couldn't see anything, or hear anything; stood there listening to the silence, which was terribly loud.

"Heather, Heather, come here, come to me and we'll have a cup of tea together. I have a headache, Heather, and I need my pills, have you seen them, have you seen my pills?"

Her voice echoed in the house, and the echo didn't sound like her at all. Could there be two Bettys in that house? Was there another Betty walking around somewhere?

Her bedroom. She groped her way down the hall to her bedroom.

It was restful, pleasant. The bedside light was on. There was a soft, yellow glow on the yellow bedspread. I should have yellow sheets, too, she thought; the white sheets don't stay white, they begin to look grey after a while. She went over to make her bed so the white-grey sheets wouldn't show in the lovely yellow glow, and then she decided not to, and lay down on her bed instead, lay down on it just as it was, unmade and white-grey. She pulled the yellow spread right up over her head and looked through it.

Everything was yellow and pleasant—that steady yellow light flowing down upon her like sunshine, like the heat of sunshine in a tropical country.

She is just lying there and breathing and watching the bedspread move softly up and down as she breathes. . . .

The light has gone off.

She heard a click, and the light has gone off.

She stops breathing, sees a shadow over her bedspread, over her, her poor heart is so terrified it starts beating loud and fast like a drum being struck by someone, bang, bang, bang, and her heart becomes more and more terrified, it is being struck over and over again, faster and faster, it can't keep up, it can't beat in its own rhythm, her blood is all confused, the blood is all mixed up, it runs this way and that, bumping into itself, making currents and eddies in her veins like a river gone wild she throws off the cover and sits up.

There is nobody there.

The light is off, but there is nobody there.

Heather has gone. She has stopped pounding on Betty's chest on Betty's heart and has gone.

Betty sits soothing her heart, calming it, and as it calms, her head becomes very clear.

She looks slowly around the room and sees that her magazines and her box of chocolates are gone. That doesn't surprise her. She sits on her bed and laughs and laughs, and then she calls out cheerily, "All right, Heather, all right, I know you are here and I know just where you are and I am coming to find you, coming to find you just like in hide and seek, you hide and I'll seek, I'll find you."

216

She is very large.

She pats and strokes her chest to soothe her heart, and then she looms up from the bed and strides from her room, ducking her head so as not to hit it on the top of the door. She walks, stooped, down the stairs, treading softly on the carpet in her red slippers.

She is much larger, but when she gets larger she gets lighter, too. She doesn't make a single sound going down the stairs, and into the kitchen she goes, and right up to the door to the basement.

She stops there, just for a second. Then she reaches out her huge hand and the knob disappears into it and she opens the door, steps down onto the first basement stair, and closes the door behind her. She chuckles, and the chuckle booms down into the basement.

"I'm coming, Heather, I'm coming, there's no door, you know, no door but this one, you can't get past me down there I'm too big, too big, I'll see you and stretch out my long arm and catch you by your white blouse."

Heather doesn't answer. Not even a laugh, not even a scuffle does Betty hear. Heather is nervous now, Betty knows; she will catch her, because she has no fear of the basement now, no fear at all.

She walks down the stairs one at a time. It is a long, long flight of stairs, the basement is deep, miles deep beneath the house, beneath the earth, and there are no windows.

She has not turned on the light at the top of the stairs.

It is dark, so dark, she can see things flitting about in the darkness, bats and cobwebs slowly making their way towards her.

There are squeakings and rustlings and creakings, and she smells choking musty smells and sees huge boxes filled with things, the tops of the boxes slowly opening and shapes beginning to drift out. . . . Why did I not turn on the light at the top of the stairs that was so stupid. . . .

Her size is changing again. She is becoming small, smaller than Heather, and now she hears a tiny giggle and sees a flash of white, the collar of a blouse, the top pearl button of a blouse, the pale throat and chin above it, the gold chain winking on the throat— Heather has flitted behind one of the boxes, and one white hand is reaching up behind it to open the top of the box wider, to let the shapes drift out faster.

217

Betty turns around and starts crawling back up the stairs, each step so tall now. Little drifts of air chill the back of her neck. I will not scream the back of my neck is wet with sweat; *the things drifting through the air make small cold breezes that change the sweat to ice.*

She shuts her eyes and keeps crawling, crawling; there is breathing close behind her, the breezes are sharper, coming faster. She hears Heather laugh like she laughs when she is with a friend, or with Jack, only this time she laughs as she watches Betty.

The anger comes back in a tired spurt, but the oozing, floating things behind her are much stronger. Her knees hurt on the slivery wood of the stairs, but she keeps going, eyes squeezed shut, hands clutching the edge of each stair, knees following one at a time . . . maybe I'm not moving up, maybe I'm just staying on two steps, going up one and down one, up one and down one . . . but now her hands bump something, she opens her eyes and sees a crack of light beneath a door, looks up, doesn't know if she can stand up, doesn't know if she is tall enough to reach the doorknob, even standing up, presses her hands against the concrete wall, pushes herself up, touches the doorknob, turns it, and falls into the kitchen.

She lies here on the floor; hears the laughter from below. Her face is pressed to the floor.

If I get up fast and slam the basement door and ram a chair under the handle she will be trapped down there.

She gets up and turns around, quickly—and Heather flashes around the corner from the basement into the living room, I see her the bitch the bitch, *see her yellow hair hanging over her white collar, see the white skinny wrist disappear around the corner, hear the front door slam.*

Betty shuts the basement door and stands still, listening.

There is nothing in the house but her.

Chapter
29

"Mrs. Perkins?"

"Heather!" Bertha waved the child over to her and hugged her. "'How on earth did you get in here?"

"I just walked in. First I phoned, and found out what room you were in. I thought maybe they wouldn't let kids in here, so I just came without asking anybody." She shrugged. "Nobody paid any attention."

"Good for you. I'm very glad to see you, and I don't care how you got here. Sit down, right here on the edge of the bed."

"Are you all better now?"

"Well, I'm getting out of here on Friday, anyway. Take off your jacket."

"But you aren't going back to your house. Mom said. When she gave me the plant. It's hanging in my room, right by the window."

"Good. That's a south window. No," she sighed, "I'm not going back home. It's too dangerous, you see. I might fall again."

"Yeah. But I thought you were all better."

"The broken bone is doing pretty well. But you see, the arthritis, it won't ever go away, I guess."

"Oh." Heather nudged her toe at the floor. "I guess that'll be better for you. To have your son and his wife around all the time." She looked up. "But I thought you wanted to be independent."

"I do, Heather, I do. But there comes a time when no matter how bad you want something, you just can't have it, for some reason. My hip. It won't let me be independent any more. Do you understand?"

"Oh yeah. I don't want you to fall again. You looked awful. Your face was all white."

219

"I'm sorry you had to see that."

"Oh no, I didn't mean that. But I wish I could've done something. You know. For you."

"Come closer, Heather." Bertha put her arm around her. "You did so much for me; you'll just never know."

Heather looked up at her. "What?"

"When you came to help me. You didn't just help me make sure the birds got fed and the plants got watered. You helped me live. Did you know that?" She pushed Heather's hair away from her face.

"No. I didn't know that."

"Well you did," said Bertha. "An old woman like me, there in that house alone. . . . You know the song about sunshine? Well, you were like that. Sunshine. After I fell down outside—you really helped me *that* day, didn't you? —after that, when you came every couple of days, regular as clockwork, well I got to looking forward to that more and more."

"So did I," said Heather. Bertha held her more tightly.

"See, a friendship, that's a pretty special thing. Mostly people have friends their own age. But I don't have them any more; not really; not anybody who's important to me. And I found it a real treat to have such a good friend who was so young, too."

"I found it a treat, too," said Heather. Bertha gave her a tissue and Heather wiped her eyes and her nose. She took Bertha's hand. "I'm really going to miss you."

"Oh Heather, I'm going to miss you, too." She squeezed the child's hand.

"I've got something important to say to you." Bertha took Heather's face in her hands. "Now this is important. Everybody," she said, "no matter how young or how old they are, needs somebody they can depend on. You can depend on me. I'm going to write down my telephone number for you—my new one, at Bob's place." Heather nodded. "Now you have to phone me if you need somebody, and your father's away, and your mother isn't feeling well. Okay?"

"Okay," said Heather softly.

"But," said Bertha, "if you should need somebody quickly, more quickly than over a telephone, if . . ."

"If there's an emergency," said Heather.

"Yes. If there's an emergency. If you get an emergency happening to you, I want you to go next door on the other side of your house."

"To Shelley's house?"

"I guess so. Is that the little girl who lives there?"

"Yeah."

"Well, I want you to go there, right up to the door, and go in and see Shelley's mother and tell her you have an emergency. Understand?"

Heather nodded.

"Emergencies can happen to anyone," said Bertha. Oh dear, she thought, I hope I'm not scaring her. "But usually they don't."

"I know. But they could. I know." Heather looked at Bertha gravely.

"What kind of thing would be the kind of thing I mean?" Bertha said quietly.

"A fire. Or somebody falling down the stairs." Heather thought. "Or somebody getting sick," she said softly, looking steadily at Bertha.

"That's right. That's the kind of thing I mean."

"I promise. I'll go there."

"Good." Bertha kissed Heather on the forehead. She stroked her hair. "Good," she said again.

Please don't let her have to do that, she thought. Please let her be able to phone me. Or not even have to phone . . . please . . .

She hugged Heather close.

Chapter
30

She took the chair she always took, the one by the window, and she tried to smother a gleam of fury when once again she found it too small. I'm my own size today, she thought, my own size, not my large size, my own size, and still this chair is too small.

She looked out the window while she waited for Dr. Jessup. The day reminded her of Heather; or maybe she thought of Heather only because of the dream, and . . . but anyway the day was pale and blue-skied and wispy. It was a waspish day. It looked warm, but of course it was not warm at all once a person got out into it. There was a wind blowing from the mountains, and it carried winter in its teeth. Chinooks were not real.

He came in and sat down beside his desk and said hello, politely, as always. She looked at him, a calculating look. She had not come to see him since before Christmas. She had not wanted to come ever again, but there was despair in her. She had to tell him both things. She did not want to, but she had to.

"Tell me what you're doing these days, Betty," he said.

"I visit, I have guests," she said, and of course he asked whom she visited, who were her guests.

She waved her hand impatiently. "I have gone to visit Sheila."

"And your friend Bertha?"

"She had an accident. She broke something. She's in the hospital."

"Do you miss her?"

"Miss her? Miss her? It does no good to miss people. Either they're here or they aren't."

"Tell me about Heather."

"Heather is the same as always," said Betty, looking at him carefully.

"Have you been to see her teacher again?"

Betty laughed. "So that's what it is. It makes you nervous, does it? That I didn't tell you about that?" She frowned. "Jack had no right to tell you. That's how you found out." She waved her hand at him, cutting off an apology, or an explanation, or a lie. "Besides, you can't just walk into a school any time you choose, you know," she said restlessly. "You have to wait to be invited." She shifted in her chair. "Why don't you have bigger chairs in here?" she said angrily.

"I'll get a bigger one, for next time. Betty, I'd like us to talk about that visit to the school. Your husband——"

"I had a dream about Heather," said Betty suddenly. "I don't know whether to tell you about it or not."

"You don't have to, of course. Unless you want to talk about it. Does it trouble you?"

"Oh yes. Oh yes, it does. But it may trouble me more if I speak it out loud. I don't know." She looked out the window again; quickly pressed her forehead against the glass. It was cool and hard. She turned back to the doctor.

"I think it was a dream. Usually when I wake up I know right away that what I have had is a dream. This time I'm not so sure. I know I didn't go to those places or see those things—but I'm still not quite certain that it was a dream. Perhaps you could tell me if it was a dream or not?"

"Yes, I think I could do that."

"Perhaps you can even tell me why I dreamed it, or what will happen now."

"I don't know, Betty. I would have to hear about it before I knew whether I could answer those questions."

His face looked rather like the bark on a tree, she thought. It was dark, and had shattered; there were tiny lines all over it. Yet somehow it managed to stay stuck together, and also to appear peaceful. She liked his eyes, which were grey beneath bushy brows. He had a great

223

deal of hair, black with grey mixed into it. He probably had children, she thought suddenly, amazed. Maybe he had even dreamt about them.

"Jack had to go to Vancouver on business, he often does that; but this time he told me to bring Heather there and he would meet us at a gorgeous hotel in Vancouver and have a holiday. I was very happy.

"I don't remember getting there," she said, straining with her eyes into the dream. "I know that we went by airplane, and it's strange that I don't remember, it's strange that I wasn't even worried, because usually I am terrified of airplanes, of any kind of travelling, and this time it was just Heather and me.

"She looked so lovely, I remember," said Betty, smiling at the wall, "dressed in a navy-blue suit with a pleated skirt and white around the collar of the jacket and white kneesocks and navy-blue shoes that tied. I was surprised that she looked so much like I did when I was her age: plumper than she normally is, her blonde hair all curly and wavy, her blue eyes looking darker, full of excitement as we walked into the grand hotel in Vancouver."

Her eyes rested on the doctor. "You may take notes, if you like," she said generously, nodding her kinky head at him, crossing her fat knees.

He looked up from his pen and paper and said, "Thank you."

"Someone showed us to our rooms," Betty went on. "There was a whole suite of them. We looked into each room. One of them gave me a dreadful shock—it had no windows, none at all, and the walls were painted green. There was no carpet and no furniture at all, just a stool. On the stool my mother was sitting." Betty uncrossed her legs. Her hands were getting sweaty and she almost wished she could stop, but she went on.

"Her hair was all white and her face had fallen apart and when I opened the door she looked up at me and covered her face with one hand and with the other waved me violently away. Her dress was wrinkled and dirty. She didn't look at all like my mother but that's who she was, all right, that's who she was. I looked around me as I closed the door; I didn't want Heather to have seen my mother like that. But Heather had gone off up the hall towards the kitchen." She drew a shuddering breath. "That's one of the bad parts," she said to the doctor, who nodded.

"It was dark, suddenly, so I put Heather to bed, she snuggled into bed with her Raggedy Ann doll. I was getting impatient for Jack to come but I knew he wouldn't be there for a while so I decided to go for a walk. I don't remember going down in an elevator; suddenly I was walking around in a kind of plaza outside.

"The night had not quite come, there was still a glow in the sky and it was warm outside. I strolled up and down amid crowds of people who were happy and smiling but not bothering me, not bothering me at all. There were little bands of people playing music. . . . "

Betty stopped and looked frantically around the office. "Oh, this will frighten me again, I know it will."

"You can stay here until you aren't frightened any more, Betty," said Dr. Jessup.

"I shall hold on to this chair," she said, gripping the arm rests.

"I stopped and looked into a store window and I remember thinking it was the most charming thing, the thing that sat there. It was a white statue of a young boy, very young, a child; there was a mirror behind it so I could see the back and the front of him at the same time. He was sitting on a rock and had one foot propped up upon the other knee, and he was resting his elbow on the higher knee and his chin on his elbow. He was gazing right at me, with a soft and thoughtful smile upon his face which made me want to cry and to comfort him, even though he looked quite content. There must have been a music box in the base of the statue—sweet tin-

225

kling music was coming from it, the kind of music that makes you want to cry, because it's filled with memories.

"I continued to walk on across the plaza, having sadness and joy together. Then I saw, black against the red sky, a small house with a peaked roof. There was a small crowd of people standing outside it, looking towards it and muttering among themselves."

She loosened her hands and clutched them again around the arm rests of the chair. "Here comes the second bad part," she said anxiously to the doctor. "There are three altogether." She took a breath.

"The door of the house opened and a wide shaft of light spilled out, and silhouetted against the light were three people—the middle one was a woman, maybe the other two were, too. The middle one was taller than the others, and she seemed to be leaning on the other two. They were walking slowly from the house towards the crowd of people. I moved closer, to see what was going on; the feeling of my dream or whatever it was had changed, and I felt nervous.

"As I watched the three women move slowly towards the crowd, on a higher level than the crowd, the middle woman suddenly toppled forward and lay still upon her face, and there was a large knife sticking out of the middle of her back."

Betty took her hands from the chair and rubbed them quickly together.

"I became terrified and began to run desperately towards my hotel, and when I got to our suite Heather was gone from her bed. Then I heard a tinkling musical sound —the sound of the white statue, the statue of the little boy."

"I ran down the hall towards the sound, and opened the door of the bedroom that was there for Jack and me. The statue was there, sitting on the chest of drawers at the far end of the room. *Two* children were there, *two* of them, sitting on a large cloth-covered trunk which was at the end of the big double bed. The whole room looked ancient and rich and was filled with a musty smell."

Betty jerked to her feet. The doctor was watching her. She turned to the window and pressed her hands against the glass.

"The two children had their backs to me," she went on, hurriedly. "Both were blonde: one had long straight hair, rather stringy; the other had hair that shone and sparkled, curling and waving down to her shoulders like it was truly made of gold. I didn't know why I was so filled with terror; the scene was beautiful, peaceful, with the tinkling of the music box and the small white marble boy watching the two children, who were wearing identical pajamas."

She left the window and sat down again. Dr. Jessup saw that her hands were trembling. She leaned towards him. "Now comes the worst part. I can't stop now."

"It's all right, Betty. You're quite safe here. You're just telling me a dream."

She sat back, and again clutched the arm rests.

"I made a sound," she said harshly. "Maybe I called Heather's name. The child with the long stringy hair turned slowly around to look at me. It was Heather; she was holding a comb in her right hand, a comb with sharp metal teeth. She turned to me and she was combing her bare chest; her pajama top was undone and she was combing her child's chest and where she combed long thin fingers of blood were running slowly down her chest and tears were falling from her silent eyes. I ran to her, picked her up, and took her out of the room and told her to run to the kitchen. Then I went back.

"The white statue had turned to look at me. The music still played. I went up to the other child and again called her name, again called, 'Heather.' She turned around to me very slowly. Her blue eyes were still bright and excited and she was smiling—a smile so cold there should have been fangs in her mouth, but there weren't, just a straight white row of child's teeth—and the child slowly stood up and in her hand she held a butcher knife. She raised the knife slowly and slowly began to move towards me; I turned around and ran and ran, I knew I was running too fast for her to catch me but I knew that she would catch me. I ran into the kitchen where the other Heather stood, tears still falling from her blank eyes, still combing her chest in jerks with that comb with teeth like knives. I took it away from her and threw it—I don't know where it went—and then I took her in my arms and held her and we waited for the other Heather to come; I could feel her coming slowly down the hall and I heard the tinkling of the music box."

Tears streamed down her face. The doctor got up and brought her a handkerchief, but she didn't look at it or reach for it. Her hands were still wrapped tightly around the arm rests of the chair. He dabbed the tears from her cheeks and unwound one of her hands gently and put the handkerchief in it. He sat down on a chair that was beside hers.

"Was it a dream?" she said to him.

"Yes, Betty. It was a nightmare. It must have been terrifying. Have you had it more than once?"

"Once. No. Only once. What does it mean? What's going to happen now?" Her face was still flooded with tears.

"What do you think it means?"

Her mouth hung open, stupidly; she could feel it. She flapped it closed, then open, trying to know what to say. She stared hard at him, at the hair hanging over his forehead, at his eyes. He was wearing a tie and a vest and a jacket, all of them.

"What do *I* think it means? What do *I* think it means?"

"Yes. What does it make you think of?"

"Make me think of? *Think* of?" She pulled away from him, leaning as far away from him as possible. "*You* tell *me* what it means! That's why I *came*!"

"You must have some idea, Betty. You must have some

228

notion in your mind of what that dream was trying to say to you. . . . "

"Why do you think I *come* here!" she shouted, tugging at one hand with the other. "Why do you think I *told* you about it! Because I thought you might want to *know*? I told you because I have to know what it *means,* if I already *knew* what it meant why would I *come*?" She had stopped crying. Her eyes were swollen; he could barely see them. She stared at him with rage.

"It's a very complicated dream, Betty. . . . "

"Of *course* it's complicated!" she roared. "I *dreamed* it!"

"You need a psychiatrist to help you figure it out, I think," he said gently, putting his hand over her two, which were twisted together.

"A psychiatrist. You can't help me," she said, her voice dead.

"Oh Betty. I'll make you an appointment right now." He went towards his desk.

"No no no!" She got up and rushed past him. She put her hands over the telephone. "*I will not tell it again!* I told it to you," she said bitterly, "because you're my *doctor,* and you ought to be able to *tell* me. What kind of a doctor are you," she said intently, hands clutching the telephone, "if you have to send me to another person? What kind of a doctor is that?"

"It's a very complicated dream, Betty. You need a psychiatrist to help you figure it out. I can help you with most things, but to understand your dream, you need a psychiatrist to help you."

She let go of the phone and looked at him contemptuously. "Then why did you let me tell you? If you knew you couldn't help me." She looked vaguely around for her purse.

"I didn't know I couldn't help you until I'd heard the dream. Betty. Sit down, Betty. Listen to me for a minute." He waited until she had sat. She saw her purse on the floor and picked it up and put it in her lap. "I think perhaps you should go to the hospital for a few days."

Betty snorted. "Hospital. Ha."

"Just for a few days. You need more help, more talking with people, than you can get here at the clinic."

"That doesn't do any good."

"How can you know that, Betty, until you try?"

"I've tried. I went to a hospital once."

"Yes, but what for? What kind of a hospital?"

"The same kind you're talking about! I know where you want me to go! I know what part of the hospital you want me to go to!" She stood up and shouted at him. "I've been to one of those and it doesn't do a person any good, any good at all, people won't talk to a person when they come out of there!"

"Betty, Betty, of course they will, of course they do. . . ."

"Not to me!" She shook her head back and forth. "I went and when I came out he wouldn't talk to me any more, he hated me then." She sat down again, exhausted.

"Betty. Tell me. Please."

"I was a child," she said dully. "I saw him fall, you see. From the cherry tree. He hit his head on a rock or something." She blinked rapidly. "Then he died. I was very upset, extremely upset," she said solemnly to the doctor. "So I had to go to the hospital for a while. And when I got out . . . when I got out . . . she was different and *he would not speak to me!*"

"Who, Betty? Who are you talking about? Your mother and father? Betty?

"Why wouldn't he speak to you? Not because you'd been in the hospital, surely. He must have been very concerned for you."

She laughed loudly.

"Your mother would speak to you, wouldn't she?" he asked quietly. "Wouldn't she, Betty?"

She looked down at the floor, leaned over to peer at it more closely. The carpet was dark blue. She saw there were pieces of lint on it.

She stood up briskly. "I will think about the hospital," she said. "I will discuss it with Jack when he comes home the next time." She turned and started for the door.

"Betty," said the doctor.

"Yes?" She raised her light brown eyebrows and pursed her small mouth.

"I want you to be helped. I care about you, Betty."

She cocked her head and smiled at him. "I know," she said, and left his office.

Chapter
31

They were in bed, which is not where Sheila had planned to tell him. She had put it off all evening, and she didn't want to go through another night without having done it.

"Ed."

"Yeah."

"I've got something to tell you."

"What?"

"I'm going to go away."

He turned on the light. "Where?"

"I don't know yet. I won't go until school's out for the spring break."

"Why? What is this?" His hair was rumpled.

"I have to go away."

He leaned against the headboard. "Jesus Christ. When did you decide this?"

"I guess I've been deciding it for a long time. I just found out I'd decided it a few days ago." She was lying on her back.

"Is there any particular reason?"

"Ed, don't be sarcastic. Please. I just have to go away."

"I'm not being sarcastic, I want to know, dammit. *Why?*"

"Oh, I feel so stupid!"

"Not half as stupid as I do. Here's my wife planning to leave me and I don't even know why."

"You *do* know why, you *do*! I don't *trust* you any more!" She lay stiffly on the bed.

Oh Christ, thought Ed. "Look, Sheila, I just can't believe this. What do you want? What do you want from me?"

"Nothing! I just want to trust you. And I can't." I wish I could cry, she thought.

"For God's sake, Sheila, you can't just run away like that! What is it, eh? Do you want me to say, don't go, don't go? Is that it? Is that what you want?" He leaned over her.

She got up and went into the bathroom. When she came out, Ed was up, too. "What are you doing?"

"Getting a blanket. I'll sleep in the spare room."

"Ed."

He turned in the doorway. "What?"

"I'm sorry. I can't help it. Maybe we'll be able to figure things out when I come back."

"Yeah." He went to the spare room.

I still don't want to cry, Sheila thought. I don't even want to cry.

Betty burst through Sheila's front door the next morning without knocking, and stood breathlessly in the hall. "Sheila! Sheila!" She heard noises upstairs, and Sheila appeared at the top of the steps.

"I didn't hear the doorbell."

"I didn't ring it, come down, come down, I've got to tell you something, it's very important, I *knew* it, I *knew* it when I went to the school. Remember when we went together, a long time ago? I knew it then." She had advanced halfway up the stairs. Sheila came down and took her into the living room.

"Sit down."

Betty sat on the edge of a chair and clutched her handbag in her lap. "When we went to the school," she said. "When I was in Heather's classroom." She looked behind her, out the window, got up and tiptoed over to the window and peered out. Satisfied, she returned to her chair. "When I went in there I knew that she does not go into that classroom every day because *I did not smell her!*" She nodded feverishly at Sheila, who stared at her.

"I don't know what you're talking about."

"I'm talking about *Heather*! I knew it then, but now I know what she *does* instead of going to school!"

"What?"

"She watches me," whispered Betty, slowly.

"What the hell do you mean?"

"She *watches* me! She pretends to leave in the mornings, but sometimes she doesn't, sometimes she stays in the house and sneaks around and spies on me. And she hides my things, my pills and my chocolates and my magazines. And pours out my tea. And makes me go into the basement!" There were tears in her eyes.

"How do you know that, Betty?" Sheila said quietly.

"Because on Friday I saw her doing it. Little flashes of her. Little sounds from her. I *know!*" She glanced back over her shoulder and whispered. "I was going to tell that doctor. But I didn't." She laughed. "I should have known better, anyway."

"What about today?" said Sheila, distractedly, trying not to look around. "Where is she today?"

"Today she's at school. Sometimes she goes to school. She has to or else they'd telephone me." She rubbed her hands together.

"Listen, she can't stay home," said Sheila. "She couldn't stay home. She'd have to take a note to school the next day, to say why she'd been away. She doesn't ask you for notes, does she?"

"No no no," said Betty. "She doesn't need notes. The teacher doesn't even know she's not there! Because she's so quiet!" She looked at Sheila desperately. "You see?"

"No, not really. No, I don't, Betty."

Betty put her arm through the handle of her purse. "Why aren't you at work? I didn't see you leave, so I knew you were here. But you should be at work. Why aren't you?"

"It's not time for me to leave yet!"

Betty got up and went to the door.

Sheila said, "Listen, Betty. Are you sure she doesn't go to school? I mean, you could be . . . mistaken, right?"

Betty smiled with contempt and went out the door.

Sheila sat still at the table. It was like seeing some-body break out in spots, she thought. I knew there was a fever, her eyes were hot and glassy, I should have known. . . .

She sat still at the table and watched the sun shine upon the snow outside. She got up and walked around the dining room; looked, surprised, at her hands, which were twisting one another. I never realized people actually did that, she thought, and untwisted them, and wiped her palms on her skirt.

What does a person do? she thought. Where is there help?

She went to the phone. 911, that's a number; but they might send cars with tires screeching and lights flashing; everybody would stare out from their windows and what would Betty say. . . .

She looked it up in the book: City of Calgary, Police, Non-Emergency Assistance. That sounds right, Sheila thought. Assistance, that means help; non-emergency, that's what we've got here.

She dialled the number. She tried to pretend she was at work, to give her confidence. "Listen, I've got a non-emergency here. A woman lives next door to me and I don't think she's—I think there's something wrong with her, you know? With her mind." Christ, she thought, and glanced over her hunched shoulder towards the dining-room window where the cold sun shone blandly and no face appeared. What am I doing?

"Could you be more specific, lady? What's she done?"

"Well, that's the problem, she hasn't really done any-thing. No, wait, I mean, she imagines things—very strange things."

"Is she being a nuisance to you or to the neigh-bourhood?"

Oh God, thought Sheila, they're the first people you think of, but they're the wrong ones. "No, well, not a nui-sance, she keeps to herself. But she's sort of an acquain-

235

tance of mine and she came over here, she tells me some very strange things." I sound so stupid, she thought, furious.

"Look, lady"—Sheila heard a sigh—"do you have reason to believe that this woman is a danger to herself or to other people?"

"Oh Christ, how the hell do I know! No." She rubbed her head. Her fingers trembled. She felt like a child telling tales. "I don't think so."

"What kinds of things does she do?" The voice was tired, but gentle. "Tell me a couple of things she's done, or said."

"Oh God, she's just not normal. She thinks her daughter sneaks around the house, hiding from her."

"Maybe she does," said the voice, dryly.

Wrong number, thought Sheila. Yeah, it's the wrong number, all right.

"Sorry, lady. I don't think we can help you. Does she have a husband? Maybe you should talk to him."

Sheila hung up, clutched one cold, wet hand with the other. How often does that man come home, anyway, she thought. My God, I can't give up, there must be something I can do.

She reached again for the phone book: City of Calgary, Social Service Department, Probation, Neighbourhood Services Division—her eyes hesitated, skimmed on down—Preventive Services Division. She dialled the number. "Hello, look, this is going to sound strange but there's a woman who lives next door to me, I think she needs some kind of help. She imagines all sorts of things I don't think are happening. She behaves strangely, you know?"

"What is your name, please?" said the female voice, briskly.

"Oh God, Sheila Dwyer. Listen, she hasn't done anything bad, it's nothing like that, I'm just worried about her. Can you send someone to talk to her, or something?"

"Could you tell me what you mean? What is it that makes you think she needs help?"

"She tells me her daughter follows 'her around the house, hiding from her. She tells me things about her past and it's like I'm not even in the room. Oh I don't know, how do you explain this kind of thing, she's sick, that's all, I know she is!"

"Does she have a family doctor?"

"I don't know, for God's sake! She must have, I guess, but I don't know who it is."

"Are there children involved?"

In what, Sheila thought blankly. "Oh. Yes. I told you, she has a daughter." Dumb broad isn't even listening, she thought. She let herself sit down on the chair by the telephone.

"Is there any evidence that the child is mistreated?"

"No no, it's nothing like that! It's the *mother* I'm worried about! Can't you send somebody around to talk to her or something?"

"Mrs. Dwyer, I'm sorry, there isn't very much I can do. We can't just appear on somebody's doorstep and ask to come in and have a look around. I'm sure you understand that."

Sheila banged her knee with a clenched fist. "Yes of course I do. But tell me," she said, suddenly calm. "What is it that can be done? Where can I find help for her? What can I do?"

"You can try to persuade her to get help on her own. Or, is her husband at home?"

"Yes, but he's away a lot. He travels, in his job. He's not home now."

"Could you speak to him, if you can't talk to her about it?"

I wish I hadn't stopped smoking, thought Sheila, without giving it a decent try.

"Thank you," she said. "I will."

She hung up the phone and leaned her head against the wall. She wished she had time to take a shower.

237

Maybe the school, she thought . . . oh Christ, how would they know anything? They teach Heather, not her mother.

Nothing of order was left in her life. She liked patterns, tidiness. She liked rushing from one familiar rut to another, back and forth from rut to rut throughout her days. They were grassy and smooth, her ruts, and as she scurried down first one, then the other, aspects changed and she saw as much of the world as she needed to see. Now they had disappeared. The earth had smoothed out beneath her feet and there were no ruts, no paths. Things looked alien, and she was without direction.

I wonder if I'll come back here. I'll have to come back, we'll have to decide what to do, how to tell the children . . . but maybe it won't happen. Maybe I'll think things out and come home all calm and just ask him, Ed . . . *why can't I just ask him?* . . . Ed, who called you on Christmas Day? And he'll tell me, it was a wrong number . . . it was a wrong number. . . .

She went to the window. She wished it were spring. I can get Shelley to find out, she thought. I'll get Shelley to find out when he's coming home again. I'll talk to him. The husband. That's what I'll do. The sonofabitch . . .

Chapter
32

Frequently she looked out from behind her living-room curtain to see if the cat had come back, to see if he would sit at the end of her sidewalk and stare at her front door and grow bigger and bigger until he could reach the doorknob and open the door and come in.

But that never happened. He never came back.

Sometimes she dreamed about him pawing through her tools and she exploded into awakeness and looked at the brown chair. But he was not there; her tools were not on the floor.

One day when another chinook had come—or perhaps it was spring, she couldn't tell—she went out of the house very, very early, before even Heather was up.

She liked to go out early and walk down the lane to look at things people had thrown away.

This day she dressed herself carefully in a navy pleated skirt that sprawled out around her waist and fell short of her knees, which were swollen with white and glistening fat. Over the skirt she wore a brown jacket with lapels, which she buttoned across her chest with some effort. She tied brown oxfords neatly over her bare feet, put on her grey coat, and clutching two brown shopping bags, one tucked inside the other, she opened the door, peered up and down the street, and ventured outside. She stood on the doorstep for a moment, listening; then softly closed the door and went down the steps. At the sidewalk she hesitated. She decided to walk around the block and look at people's front porches and their curtains, and then she would go into the lane.

She tiptoed up the street, holding the shopping bags in both hands. She crept along the slushy sidewalk with great care, hunching as though she were making her way behind a fence, stopping every so often to swivel her head quickly around and stare fixedly at the curtains in somebody's window.

The curtains did not shudder at her stare, she noticed. They just drooped dreamily from their rods, unmoving, hiding without rancour the rooms behind them.

She progressed with skill up the street, one toe leading the other, on and on, small steps and quiet, hardly disturbing the stillness of the morning.

She had walked to the third house past Sheila's when she saw the cat.

She pulled her large body backward when it was poised to go forward, toppled onto the pavement of the sidewalk, and scrambled in terror to her knees. Holding the shopping bag in front of her eyes with one hand, she crawled with the clumsy speed of a crab behind a leafless bush in somebody's front yard. The lower branches of the bush quivered in their effort to hide her; she separated them and peered out, round blue eyes scurrying around on the ground, combing the snowbank, fixing on the cat. He was lying at the edge of someone's yard.

She tried to pretend she was very large—large enough to step on a thing as small as a cat and crush it and look down and not even be able to see it sticking out around her foot. Crouched behind the bush, the faint scent of the slowly stirring earth in her nostrils, she tried to collect herself, calm herself, and change her size.

But the cat stayed the same size and the bush behind which she tried to hide stayed the same size and the street lamps were still tall against the early-morning sky and she knew it hadn't happened, she was the same size, too.

She stood up behind the bush. Not taking her eyes from the cat, or her shopping bag from its position over her mouth and chest, she advanced cautiously around the bush and down the walk.

Her whole body was averted slightly from the cat, ready to flee, to run, to crawl, to roll down the sidewalk away from it towards her own front door.

With mincing, sideways steps she inched her way closer to the cat, which did not move.

She stood beside it, hunched over it, peering above the top of the shopping bag at the creature with long, grey, matted fur who lay there, relaxed and quiet, upon the melting snow.

He was so still. He had stopped breathing, she thought. He was hoping she would go close to him so that he could scream and throw himself at her with all four of his paws, claw her until blood was coming out all over her, like that last time.

She stood for some time, unmoving. He lay perfectly still. He did not have his electricity back, she thought. She nodded, staring at him. His green eyes were open, but he was not looking at her.

Holding the bag before her with her left hand, she slowly reached her right hand down, down, towards the grey fur; she touched it, leapt back in a lurch, stood trembling with her eyes riveted on the cat.

It did not move. Even its green eye, open and staring, did not move.

She slowly lowered her shopping bag. Absentmindedly standing first on one foot, then on the other, she cocked her head and stared at the cat. She scratched the back of one leg with the other foot. She reached out a foot and nudged the cat with a brown oxford. It moved; she jumped back; it settled into itself again; she moved forward and watched it intently. Its ribs did not move gently up and down. Its tail did not flick lazily back and forth. Its eye stared only at the snow.

She reached down again, knees bending only at the last second, only as much as was absolutely necessary, and opened wide her hand; and as a bird sang joyously near by, Betty slid her open hand beneath the cat's tail

241

and slowly tightened her fingers until the tail was caught in a tight fist. Still the cat did not move.

She stood there, bent over, staring at the cat's open eye, clutching her shopping bag in one hand and the cat's tail in the other, and she didn't lift the cat because she could feel that he was dead.

She put the shopping bag down and squatted beside the cat. He looked just the same, with grey fur and green eyes and his lips pulled back in a snarl. She couldn't understand why he was dead—how he had died. But she knew that she had done it.

She pulled the cat partway up, carefully, letting his head stay on the ground, and moved her staring eyes from its head to that part of it on which it had been lying. Her mouth opened; she dropped her bag and peered with intense curiosity at the underside of its body, matted and sticky, the body split in a dozen places, and she saw oozing dark blood and bright blood upon the cat's fur and upon the snow, and the earth beneath was a dark deep wound. She tried to think what was familiar about this; what was wrong with it. He shouldn't have been a cat; that's all she could remember. And his eyes should have been closed.

Still grasping the tail, she dropped the cat back exactly where she had found it. She looked all around its edges; not a sign, not a drop of blood. Experimentally, she lifted it and dropped it; lifted it and dropped it, gently, taking care that the head did not move from the ground, that each time it dropped it fell in precisely the same spot.

She stood up, looked down at the cat, and laughed. She leaned over, slapped her knees, and laughed. She picked up her shopping bag and headed back towards her house, stopping every few steps to look back at the cat and giggle.

When she reached her own doorstep she craned her neck to see down the street; the cat was now out of sight. She hurried back to the sidewalk and strained and strained until she could glimpse it lying there, grey on the white snow, hiding its own red blood. She ran into her house and slammed the door.

"You're going to have to tell them," he had said. "Not me. I'm not going to tell them. It's up to you."

He was right, of course. It won't *happen* until I tell people, Sheila thought, wandering around the kitchen, touching the blender, the toaster, the broiler-oven her mother had given them for Christmas. I won't *go* unless I tell people. I've got to tell them at the office. My God, I'm planning to leave there in just a couple of weeks and I haven't even told them yet. I've *got* to.

She sat down and ran her finger along scratches in the top of the table. If I can do that today, she thought, give my notice, if I can tell them at work today, then I'll have to tell the kids. I'll have to. She put her hands in her lap and sat still. Her insides felt shaky. Her hands were cold. Maybe I'm getting sick, she thought.

No, it's that cat. That's what it is. That cat, Shelley's tears . . . at least Peter had already left . . . they'll be all right, Ed loves them so much.

She got up and stood in the living room, looking out at the trees and the yard where she had had the garden last summer.

Betty hurried next door. She scooted, eyes turned away and hand up over her face, so she wouldn't inadvertently glance beyond Sheila's front yard. A few minutes later she was sitting, agitated, at Sheila's dining-room table.

"Betty," said Sheila.

"What? What is it?" said Betty sharply.

"I just want to tell you—I'm going away soon."

"Away? Why? Why are you going away?"

"Oh, I've got to think about some things. I'll come back. But I wanted you to know."

"What things? What things do you have to think about? Why can't you think about them here?"

243

"I have to be by myself," said Sheila. "You know."

"Oh yes, I know, I know about being alone." She laughed. "But you can be alone in your house, you know," she said craftily. "I don't like it," she said. "I don't like it that you're going away." She banged her cup down in the saucer. "I didn't want any coffee. Why do you always give me coffee?"

She picked up her purse, then put it down again.

"I saw something," she told Sheila. "This morning. A cat. A dead one."

"I know. We buried it." Sheila stood up. There's something I have to do, she thought.

"Who buried it? What are you talking about? It wasn't your cat."

"The kids and I buried it. Heather and Shelley and I. Heather found it on her way to school. She came running over here. She cried, too. Has she ever seen anything dead before?"

"What do you mean, Heather found it. *I* found it. *I* did. When I was out. Earlier."

"It must have been hit by a car. The streets are so dangerous. So are playgrounds. Peter got hit in the forehead by a swing once."

Betty was shocked. "How do you know that? How do you know it was hit by a car?"

Sheila sat down and slowly raised her hands to her cheeks. What is it that I have to do? she thought, and the thought seemed far away.

"I have a headache today," said Betty. "This is such nice coffee, you do make such good coffee, it's so pleasant to sit here calmly and hear the clock tick and drink coffee with you." She took a big slurp. "My what a lovely fern, it's new, isn't it, hanging here over the table, how nice, but ferns drop leaves and bugs, I know, I know." She nodded her head vigorously.

"Was there much blood?" said Betty suddenly.

The clock ticked. The refrigerator hummed. Outside Sheila heard a child shouting. "It didn't seem to be damaged at all, at first," she said. "It didn't show, at first. The damage." She looked at Betty. Betty smiled. "They wanted to bury it," said Sheila slowly.

"I never saw him before," said Betty loudly. "I never saw this cat you're talking about. Not until this morning, not until I saw him lying there this morning, sleeping on the snow. I saw no blood. No blood."

"I didn't either, at first." Sheila felt sick again. She looked at Betty's face and wanted to cry. "When I put the shovel under him . . . then we could see the blood, and the kids started to cry again and shriek and they both grabbed at me and buried their faces. . . . " Sheila felt tears trickle down her cheeks. She bowed her head and let them fall upon her hands, which rested limply on the tabletop.

Betty laughed. "I'm sorry," she chuckled. "But if, after all, a cat is, as you say, hit by a car, then of course there will be blood, won't there. I couldn't see why you didn't see it right away, but of course now I understand. So you took your shovel and you shovelled him into a box. Then what did you do?"

She leaned forward. Sheila raised her head. Betty looked at her face with interest.

"We buried it in the back yard," said Sheila. "The earth's getting softer, now. We dug a hole near there and put the cat in. They're going to put four pansy plants on top of the grave, later on." Tears continued to fall, getting her cheeks wet.

Betty nodded sympathetically. "My, you've had a busy morning, haven't you, and you haven't even gone to work yet, could you show me, do you think?" She stood up and came around the table to Sheila. "Where you buried him?"

She's very big, thought Sheila. She led the way into the back yard, through the melting snow. She heard water from the snow on the roof streaming down through the eavestroughs. She walked with Betty to the corner of the yard and looked down at the raw earth.

"He's under there," she said.

Betty swivelled her head around to look at Sheila. "Under there."

Betty nodded and there was a little smile on her face. She walked slowly away.

Sheila remembered what she had to do; she called out. Betty turned around.

"When will your husband be back?" said Sheila pleadingly, clutching the sides of her skirt, shivering, still crying. "When will your husband come again?" she said in a high voice.

Betty looked at her thoughtfully. "Soon. Soon." She walked away, back to her own house.

I'll watch for him, thought Sheila, crying. I'll watch for him every day. I'll get Shelley to watch, too. And Peter. We'll all watch for him. . . .

Chapter 33

"Hi, it's Jack Coutts. I'm going to have to keep this short. I'm calling from a site, and I can't tie up the phone. Just want to be sure she's, uh, keeping her appointments again." He laughed self-consciously, perched on the edge of a desk, body slightly tense, eyes alert for somebody wanting to use the phone. The place was empty except for a couple of men drinking coffee out of the cold, but the foreman could come in any minute, wanting his desk back, wanting his phone.

"We've hit a snag," said the doctor. "Nothing to worry about, I'd say, but I think we should call in a consultant."

Jack wanted to hang up the phone.

He stood up. He turned around, his back to the two men murmuring and laughing at the other end of the ATCO trailer that served as the office. "What do you mean? What consultant?"

"I repeat, it really is nothing to worry about. But your wife does seem depressed. She had a frightening dream. I think it would be wise to call in a psychiatrist at this point."

"Doctor," said Jack steadily, "I'm not understanding you. You are not getting through to me. Why do you want to call in a . . . consultant. Because of a dream?"

"It was an important dream. I think if she were to discuss it with a psychiatrist we might learn a great deal. I suggested that she, ah, consider spending a few days in the hospital, where she can . . . "

"A hospital? You mean the psychiatric ward? What the hell's going on!" Jack stared at the small window in the wall at the end of the trailer. The men behind him had stopped talking. He didn't know whether they'd left, and

247

was surprised to realize that he didn't care.

"Mr. Coutts," said the doctor wearily. "It was just a suggestion. Your wife didn't take it very well, I'm afraid. I wish you'd been there. . . . "

"I'm not goddam surprised! What's all this bullshit about she's doing so well, making progress, all of a sudden you're helpless or something! What's so special about a psychiatrist? What the hell do *you* do!" He was trembling, and took hold of the back of the chair behind the desk.

"I've explained that. I explained it to you when your wife first began seeing me. I tried to explain it to her again on Monday. Listen. You go to your family doctor; he looks after you. Then one day you get something wrong with your stomach. He does what he can. It doesn't get better. So he sends you to a specialist. It's the same thing. This is not an unusual situation."

"But what's this about the hospital, for Christ's sake?" He was calmer, but not calm. The doctor was calm. That's his goddam job, thought Jack.

"It might not even be necessary. I just asked your wife to think about it, that's all. Discuss it with you. Obviously we can make strides more quickly if she sees somebody every day than if she sees me every week. That's why I suggested the hospital." The doctor took a deep breath. Jack wanted to put his fist through something. "I've been in touch with a psychiatrist, a very good man," said Jessup. "He's agreed to see your wife as soon as we can set up an appointment. Will you be home during the next few days? I'd like to discuss it with you in more detail."

Jack carefully put the receiver into the cradle of the phone. He turned around. The men were gone. He sat in the foreman's chair.

His car was loaded and gassed up. He figured he was about four hours from Calgary. He felt completely hopeless, and he didn't feel at all like going home. He wondered, with not much interest, whether she would have written on the walls again.

I've had it, he thought, resting his elbows on his knees and his head in his hands. I've finally really had it.

Chapter 34

When she got home from Sheila's house she took out her tools, and this time she knew that she would use them, she just didn't know yet how she would use them.

She spread them carefully upon her bedspread, and her heart beat fast in anticipation of something. She slowly, ceremoniously, took off all her clothes and looked in her closet. At the very back she found the yellow robe she had gotten some time earlier, and the yellow slippers, too, and put them on. They felt stiff and new and awkward upon her body. She would have to wear them for a few hours before they felt comfortable. Then she would do whatever she was going to do.

She left her tools displayed on the bed. That cat would not come back. He was lying dead under the earth in the yard next door, and he could not crawl out and sit in front of her door and maybe get bigger and turn the knob. And Heather had gone today, too, really gone. She knew it; she had listened; the house breathed back, but it was not Heather's breathing. Nobody could disturb her. Nobody.

Bertha was not there any more. That house was empty. It was sold, but new people had not moved in. She was glad of that.

Sheila had left for her work. Betty had watched, patiently standing on one foot and then the other, and finally Sheila had come out and slowly locked the door and slowly slushed along the sidewalk past Betty's house to the bus stop way up at the corner. She didn't even look around; she just walked, slowly. Betty watched her dispassionately from behind the curtain.

She walked around the house, her yellow robe moving stiffly around her body and the yellow slippers slapping at her feet. She walked cruelly in her slippers, wanting them to break and mould themselves around her feet. She felt within herself; there was nothing wrong there today. Her shape would not change. She was locked into her ordinary shape today. And she didn't even have a headache—she had lied to Sheila, of course, just for something to say. It was difficult to find things to say that people would listen to. They listened when she looked backwards inside her mind and said what she saw there, or when she talked about the dreams in her head; they listened then. But nobody had really listened to her for years and years. Today somebody would pay attention. . . .

She had listened. She remembered listening. It hadn't done any good. Things spoke to her from inside as well as outside, and finally she trusted her own head more than anybody else's—even hers, even her mother's.

She walked around the house, enormously pleased with it. She closed the curtains in the living room, to keep out the brilliance of the sun, to let in only its muted light. She closed the curtains in the kitchen, blocking off the back yard. She went around the house closing all the curtains until she was alone in the house with the filtered sun. Nothing else came in from outside, and nothing inside could escape.

She made herself a pot of tea and sat in the kitchen drinking it, not moving except to lift the cup up to her mouth and down into the saucer. She was thinking, letting thoughts come into her head and go out again. She didn't keep anything out of her head. She let anything come in there that wanted to come in. Her robe felt softer. It had become just a little limp.

She went upstairs and looked again at her tools. She thought and thought. She went into the bathroom and took down the plastic bottle with the headache pills in it. She had just got some more the other day and had used only one. There were lots and lots of pills in there, small and light green. And there was a glass in the bathroom. She didn't want a pill now. She didn't need one.

After a while she sat on her bed amid her tools and took a magazine and read it, and dragged a box of chocolates from underneath her bed and ate some. The magazine was incomprehensible, filled with photographs of strange-looking women wearing strange-looking clothes, but she looked at it raptly and ate her chocolates. Soon there was chocolate smeared all around her mouth. She wiped her mouth with the back of her hand and saw the chocolate all over the back of her hand. She looked at it for quite a while before she wiped it on her yellow robe and began to read and eat some more.

Finally she put the magazine and the chocolates on the floor beside her bed. She stood up and tied the robe firmly around her middle and pushed her feet firmly into the new yellow slippers. She gathered all her tools together and put them in a straight line upon her bedspread and she stared at them, frowning. She picked up the tweezers she had found in Sheila's house. She walked into the bathroom and turned on the light.

She stared into the mirror and carefully with the tweezers began to pluck hairs out from her eyebrows. Each time she pulled one out she felt a little sting, and she remembered that cat and his claws in her nose. She kept pulling them out, one after another, for a long, long time, until the sink was full of hairs from her eyebrow and her eyes were filled with tears from the stings and one eyebrow was completely gone. She liked the way her eye looked with no eyebrow above it. Her eye was naked and astonished. She started to work on the other eyebrow. This time the stings hurt more, and her eyes kept filling up with tears, but she knew she wasn't crying, not really, so it didn't matter. One after another she pulled out the light brown hairs above her left eye, until finally that eye, too, was bald. She looked into the mirror at her red and watering eyes and laughed through her tears, feeling the stinging. She wet a washcloth and put it on the places where her eyebrows had been. The places were red and raw-looking, swatches of red cut across her face right above the eyes. She laughed, and pressed the cloth on her face again. Then she went back to the bedroom and dropped the tweezers into a garbage bag and sat on the bed to look at the rest of her tools.

She picked up her sewing scissors and began cutting off her hair. She clutched a handful and put the scissors into it and felt them right next to her scalp and then she cut. Light brown curls cascaded down onto the yellow bedspread. She cut again and again. She ran her hand over her prickly scalp, and everywhere she felt a piece of hair that had escaped she said "Aha!" and grabbed it and cut it off. She went to the mirror, then, with her scissors, and looked at herself. She admired the shape of her head, which she had never seen before. She clipped off the hairs that still clung to her head. She went back to the bedroom and dropped the scissors into the garbage.

She hung the glasses over her ears and on top of her nose. She squiggled her nose until they fit just right. She peered around through the glasses. They had no glass in them and she saw perfectly through the holes. She looked at what was left. The big kilt pin. She pinned it to her robe.

That left the long hat pin with the pearl knob on the top; the jackknife with the leather handle and the leather pouch to hold it; the long-handled two-pronged fork; the screwdriver with the bright orange handle; the pliers. She stared at them, absorbed.

She looked in her closet for a hat but couldn't find one she wanted to wear. She sat on the bed and undid the tie around her waist. She saw her stomach; poked it. It shook and trembled, filling her lap. She frowned. She saw her thighs, wide and strong. She poked them. They moved, but not much. She picked up the hat pin. Delicately, she traced a line on the farthest left side of her left thigh. She took away the hat pin. The line disappeared. She pressed harder. She felt a sharp squeal from her skin but she went on. One letter after another. Blood raced to the faint fragile tears in her skin, and the skin squealed more loudly. Impatiently she shook the pain out of her head and plodded on. After a while she took away the pin and looked at her thighs. "B E" was on the left one and "T T Y" on the right one. She liked the look of it. Her thighs were hurting a lot so she hunched into the bathroom with her robe open, stomach flapping, and there she wet the washcloth and pressed it onto the letters on her thighs. She patiently waited and pressed it down again and again. Finally the weak, thin trickles of blood stopped coming. She thought about putting some ointment on her thighs but decided not to. She went back to the bedroom and dropped the hat pin into the garbage.

She picked up the long-handled two-pronged fork. She pushed up the left sleeve of her robe and dragged the fork up her arm, from wrist to elbow. Two pink streaks appeared. She stared at them critically to see if they would stay, and when they began to fade she did it again. Altogether she did it four times, and then four more times on the other arm. Both arms were screaming at her now, along with her thighs, moaning and groaning down there, and the places where her eyebrows had been were still stinging mutinously. She was getting impatient with her body.

There was the jackknife left, and the screwdriver, and the pliers. She sat on her bed and thought. She couldn't think what to do with the screwdriver or the pliers that wouldn't incapacitate her. She didn't want to be incapacitated. Sadly, she threw them into the garbage, where the orange handle of the screwdriver winked up at her in relief.

She took the jackknife and went into the bathroom, where she picked up her pills and the glass. Downstairs, she put the knife on the card table and pulled the table close to the end of the sofa. She went to the kitchen and filled the glass with water. She put it on the card table, and put the pills next to it. She looked at the bottle of pills and then at the glass of water, calculating. She walked back into the kitchen and found another glass and filled it with water, too, and put it next to the first one. Then she sat on the sofa to wait.

She tried to think which hurt most, her thighs or her arms or where her eyebrows had been. They all yelled at her in anguish of one kind or another, none of them realizing that she was getting the same yells from other parts of her body. She chuckled amiably as she listened, and wondered whatever her mind thought it was doing, sending out so many different messages, conflicting messages sometimes, or messages that were irrelevant to each other —sending them all out at the same time, some having to do with her body, some having to do with things outside herself. She had not much respect for her mind. Sometimes she felt contempt for it. She was amazed that other people appeared to live so comfortably with their minds. Some people could perhaps turn off parts of their minds at different times—but not her, not her. Hers was too strong a mind, or else she was too weak.

She heard the door open and close, and she sat still upon the couch. But when Heather entered she quickly stood and whirled around and said, "Boo!"

She knew what she looked like, oh yes, but Heather couldn't see it all, no no, some of it was covered up by the robe, the sticky yellow robe Jack had given her for Christmas. Heather looked at her and screamed.

She ran to the child and threw her arms around her and buried Heather's face in the front of her robe.

"How do you like it, it's me, just me, Heather, just me. It's all right; look, it's just me. I'm going to let my eyebrows and my hair grow out again, and maybe it'll all grow out yellow like yours, maybe then I'll have yellow hair again like when I was young, like you, see? See? Come along now, don't be silly, come along."

She dragged her over to the sofa and sat down. She pulled Heather onto her lap.

Heather's face was white, which Betty thought she had probably expected to see, and the skin was pulling away from her face in a most unattractive way, and her lips were pulled back, too. She looked almost like she was snarling. Her hair fell back from her head. Betty grabbed it with one hand and lifted her right leg—both her thighs were screaming at her now, because they were being rubbed. But Betty ignored that and lifted her right leg and threw it over the bottom half of Heather's body. She reached for the bottle of pills, which she had uncapped. She told Heather to open her mouth, but the teeth clamped shut. The eyes were twice as big as normal. Betty marvelled at that. There was white all around the blue part of her eye, the whole way around, the eyes were open so far. She was sure Heather's eyes had never been opened so far.

Outside the wind started to blow. She stopped and cocked her head and listened to his eager rustling around the bottoms of the doors, around the windows. He wanted to get in, for some reason. But she wouldn't let him, oh no.

Heather screamed again and quickly, deftly, just like that, Betty dropped half the pills down her throat. She let go of Heather's hair and clutched her chin with her left hand, holding her mouth closed. She counted to thirty while Heather struggled and kicked and choked. Then she opened the mouth just a little and poured some water down. Heather choked and coughed and swallowed. More water. Choking, coughing, swallowing. Betty did this again and again—pills, jaw closed, choking, water, coughing, swallowing. Heather kicked and struggled. Through the fat fingers of her strong hand Betty felt Heather's tears, warm and languid, and the liquid from her nose, warm and sticky.

When she took her hand away Heather's eyes opened; she struggled still.

It would take some time, Betty knew. But she could wait. She sat back on the sofa and held Heather in her two arms. Her face stung and her thighs and her arms continued to scream in pain, but stoically she held her daughter and felt herself weeping. She held her and rocked her and wept and waited.

If the jackknife isn't long enough, she thought, there's a bread knife in the kitchen; if the jackknife doesn't go all the way, the bread knife will.

It was very important that her actual heart be touched.

The station wagon entered the city and found its way to Memorial Drive, which followed the river; and the trees lining the drive moved jerkily in the wind, their angular branches slapping awkwardly at the sky. The station wagon moved beneath the trees, changing lanes impatiently, and sometimes it had to stop because of red lights, but always they became green again, and the wagon moved on stubbornly, ignoring the wind.

The wind howled around the station wagon and slapped at the doors; it followed when the car turned north, and west, and it rose high high into the sky and hovered there as the station wagon stopped in front of a slightly rickety house which needed to be painted but which had a tree in its front yard.

Jack got out and closed the door, and as he watched his hand turn the key to lock the door he felt the absence of the wind. He looked up, into the face of his house. Drawn curtains had closed its eyes.

Jack looked at the tree in his yard. The tree stood straight, staring at the sky, where the wind had hidden itself.

He looked at the tree and at the face of his house and began to walk towards it and he felt extremely light, and agile, and if he had had a headache it was gone. All he felt was weightlessness and all he heard was silence and all he hoped was that the world might start to turn

257

again when he opened his door. He reached out; his hand turned the knob; he stepped into the silent hall and opened his mouth to call, "I'm home."